# WEIRD TALES OF HORROR

## DAVID J. WEST

# DAVID J. WEST

## LOST REALMS PRESS

## TABLE OF CONTENTS

**DAVID J. WEST**

Dedicated To My Inspirations

## GARDEN OF LEGION

The McHenry wagon train, bound for California, persevered through prairie fires, buffalo stampedes, Indian attacks, and even a bout of embarrassing dysentery, but their greatest struggle was when that flower of the prairie, nineteen year old Fannie Burton, became possessed.

Some recollected the pretty little blonde dabbled with an ensorcelled Ouija board stolen from a New Orleans juju man. Her mother claimed the girl was bewitched by a Navajo skin-walker, and still others said she had taunted Satan himself late one night around the buffalo-chip campfire after refusing to say grace. Regardless of the sinister origin, something hideous held the girl in demonic thrall.

The once shy and reserved Fannie swiftly took a rough frontier situation from dreadful to dire and finally to disastrous. She ripped apart the Conestoga's, devoured the pitiful food supplies, guzzled or smashed their water caskets and, astonishingly, ate a pair of oxen...alive! The company attempted to subdue the normally weak girl many times, but even a dozen of their most able-bodied men were overpowered by the maiden with a newly developed voice that was deep as the pit of Gehenna.

She, or *It*, or *Them,* seemed determined to force the desperate McHenry party to die in the wastes, reveling in their cries of desperation and misery. Each day they grew weaker and she, *It*, or *Them* grew stronger. All hope seemed lost in the blossoming desert of the American southwest. Tormented by a devil in a black dress, it seemed the party's bones would soon bleach under a merciless sun.

Being good Christian folk, they prayed for deliverance and a man they later called the desert prophet materialized. He appeared to be of late middle-age, medium height and build, walking barefoot upon the scorching earth and, most important, he could exorcise little Fannie Burton of her demons.

Spying the holy man's approach, the girl cried aloud and wallowed in the powdered dirt, frothing, vainly trying to hide in a baptism of cinnamon-like soil.

The entire wagon train listened in hushed amazement as the

desert prophet communed with the throng of evil spirits inside Fannie. "You don't belong here. You must leave. I command you in *His* name."

"Suffer us to enter into another set of the living," came the bottomless well of a voice from the convulsing waif. "Even, *He,*" it gnashed, "was so accommodating."

"You may enter into whatever lives on the other side of that nearest mountain," allowed the mysterious holy man.

A vile grin split the girl's face as her body shook one last time. An almost imperceptible mist spouted from her frame and flew like a swarm of ravenous locusts to the far side of the mountain.

Her own true voice restored, Fannie spoke hoarsely, "Thank you stranger, but who're you?"

"One of three who tarry," he answered, drawing her up from the baptism of fine powdered earth. "The demons shall not trouble you again. Go your way in righteousness."

Fannie ran to her waiting mother and father. As the rest of the McHenry caravan came out cheering from behind their wagons, a dust devil sprang up out of the dunes and the desert prophet vanished.

The McHenry party never caught his name, his tracks vanished into the shifting sands. Their problems were over, but two mountains away, the hell on earth was about to begin.

\* \* \*

Port trotted to the top of the pass, the dust swirling about his horse's hooves like the phantoms of nipping dogs. The horse stamped at unseen ghosts and Port clicked his tongue softly to calm the beast. Grey clouds loomed on the horizon. Rain would strike the desert soon enough, drowning as much as quenching, and Port had no wish to get wet.

Port was a broad-shouldered man with long dark hair and a short beard. He wore a stained duster which canvassed the flanks of his dun horse. A brace of pistols jutted from his vest as he glanced back at his unwilling companion.

Lashed to the trailing mule's saddle was a scrawny, red-haired kid with a face so sun-burnt it almost matched his curly locks. A thousand bitter curses were written in his gaze.

Neither spoke. Port, a gunfighter turned lawman, had nothing to say to the horse thief. Likewise, the kid had nothing to say to his captor. At the top of the pass, each looked down into the canyon before them. A small reservoir collected precious runoff from the mountain peaks, while a town lay jumbled a little farther below like a half-shuffled deck of greasy cards that had been played too many times. A wretched sign designating the town leaned at Port's right. The name made Port crack a smile, it had to be someone's sick joke.

The ruinous sign read, *Eden*, pop - 37. The number had been crossed out many times. With each scratch, the population had decreased until there was no space left for the last few numbers. Someone had tacked an extra board on the side to accommodate the count.

The mountain looming on the south side was covered with as many pockmarks across its face as the ne'er do well horse thief. Tailing's from mine shafts spewed out discoloration and Port noticed few, if any, were working claims.

The town itself had two dozen buildings in various states of decay. There wasn't a single tree and no plants except a desiccated tumbleweed passing by in the ever-present wind. The only other sign of life was in the murky reservoir. Insects skeetered by, but not a single fish jumped.

Porter had seen less promising towns but not by much. This was a town of broken promises, failed dreams and dead hope. Still, maybe he could get a drink.

Riding in, the breeze seemed to pick up and whine at this desert oasis. Port thought he heard a fell voice on the wind but he paid it little mind. He rode straight for the faded yellow star, bleaching upon the front of a peace officer's shanty.

Port tied his horse and the mule to the rail, and dragged his prisoner inside, bringing a cloud of dust with him as he opened the door and shoved the kid through it.

"What can I do ya for?" asked a portly sheriff, startled from his late afternoon nap.

"I have a prisoner. I want to lock him up secure for the night. We'll be moving on in the morning to get before the territorial judge by tomorrow night. I have a badge, my name is—"

"I know who you are, Porter," the sheriff interrupted. "I suppose we can hold your prisoner."

Port removed the kid's bindings and pushed him to the sheriff, who put the kid in the tiny jail.

"What'd he do?"

Port stepped to the door, remarking over his shoulder, "Horse thief and murderer, he'll hang soon. Where can I get a square drink?"

"Lulu-belle's, it's the only place still open."

"Much obliged." Port shut the door in the face of the gale and strode across the cactus dry street.

Inside Lulu-belle's a hairy-knuckled barkeep wiped down unused glasses as an off-tune woman sang an off-color song. The carnival of patrons looked Port's way as he entered, then went back to their previous distractions. He went straight to the bar, thumping down two bits.

"What'll ya have?"

"Whiskey," Port said. "The wind ever stop blowing around here?"

"Not usually. The miners like it. Helps keep 'em cool. It's hot as hell most days."

Port's gaze tightened. "Wait, is this the cursed town I heard about?"

The barkeep smiled, "It is indeed. That's our claim to fame. The territorial governor cursed Eden as the wickedest city in the west and said we'd fade out, but were hanging on. We ain't hardly licked yet."

Port chuckled to himself. He doubted the town would last another year unless the miners struck something. Everywhere death and decay lurked, whitewash peeled leaving flakes like dandruff on the ground and a certain stink never left the air. It was a dead and bloated town, with inhabitants like fleas still clinging to the lifeless dog's warmth.

Something banged near the back of the saloon and distracted the barkeep. "Sadie, will you serve this gentleman?" he called, "I have to see what that was."

Port looked out the window as a single tumbleweed rolled by, helped by the ever present wind.

A homely saloon girl with a whiskey bottle and glass sidled up to Port, "Well howdy stranger, doesn't it get lonely on the trail all day?" She batted her eyes like a butterfly gathering nectar.

He gave her a dirty look. "I ain't looking for company, just a drink."

"Everybody likes company," she said through overly red lips.

Port grinned. "Maybe so, but not me." She offered Port the glass but he declined and took the bottle.

"You're funny," she said. "I'm Sadie."

"Howdy Ma'am, I'm Porter."

"You from nearby?"

"A bit up north." He noticed a pair of tumbleweeds ramble by on the street. He took another swig watching the sky turn azure as Venus appeared.

Sadie coaxed, "I hear it's nice."

"I expect you'd like California better," Port said offhand.

The barkeep hollered for Sadie again and she shrugged. "Anything else you need, just you holler."

Port gave a half charity smile and focused on his drink instead of the next tone-deaf song. Dusk was falling and the wind grew louder with a moan like a dying man's last gasp.

Port rubbed a broad hand over his face and pondered the ride in the morning. The kid would hang in another night. It bothered him. The kid was young. Still, that he deserved it couldn't be denied. What would the parents say when Port brought their son home? Wouldn't likely be thanks. Nope, not a lot of appreciation for his service out here. He took another long pull on the whiskey bottle.

The wind moaned again and the rapid sound of a boot heel kicking the boardwalk shook Port from drowning his troubles. He stood and stalked to the saloon doors, hand on his navy colt.

Not six feet from the swinging doors lay an old man with the blue face of one who'd been strangled.

Glancing around the corner, Port looked left and right. Not a soul was on the street, just those blasted tumbleweeds rolling in the wind.

"Someone give me a hand," he ordered.

The bartender and Port brought the dead man inside. His clothes were dirty and disheveled, food stained his shirt and jacket precisely where a napkin bib wouldn't cover. Tight red gouges across the neck revealed the cause of his murder.

"Who was he?"

The hairy-knuckled bartender answered, "Quinn Cleary, town lawyer."

Port gave the bartender the stink-eye.

The bartender gulped adding, "And town drunk. There hasn't been a lotta need for a town lawyer last few years."

"You don't say? Who'd want him dead?"

Shaking his head, the bartender said, "No one. He was harmless."

Wheeling, Port looked upon the rest of the motley group of patrons. "Anyone?"

No one volunteered anything. Most seemed in shock, but Sadie stepped forward, "He was liked by everyone, there weren't no bad debts or dissatisfied miners if that's what you mean?"

Port nodded, "I'll get the sheriff." He went out into the night, the dark wind whipping about him like a scorned lover. With the wary sense of a predator, Port kept an eye up and down the street and while a sense of dread filled him, he couldn't see another soul. He convinced himself the dread was merely the aura of the town in general. He struck a match to light his cigar but the wind blew it out.

A rather large tumbleweed rolled in front of him and stopped abruptly despite the wind.

Port looked at the noxious weed, rubbed his beard and gave it a kick, sending it flying into the darkness.

He continued across the street, looking over his shoulder several times. Lamplight flickered through the shuttered windows of the sheriff's office, and a hint of laughter filtered out against the moaning dirge of the wind. Port frowned, what could there possibly be worth laughing about in this stinking town?

The sheriff sat at the little wooden table playing cards with the kid. Each looked up in shock at Port.

Port barked, "This the kind of town you run sheriff? Granting the opportunity for a horse thieving murderer to escape?"

"It ain't like that. We was just playing cards."

"Yes, sir," the kid agreed, "jus' playing cards. I wasn't gonna try and escape . . . honest."

Port picked the kid up by the scruff and threw him into the jail cell. "He has killed three men already, for six dollars and a slow horse."

The sheriff looked indignant at Porter, as if he didn't believe him, while the kid gave his most innocent look.

"I suppose I can keep him locked up," muttered the lawman.

"You suppose? You got more problems. Someone strangled your town drunk, and *that* murderer is still on the loose." Port struck another match and lit his cigar.

"Cleary's dead?"

Port nodded, smoke flared from his nostrils. "Strangled with wire. We got him over in Lulu-belle's."

Putting on his gun belt, the sheriff wheezed and said, "I'll be over in a minute."

Not waiting any longer, Porter went out the door back into the blasting wind. More tumbleweeds rolled by. Several weeds were massed up against the open saloon doors. The wind extinguished his cigar, and he prepared to light another match. Port kicked the tumbleweeds aside and went in. The lamps were blown out.

Everyone was gone.

Port spun around wondering if it was some kind of joke, but the saloon was deserted. No one was behind the bar or on the low stage. It dawned on him that the dead man's body was gone too. Going up the stairs with his navy colt drawn, Port was ready for anything. A tumbleweed had been blown up to the landing. Port knocked it aside.

There were four small rooms. Two had doors cracked open. No lamps burned, but a hint of moonlight crept through the narrow windows.

No one in either room. Port opened the first closed door, standing as far back as he could reach and still turn the knob. He half expected a gunshot to explode through the door, but none came. Each room was empty as well, though the last had an open window with the wind whipping the sun bleached pink curtains like a banshee.

Port came back downstairs and puzzled. It had been at least five minutes. Where was that idiot sheriff?

He went back outside. Somewhere in the cold distance a horse screamed. Porter gave pause. The street was nearly covered with tumbleweeds, and his horse was gone too! "Wheat in the mill! That damn kid!" He waded through the sea of weeds that almost acted like they wanted to grab and hold him. He puffed on his cigar extra hard to keep it lit against the wind. The orange cherry flared and the weeds seemed to part a little. The door stood open. Expecting to see the incompetent fool dead, Port leveled his six-gun at the ready.

But the sheriff wasn't there.

The kid was. Hunched in his cell in the darkness, in a fetal position, he sobbed and jerked as Port entered.

"Where is he? What did you do to him?" Port demanded.

"I didn't . . . do anything. It was them."

"Them who?"

"The weeds, they came to life. He opened the door and they rolled in. They took the sheriff. He screamed 'til he couldn't breathe no more."

"Horse chips!"

"They drug his body out the back. They tried to reach me but couldn't through the bars."

"You damn liar. Do you got friends trying to bust you out? Tell me or I am gonna shoot you here and now!"

"Better that than those things getting me."

Port wheeled and looked out the slit windows. The wind was forcing more tumbleweeds up against the door. Their scratching was unnerving. It almost looked like their myriad tiny branches were moving in a uniform, crawling chaos.

Port wrinkled his brow. The whiskey must be too strong here.

"They are trying to get in," moaned the kid.

Port puffed his cigar and said, "You're one defective bullet kid."

"It's true. Open the door and find out, you cold-hearted bastard."

"All right." Port opened the door, wary of gunmen on the street. He puffed on the cigar, looking with disdain at the weeds which fell back away from the door. "Yeah, kid, they're alive, either that or the wind moved them."

But the kid was as far back in his cell as he could be.

"Porter!" came a woman's voice.

Port looked and there on the roof of the saloon was Sadie and a handful of others.

"Run! Run! You've got to get away!"

Port looked each way down the street. "From what?"

"The weeds!"

He furrowed his brow again and the wind blew out his cigar.

The weeds closed in.

"Horse chips."

He leapt back into the sheriff's office, slamming the door as he did so, but the weeds clogged the threshold, keeping it open. So many rolled atop each other, that the pile was as tall as Port.

He did the first thing that came to mind. He shot the mass with his navy revolver. Smoke belched from the six-gun but the weeds were unaffected beyond a moment's respite.

The kid screamed in his cell.

"Shut up!" Port kicked over the card table, which did nothing to the weeds. He flung at chair at them. It crushed a few, but against the mass it was useless. Taking the other chair, Port smashed out the window behind him and dove through.

He landed hard on his elbows and knees, rolling to get up.

Weeds tumbled around each side of the office and out the lip of the window.

Port was on his feet racing to the next building, a dilapidated Smithy's. Scrambling up a post, covered with tools, he managed to get several feet off the ground and above the weed's reach. He climbed up to the narrow slanted roof.

The weeds thrummed in unison and surrounded the tiny structure.

From his new vantage, Port could see thousands of weeds covering the town. Across the street, Sadie and a dozen others sat on the saloon's roof. The wind moaned and Port sat precariously for what he deemed one of the worst nights of his life. He chanced throwing matches at the weeds, but they rolled away until the matches died in the blustery night. Port knew there was no way he could burn the brush while they were so spread out.

Several times individual weeds attempted to climb the post after Port. One on one he could knock them away, but what about when sleep would eventually take him? He couldn't stay awake forever.

Dawn's light only revealed a greater nightmare. There were more weeds than Port had guessed. Not a single horse remained. There'd be no way to outrun the horde, and still the hurtling wind blew fierce as the devil.

He kicked another tumbler that clambered up. Sadie and the others above the saloon did the same with their climbing invaders. Port knew that eventually they would lose. He had to take the fight to the weeds. Looking across the lay of the land, the narrow sloping valley, the reservoir sat above the town. Port chewed his lip and hatched a plan. As much as he didn't like it, he would need help.

"Sadie," he called, "Are the miners still using their powder magazines? Do the mines go deep?"

"Yes. It's there past the east barn," she shouted, pointing to a lone shack at the far upper end of town. "But so what about the mines depth? The weeds can go anywhere a man can go."

"Much obliged."

She puzzled over his intentions and frowned, shielding her face.

Tearing off another, ascending tumbleweed, Porter snagged a blacksmith's hammer from the post. He tossed it to the roof of the sheriff's office. He gauged the distance between the two buildings. It would be a long jump, especially since he didn't have much room to start with.

He didn't like heights, and while this wasn't that high, the weeds waited below, hungry as rabid dogs. They seemed to sense his intent and gathered thickly underneath him. It was now or never. More weeds were crawling up the post.

Port reached with all he was worth, whispering a prayer as he jumped.

His fingers grasped the lip of the sheriff's office as the wind was slammed from his lungs. Still, he didn't let go. He struggled over the lip of the flat adobe roof. Port lay on his back a few moments, breathing hard.

"Are you alright?" called Sadie.

"Yeah, never better," he panted.

Porter slammed the hammer at the roof of the jail cell. It was hard work and took longer than he would have liked. By the time Port burst through the ceiling, the kid below was screaming in terror.

"Shut up, it's only me."

Dumbfounded, the kid nodded and let Port pull him up to the roof.

Port whispered, "We got two things we can do. Nothing and die, or act and perhaps live."

The kid nodded.

"I know you can run, so I got a job for you. I need a distraction. I need you to get the weeds' attention while I charge up to the powder box and blow the reservoir wide open. It'll wash this town clean."

The kid shook his head, "I'd rather wait here. Get someone else to do it."

"Look kid, I can't be yelling these plans across the street for the weeds to hear. I don't know how smart they are. Wheat! I don't even know how they are doing this. It's gotta be you."

"It could be you. I can run faster than you. Let me light the powder and blow the dam."

Port grimaced. He knew the kid was fast, he'd been awful hard to catch. "Here's my matches. There will be some powder kegs. Take one or two, whatever you can still move with. Get up to the reservoir put the keg next to the drainage channel, light it and get the hell away. Once a hole is knocked in that dam, it'll be like a river in flood. Get clear. You hearing me? These things will come tearing after you, so you gotta do it quick."

The kid nodded, "But what about after? I do this, you still gonna take me to get hung?"

Port narrowed his gaze. "No. But you're gonna head to Mexico."

"I don't wanna go to Mexico."

Port cocked his head and gave a wicked grin.

"I'll go to Mexico."

"Good lad. I'll lead the weeds south as best I can. You run north fast as the devil on your tail. Make sure this wind don't blow out your match."

Port dropped down to the slopping roof on the front of the office. He tore the sign from the rusted brackets and tossed it, smashing weeds beneath. He jumped down and ran serpentine through the streets of Eden. Weeds rolled after him like a pack of dogs.

\* \* \*

The kid watched a moment, eased down the backside and made for the powder magazine. On the ground he peered around the corner to determine if the weeds would even see him. They appeared taken with Porter and paid no attention to him or the others on the saloon.

Porter dodged the few weeds that rolled to intercept him and booted a few, but more came on until they were so thick on his heels that kicking would only waste his time. They lashed at his ankles and no amount of shooting or struggling would avail him.

The kid moved behind the ghost town shops to avoid being seen, but Sadie saw him. "Where are you going?" she shouted. "Help us!" He signaled her to be silent.

While they watched, weeds with a thousand tiny arms grabbed Port's heel and tripped him. He flailed and sent dozens spinning away, but for every one he threw a dozen more took its place. The weeds piled, reaching to strangle the human life they envied and hated.

Through some eldritch means, or from understanding Sadie's shouting, the weeds sensed the kid. A number of them, too far from reaching Porter, stopped and rolled north after the young blood.

The kid glanced from the edge of the hotel and saw them coming. He turned and ran for the powder magazine. He pulled matches from his pocket.

Port reared up, tearing weeds from his throat. He roared like a mad bull and swatted the balled weeds away. Like an infinite hydra they attacked from all sides.

The kid saw a hundred or more weeds rolling. He reached the powder magazine and threw back the door. Inside were a half dozen powder kegs. He picked up the nearest and ran for the reservoir. "This had better work," he muttered through clenched teeth. The weeds were gaining on him.

At the drainage ditch, the kid dropped the keg and fumbled with the matches. The wind blew out the first three—only two left. He looked over his shoulder. The weeds tumbled closer and closer. A light and the fuse went quick. He shielded the delicate blaze with his hands. The weeds rolled. There would be no time to escape and keep the fire alive. This would be his redemption.

"Sorry Mama," he whispered.

\* \* \*

The keg exploded in raucous thunder. Black smoke, brown earth, and gray water spit in all directions.

The pursuing weeds stopped and backed away from the spilling reservoir.

An arm reached out from the mass of weeds, and Port was free for a moment before he was sucked back down by the malevolent force.

A torrent of water become a river, as chunks of the dam broke free in a mighty domino effect.

Porter knew he was turning blue from the vine's deadly grip on his neck. With eyes barely open, he fell to the dust. Torn in all directions, his tongue lolled in hot earth, then felt cool relief.

Water ran, slick and cold, as the weeds let go.

Porter struggled to his knees and saw the wave coming. He moved like a crippled locomotive and just managed to grasp a sturdy post as the river hit. Weeds were drowned and taken away past the corrals and abandoned bordello.

The tumbleweeds tried to hold to one another and again and again were washed downstream from the town.

Sadie and the others atop the saloon cheered and whooped. Port held to his post like a rod of iron, fearful of being carried away. When the water at last subsided to a few feet deep, he looked behind and saw a clumped mass of the drenched weeds.

They moved as one.

Forming together, they rose out of the ebbing waters, rounded like a head with hollow spots for colossal eyes and mouth. Shoulders appeared then arms, fingers, and a hideous weed-bodied torso. Thousands of wet tumbleweeds fused together to fashion a giant weed golem. The vines interlaced, wrapped and knotted about tenaciously. An inhuman cry echoed from the cavity of a mouth and the thing stood up, over three stories tall. It shook the wetness from itself and stepped forward with a ponderous gait.

Sadie screamed. The others ran for their lives to escape the colossus's awful gaze. Port shuddered, but still his mind sprang like a steel trap to find a way to defeat this demonic foe.

Coming closer, the awful giant stepped on the bordello, crushing it asunder. With the waters gone, the town was a mud track. Some of the structures had been knocked off their foundations and were laying haphazardly. The street in front of the saloon was the biggest clearing the town had left.

"Wheat! I'm a fool," Porter said to himself. "Now I got him."

"We have to get out of here," the barkeep shouted, tugging on Port's shoulder.

"You think you can outrun that?" Sadie asked.

"We just gotta outrun the others," the barkeep answered.

Port grasped his shoulder and swung the man around. "You wanna live? Get me a lamp! All of 'em! And be ready when I am! I gotta buy some time."

The barkeep stared at him like he was insane but dashed back inside.

The colossus was almost upon them and Port stepped into the muddy streets to face it.

18

"*Porter,*" it echoed.

"You know me, but I don't remember meeting you before."

"*We are legion. Ours will be a place of honor in Gehenna, when we destroy your body,*" the voice came, deep as the pit.

"That's where we have our feud. I doubt I'll get anything for destroying yours."

The hollow eyes looked down on Porter, and an ominous sound that he believed was laughter echoed.

"*You have no power over us.*"

"That's where you're wrong. I do have power over your chosen body."

"*We were tricked. But it serves us well enough. We cannot be shot. We cannot be drowned. We cannot be blown apart.*" It leaned in closer to Port. "*We cannot be kicked now.*"

"You forgot one," Port caught the oil lamp the barkeep tossed him. He threw it into Legion's mouth and shot.

Fire erupted and an inhuman cry rocked the town. The whipping wind gave the behemoth a tongue of flame, and it laughed again before shooting witch-fire back at Porter like a blast furnace. "*You have only given us more power to destroy you! Embrace your doom!*" Still sopping wet, the Legion thing was not burning.

The front of Lulu-belle's burst into flames, but the wily gunman dodged and ran about the slick street, taking cover behind the ruins of the blacksmith's.

The tongue of fire blasted again, igniting the forge and structure. Port crossed to a ramshackle house. Again the fire tore into the dry wood. Port faked left and went right, taking cover in the collapsed bordello. "You have to do better than that," he taunted.

The weed golem swung a colossal fist at Porter and shot its witch-fire tongue as he dodged yet again. Smoke obscured him, but as he chanced a look, the edges of the Legion's mouth blackened.

Sensing that its protection of wetness was wearing off, the golem brought up a hand and suffocated the fiery tongue. It cast its wicked gaze for Porter and realized too late it was surrounded by the flaming ruins of the town--a second sacrifice it never could have understood.

Sadie and the remaining others threw more oil, and the flames grew. Porter backed away through burning wreckage, choking on the smoke. The Legion thing was trapped, and its weed body sizzled and smoked as the wetness boiled off. Every path was blocked. It twisted and turned looking for escape, finding none.

"*We won't forget this!*" it roared, before dropping to the mud and writhing as dry weeds were burnt to skeletal ash. Dark things flickered amongst the smoke, and it seemed evil spirits, free of any mortal coil, fled up into the ether.

"The thing burned awful fast for being so wet," Sadie said.

"Yeah, it did," Port answered. "I'm glad at least one element was on our side."

A barefoot, middle-aged man of medium build stood beside them as if he had been there the whole time. "With every blessing comes a curse," he said. "And vice versa."

Port cocked an eyebrow and shrugged, "Horse chips."

## THE KING IN THE WOOD

A brisk wind, like groping hands shoved Nikki through the doors of Ye Olde Curiousity Shoppe almost knocking her into a glass display case. It was a blustery day but she looked behind just to be sure it had not actually been a person pushing her.

Nothing but the flying leaves clinging to her hair and the rolling grey clouds bringing sleet.

"Goodness. You all right?" asked a bespectacled old clerk. "I was afraid that gust was going to knock you over."

"It almost did," said Nikki. She stepped back and looked around the store at the myriad trinkets that filled the room. "You certainly have a lot of interesting things here."

"Yes, we do. It has been our life-long hobby to collect and travel. I only just recently brought in most of my personal collection. Decided it was time to share, see what other people might like to have a look at. Quite a few things here are one of a kind."

For all his verbal enthusiasm, he remained seated behind the counter looking down at his crossword puzzle.

Nikki wondered if it was simply a tired old sales pitch. She had walked past the shop many times before, it wasn't until today that the wind had decided her fate, regardless of how little money she had to spare.

Sun-bleached toys, rusty bicycles, and vintage signs hung about the walls. Embossed books with curious gold lettering on their spines and magazines older than her parents were stacked reaching to the ceiling. Basket-hilted swords leaned in the corners beside old brass instruments. Glass cases sat in the center of the room, crammed with more than they were ever made to carry. Instead of jewelry there were a multitude of carven images; some Chinese jade figurines, an African mask, a waxen Thai bust of the Buddha and a scowling Mayan warrior; even an Aztec sun disc with its central face and protruding tongue. There was also a wide assortment of Celtic green men with leafy green beards made of both stone and wood.

But what truly captured Nikki's eye was an oddly shaped fiddle made of light green wood. It had five multi-hued strings and was unlike any instrument she had ever seen. Somewhat pear shaped with a short stout neck, it defied expectation. Strange glyphs faintly visible along the neck made Nikki think of Egyptian hieroglyphs or Sumerian cuneiform, perhaps even Mesoamerican pictograms.

Most intriguing though was the bushy face not unlike the other green men perched at the head of the instrument. Twisting leaves upon his beard would tune the strings. The carving itself was minimalist but intense, with black staring eyes and a roman nose. The face was both fierce and proud, though not malevolent, it seemed royal, that was the first word that came to Nikki's mind.

She found herself pressing a hand against the glass to reach it, to play upon it, though her years of piano gave no real semblance on stringed instruments.

"See something you like?" asked the clerk, startling Nikki.

"What?"

"You've been looking for a very long time, so I thought to ask if you saw anything you liked."

"A long time?"

"I'm not trying to rush you. No worries, but we close at five."

"It's only a quarter to four." She looked at her phone, as she had only moments before stepping inside. It read four forty-four. "It's not daylight savings time yet is it?"

"That's next week."

"I must have read something wrong."

"Quite all right."

"What can you tell me about this . . . violin?"

The old man peered down. "Not much I'm afraid. It was my wife, Deborah's. I can't recall where we purchased it. I want to say Mexico or Egypt. I remember pyramids as she showed it to me, but that was a long time ago. It's very old. I've never seen another like it."

"So it's expensive?"

He smiled. "What would you like to pay for it?"

Nikki smiled back. "I don't know what I could afford right now. I'm trying to write my thesis but I don't play enough anymore with school, but something about it. It's very majestic, magical even. I would like to learn to play it. To let whatever is inside . . . out."

"Take it."

"I couldn't."

"Take it. You need to write, you need to play in this life before your time is gone. Deborah wanted to play it too and she never did find a way to release the song within. It needs to be heard, not just hung on a wall, forgotten."

"Are you sure? Mr.?"

"It's Mr. Christy. You were staring at it long enough. No one else has expressed half as much honorable interest since my wife did."

"Thank you," said Nikki, though inwardly wondering how he still thought she could possibly have been there for more than a few minutes.

He wrapped the fiddle carefully in long brown paper and tied the ends with string. "Take care. The song must be released," he called.

She thanked him and stepped out the door.

*　*　*

The wind still whipped down the avenue, sending leaves aloft like notes in every direction. The sky was noticeably darker beyond just the threatening clouds. Nikki doubted her own conviction of being confused on the time, she had been inside for an hour at the very least but how?

A svelte dusky man in a smart dark suit approached her with purpose saying, "Greetings. I understand you just bought an instrument that I want very much."

Regardless of his tone and demeanor, not to mention his suave manner of dress, Nikki did not like the aura he gave off. Something about his unblinking eyes made her uncomfortable.

"How much? Sell it to me."

The fiddle strings seemed to twitch beneath the paper at his very approach and Nikki wondered if it was just the wind on the wrapping paper, but still . . .

"I'm afraid I couldn't do that. It has sentimental value to me."

"Maybe, I didn't make myself clear," he said, gripping her shoulder and reaching for the package. "I will have the instrument. It rightfully belongs to me. I made it!"

"Hey!" shouted a policeman from across the street. "There a problem?"

The dark suited man let go of Nikki's shoulder and gave a wicked half-smile. "I can offer more than you can possibly imagine. I will see you again." He strode around the corner before the officer could cross the street.

"That guy bothering you Miss?"

"Yeah, he wanted my package."

The officer grinned, nodded and ran around the corner.

Nikki felt stupid about the exchange, had any of this really just happened? Did she just say, 'he wanted my package?'

The officer promptly turned back. "He's gone. If you see him again an' he's threatening, give us a call. Good day Miss."

Nikki nodded. She had never before been so grateful and disappointed in having an officer close by, and none of this strange occurrence explained her time lapse either.

Worried she was feeling ill or worse, she sat on the bus-stop bench to compose herself. She called her sister. "Maria, how long ago did I leave your place?"

"About an hour and a half. Why?"

"I have been in a curio shop all that time."

"Seriously?"

"The gentleman inside told me I had been standing there the whole time, but I thought it was only a minute. Then a handsome weirdo demanded I sell him the fiddle I bought."

"Gentleman? Fiddle? Was he some kind of pervert? Did he drug you?"

"No, not him. I just can't believe the time went by so fast."

"Were you reading?"

"No. Just looking."

"Right. Maybe you should come back here. I'll fix coffee."

"No, I'm going home. I want to relax."

"I wouldn't go back there again if I were you."

"Thanks' Sis."

Nikki felt fine, just confused. She had to catch a later shuttle than usual and at first saw only unfamiliar faces. Then toward the back she recognized a friend, Professor Carlson from the University. He wore his usual sun-bleached fedora and brown overcoat. Nikki always thought he looked like the actor Donald Sutherland. He had a mess of papers hanging from his accordion like folder and several books beside him on the seat along with his laptop. He almost never used his Mac but he was never without a book.

"Good evening Professor."

"Good day," he said, without looking up.

"It's Nikki."

"Oh, hello Nikki. Good to see you. I didn't expect anyone I knew to be here. I was grading papers later than I meant. You're not usually this late either." He picked up his books and she sat down beside him.

"I want to show you something." She unwrapped the paper and produced the fiddle.

He glanced at it, took it in hand and tried to read the glyphs upon the neck. He flipped it over scanning the entire body for any trace of identification. "Where is this from?"

"The Curio shop on the corner."

"When did you get it? It's been closed for months, since the old couple running it were held up."

"No, I just bought it. I talked to an old man."

"Trust me, I used to go in there every other week just to keep an eye out for rare books. The Curio shop has been closed since last March. The old man that ran it is dead."

"Someone was in there."

"Strange, but this . . . this is a unique piece. What do you know about it?"

"Nothing. I was hoping someone . . . well you, could tell me more, or at least point me in the right direction. Some weirdo already offered to buy it. Not that I feel like selling. I want to hear its song."

"I can tell from the grain and desiccation here, it is very old. Not sure what kind of wood though, strangely green. But several of these marks don't make sense. These almost seem like cuneiform, but this one looks Hebrew, and that one is Toltec. And this head looks like the Green Man from Celtic myth."

"That's what I thought. I love the leafy tuning fronds."

"It is remarkable," he agreed, turning the fiddle over again. "I hate to make a call sitting here on the bus, but either it is a phenomenal forgery or a truly history altering piece."

Nikki's eyes grew wide.

"Of course I can't really say more and must lean toward it being a bizarre chimera perhaps at the least three hundred to four hundred and fifty years old. Maybe something truly unique from Renaissance Italy? Or maybe just a hoax. Nothing should have this collage of old and new world symbols."

"But this . . . "

"It is remarkable, but where is it from? Who made it? Hoaxes ruin it for everyone," he said, shaking his head.

"I don't know anything about it, but I don't think it is a hoax either. It's too beautiful."

"Did the shopkeeper say who brought it in?"

"He said it was Deborah's, his wife."

Professor Carlson rubbed his chin and curled his mustache. "It can't be Mr. Christy, but I suppose Deborah could have remarried, if she has been released? Last I heard she was still in St. Pat's, almost comatose. I only visited once, time goes by too quickly. Very odd that. Someone else must be running the shop."

Nikki shrugged.

"This is my stop. Let me know what you find out. I'll have to go visit the Curio shop tomorrow too," he called, waving as he got off the bus.

Nikki couldn't help fixating on the fiddle, especially that leafy green face. She would find out more tomorrow.

\* \* \*

Inside her tiny apartment, Nikki fed her cat, Bagheera, ate a little herself and stared at the fiddle. She dared to pluck at the strings but proceeded only in creating discordant notes. She played with the tuning fronds but never quite found the harmony within. A proper bow must be needed to truly play.

She went to bed with Bagheera at her feet and moonlight shining through the curtains and onto the fiddle that sat facing her upon the chair. Did the dark eyes sparkle? Did the imperious scowl hidden behind the beard actually grin? Sure she had imagined it, she rolled over, clutching her pillow.

Nikki drifted into the realm of sleep when the throb of drums opened her eyes. She was no longer in her bedroom, but instead a vine covered forest.

Laughter and haunting music echoed throughout and a bearded man painted vibrant green, danced through the woods. Children followed him into a great courtyard, past massive stepped pyramids and finally before the largest tree Nikki had ever seen. Crowds amassed and played all manner of harmonious music, food too spilled across wide tables, every manner of good green thing from the ground or vine was available for the taking at this wondrous feast.

A crown was placed upon the green man's head and a sense of peace and prosperity extended as Nikki danced with the people in celebration of the coronation. The music continued into a wilder beat as the Green King danced in ecstasy.

But a discordant note sounded from out of the cyclopean pyramids, as black smoky tendrils extended and strained to reach the King. They engulfed him, coiling like serpents, driving the life force from him while also choking out the great music which had so recently filled the void. Desperate green hands reached out for aid, but were laid low against the choking amorphous doom.

While still just a spectator in what seemed a vast crowd, Nikki knew he was not dead, but venomously asleep.

Time passed swiftly and the Green King was buried beneath the sacred tree and winter came. Somehow, entombed in the cold dark ground, Nikki yet saw his still serene face, just like the carven fiddles head, but dusted with earth and shadow and covered in tangled roots.

Suddenly his pale eyes opened.

Nikki awoke with a start, to the sun shining through the curtains and the disinterested look of Bagheera.

She was late for class.

* * *

Nikki was busy copying notes in the lounge out front of the University Bookstore when Professor Carlson walked up, a frown across his face. "Are you laughing? Having a good joke at my expense?"

"Hello, to you too, Sourpuss."

He folded his arms and just looked at her.

"Ok, I'll bite. What are you talking about Professor?"

"Nikki, where did you get that viola? That shop is as closed now as it was eight months ago."

"No, it was open yesterday."

Carlson looked deep into her eyes and cocked his head. "Seriously. You're not messing with me are you? This isn't some joke, you're pulling on your doting old Professor is it?"

"Of course not. I was there yesterday. The old man, he said his name was Mr. Christy, he gave me the fiddle. He said something like, better I should learn to play it than it sit unused on a wall somewhere." She sipped her juice looking at Carlson. "What? I'm not lying."

"How did you get the viola?"

"I just told you. Mr. Christy gave it to me. There is no way it's closed. There must be some kind of mistake."

"You swear?"

"I don't need to swear, but yeah. What the hell Professor? I'm too busy with my essays to make this up. I think I saw that creep who wanted me to sell it hanging around here earlier too."

"Would I recognize him?"

"I doubt it. He looked thirty to fifty. Maybe kind of Latin or Indian, maybe not."

"Thirty to fifty? How old do you think I am?"

Nikki grinned. "He was dressed in an expensive looking black suit. Kind of handsome but creepy. Piercing eyes."

"All right, I'll watch for him too. Would you like to go with me to St. Pat's this evening? I want us to go see Mrs. Christy. We could try and ask her about the viola."

"Sure, if you think it's all right. If people weren't looking at us already, they are now."

He grinned at that. Their platonic friendship was still flattering. "I'll pick you up at five in front of the Bedford Building. See you later."

As Professor Carlson walked away, all the business and stress of the day faded and the haunting dream came back to Nikki in full force. Those pale eyes opening in the gloom, how could she see those pale eyes open in the dark? The clock tower gonged and she went to her next class, unwilling to think on anything but the fiddle.

\* \* \*

At four in the afternoon, Nikki walked around the corner to the Curiosity shop. She reached for the doorknob and twisted, expecting it to easily turn and was surprised that it remained immobile. Glancing up, the sun-faded closed sign had cobwebs lilting from it. Dead flies littered the inside of the window sill. Inside the macabre scene was repeated with more dust and webbing.

Surely this place had not been open in months. Nikki stepped back and looked again to be fully sure this was indeed the place she had visited yesterday.

Stepping forward once again she rapped on the glass, eliciting no response. Poking her face against the pane and shielding her vision to adjust she looked deeper.

It was the same as it ever was, albeit dustier, but, there was a pear shaped spot in a glass case where the fiddle had rested, a spot where the green velvet felt was visible like an island in a sea of dust.

"Did you change your mind? Do you now wish to sell Madoc's fiddle to me?" asked the black suited man.

His presence intimidated her. She had not heard his footsteps on the walk. At least he refrained from touching her this time.

"No. I just wanted to ask the shopkeeper about it."

The man gave a wide flat-toothed smile. "He knew nothing. It is a sentimental piece for me alone. Do not be cruel, you received it for free, extend the same courtesy to me—its true owner."

"I don't think so."

His smile dropped. "You are a wicked child. Give me my lost treasure. It has no real value to you but means everything to me and my kingdom."

"Kingdom? Where are you from?"

He shook his head. "They have let it collect the dust of ages but it belongs with its master."

"Uh-huh. Tell me again how it's yours? Who are you?"

Encouraged by her response he took a step forward. "I crafted the instrument long ago. To play upon it at my leisure. It is mine to do with as I so choose. I don't need to answer to you child."

"Child? Ha! I'm the one who has it. You answer me. How did you lose it?"

"It was stolen a long time ago by a thoughtless priest who traded it away to a woman he could never have."

"Look. I know you're attached and all, but none of this shtick makes me want to just hand it you."

His face darkened again and he reached inside his coat pocket.

Nikki felt trapped against the doorway, thinking he would draw a weapon.

He pulled out what looked like a checkbook. "How much?"

"So you try to get it for free first, now you offer money? Get real, it must be worth an awful lot and you're just a freak!"

He slammed his hand against the brick. "Do not mock me."

Putting on her bravest face, Nikki asked, "Who are you? And why should I care?"

"I am Tezcatlipoca. I am from the Land of Reeds in Tollan. Sell it back to me!"

Nikki smiled and looked agreeable just enough to slide sideways and get back out on the sidewalk. "No. I don't know what your deal is Tezz, but I'll never sell it to you."

Visibly furious, Tezcatlipoca stood his ground, "I am Tezcatlipoca and it is mine alone to play upon!"

Nikki backed away down the sidewalk, a few other pedestrians staring at the interchange gave her courage, but as she took a dozen steps and looked back, Tezcatlipoca was gone. How could he have been so swift?

\* \* \*

Professor Carlson was early, and in the twilight this time of year

Nikki was relieved. He rarely drove his personal car, but tonight to go across town he would. Nikki got in, buckled and said her hello's.

"You all right? You're pale."

"I'm fine. That handsome weirdo demanded to buy the fiddle again, and you were right, the shop is closed. It doesn't make any sense."

"Of course I was."

"I thought we were mixed up on which shop it was. I didn't dream it up. You saw the fiddle too."

"I did."

"So it doesn't make any sense."

Carlson shrugged. "Maybe sometimes things are outside what we think makes sense and always will be."

"You're a professor, you're not supposed to say things like that."

"I don't have all the answers either."

Nikki smirked. "You sound like you do in class."

"You're mistaking my opinions for answers."

"At least you're honest."

"Did the handsome weirdo say who he was? Why he wanted it?"

"He said his name was something like Tez-Cat-Lee-Polka and he was from the place of reeds, Too-Lawn?"

Carlson looked away from the road and raised his eyebrows. "Tezcatlipoca? Tollan and the Land of Reeds?"

"Yeah, that's it. He claimed the fiddle was his, he made it or something and that it was stolen."

"Anything is possible, but I'd still like to hear it from Mrs. Christy if she can tell us anything. The old man, what did he look like? Take a look at this newspaper clipping from my files. Section D, page 3." He gestured to a vanilla folder on the seat between them.

Nikki picked it and thumbed through saying, "That's him!"

"You're sure?"

"Positive. But I thought you said he died months ago?"

"He did."

\* \* \*

The elevator opened to reveal a life-size statue of St. Patrick.

Carlson tipped his hat and gestured Nikki on. He spoke quietly to the nurse at the desk and beckoned Nikki on to room 101.

Inside, a mute TV displayed the home shopping channel. An old woman with ivory wisps of hair lay in bed.

"Deborah? It's Bill Carlson," he said softly.

She didn't move except for her eyes, the lids tilting upward ever so lightly and flickering like moth wings. "Bill?"

Carlson took off his hat and smiled. "You used to call me the book worm."

"Ah, yes. Who is your friend?"

"I'm Nikki, I was given your violin by—I think your husband."

Carlson looked sharply at her for that remark, but Mrs. Christy sat upright a little more and gave Nikki a curious look. "Are you in trouble?"

"I don't mean any harm, I—"

"No, listen child. The song must be released. But I couldn't discover it. Lord knows I tried."

Professor Carlson held Deborah's hand asking, "Where did it come from? What can you tell us about it?"

"We bought it somewhere in the Chiapas back in the sixties on our honeymoon. I always loved to travel with Burt. Some rude man tried to get me to sell it. We had to cut our vacation short because he said we stole precious relics, but the violin is unlike anything I've seen before and was not wholly Toltec, it is also Welsh, probably from when the great prince Madoc came."

Nikki looked at Carlson. He shrugged, "There are unverifiable rumors that a Welsh prince sailed to Alabama, returned to Wales, and came back and became king of the Toltec's in Mexico. Some say the winged serpent Quetzalcoatl is based upon the Welsh dragon."

Deborah nodded lightly at Carlson's tale, while a tear welled in her eye.

"What's that have to do with my violin?"

"It might explain the Green Man head and now that I think about it, those markings aren't cuneiform but possibly Ogham, an ancient Celtic script."

Deborah took Nikki's hand, "Tell me what my husband said."

"He said the song needed to be heard by someone who cares. That it shouldn't just be hung on a wall, forgotten. That he wanted to hear it."

"That was for me. He always said I needed to follow my true inspiration and release the music, to release the king within. But after years of not finding the song, I gave up and hung it on the wall. A piece of art in limbo, appreciated by no one."

Carlson took her hand in his. "Are you all right Deborah?"

"I will be soon. Release the song, don't give up as I did. Release him, release the king within." She rolled over whispering, "Goodbye, I need to rest."

\* \* \*

"How can I release the song? The king she called it?"

"I don't know. This is strangest diffusion I've ever been a part of."

"Diffusion?"

"The cross cultural diffusion of Wales and Mexico. There have been rumors for ages, Vikings, Irish Monks, Romans, Hebrews, Chinese, all well before Columbus; but this would be the first 'proof' I have ever been a part of. If I could even dare call it proof."

"I have to find a way."

Carlson nodded. "I suspect there must be something we need to understand about the fiddle beyond just playing it. Deborah was an accomplished musician in her time, she must have tried every bow and tuning fork imaginable and none of that worked."

"What can we try then?" asked Nikki incredulous.

"When we have exhausted all the rational we must go with the irrational. I'll get you some occult books tomorrow and we'll both research and run down any ideas we can. I want to hear this song too."

Nikki grinned, "I can't believe I have a professor that is actually suggesting magic."

Carlson shrugged.

\* \* \*

Twice over the next day, Nikki saw the dark man, Tezcatlipoca, skulking nearby at the University. Each time she made it known she saw him as well and was not openly afraid.

He looked exasperated but kept his distance.

Professor Carlson gave Nikki a stack of books saying, "If we can find the answer it will be in one of these books—I think."

The titles were varied and strange but covered a wide gulf of arcane knowledge, from Frazier's *Golden Bough* to Von Junzt's *Nameless Cults, De Vermis Mysteriis,* and even the Mayan *Popul Vuh.*

"I was reading in this one about the sacred violins of Adygea," Carlson said, "that the very sound was endowed with mystic features that alleviated pain and granted nobler qualities upon all who heard it. They had to be contained in a special fabric when not in use so that evil spirits could not steal its magic sound."

"That's all interesting, but doesn't say how to make the sound."

"What if the sound has already been stolen?"

Nikki sighed, "I don't even want to think about that. Besides if it had, would handsome there still want it?" She pointed across the library just as Tezcatlipoca disappeared again.

"I suppose not. Let's keep looking though."

"I'm exhausted and need to go home and feed Bagheera."

"All right, but take a few of these with you," he said, pushing a stack of weighty books her way.

"Of course, nothing like curling up on a Friday night with my cat and books. I'll get my degree in crazy old cat lady in no time."

Carlson smiled. "Count this crazy old dog man as your warning to solve this mystery and have a date next week."

\* \* \*

Nikki sat in her threadbare recliner reading *The Golden Bough* while a classic rock station played softly on the television. She was in the mood for classic rock after realizing that Jim Morrison had borrowed lyrics from Frazier's opus.

"Not to touch the earth, not to see the sun," she mused.

She also perused a massive tome by a Hugh Nibley about Egyptian Papyri and both books mentioned the sacredness of trees and the ritualistic killing of the king. None of this would have seemed like the proper course to play the fiddle but for her dream, the haunting vision of the green man buried beneath the great sacred tree.

The cross-cultural ties seemed to bind a lost knowledge of wisdom and sacrifice, beauty and terror. Could a king return and set things right?

Nibley's book also mentioned smashing the tree to kindling to release the trapped kings spirit. Nikki wondered if crafting the violin had done just that, a musical tribute to a magical Green King? A line in particular translated from Egyptian stood out.

*"Lift the stone and there you will find me, split the wood and there I am. In the pillar and in the tree."*

A loud knock at the door broke Nikki's wandering muse. "Who's there?" she asked with a chuckle because The Who were now playing on her television.

"Nikki," came Carlson's weak stammer.

Surprised, she jumped up and answered the door.

As the lock unlatched, the door pushed hard and Nikki was thrown backward.

Bagheera screeched as The Who roared into their climax of *'Won't Get Fooled Again'*.

Tezcatlipoca thrust Carlson inside and to the floor. He bore no weapons but had already bloodied and bruised the older man.

"I am welcome, yes?"

"Get out!" screamed Nikki.

"Not until you give me the instrument."

"Or what? You'll beat up an old man?"

"Hey!" protested Carlson.

Tezcatlipoca laughed.

"I'm calling the cops!" said Nikki, dialing.

"Call them. They cannot catch me and I'll come back."

"What do you want?"

"You know. I want the instrument."

"How do you play it?"

"It is for my ears alone."

The phone answered, "911, what's your emergency?"

Carlson struggled to stand, but Tezcatlipoca struck him again harder than Nikki would have believed possible. "Hang up. I will kill him, give the instrument to me."

Nikki hung up the phone but picked up the violin.

Tezcatlipoca reached.

Nikki held the violin in her hands and looked at the green man's face. "What would happen if I could release the song, release the king?"

"You don't know how to play it," he said, smirking gesturing with his two forefingers.

Behind Tezcatlipoca, the television gave a vision of Pete Townsend smashing his guitar onstage.

Inspiration from Nibley's book and smashing the sacred tree to kindling washed over Nikki.

"Would the Green King destroy you if he was released?"

Tezcatlipoca said nothing, but the fear in his eyes gave answer.

Carlson looked at her through bleary eyes and nodded.

Nikki raised the beautiful fiddle, just like Townsend and brought it down.

Song rang out like thunder and the Green King was released in splendid emerald light. Righteous strength returned and his arm stretched forth taking Tezcatlipoca by the neck. The demon man struggled in vain, caught in a grip strong as the tide.

"Mercy, Lord," croaked Tezcatlipoca.

The Green King retained his grip on the foe and looked to Nikki, "My thanks, daughter of Eve for releasing my song and spirit."

Stunned, Nikki could only answer, "Anytime."

"I return to my hallowed place and take my blood brother with me. The gift of my song will be yours always." The Green King shifted and his visage warped and twisted and he stepped into another realm, still holding Tezcatlipoca by the throat. They faded from view.

"Are you okay?"

Carlson got up from the floor and slumped in the chair. "Yeah, I've had worse, been a very long time but I've had worse."

"Did he call me daughter of Eve?"

"Yeah, he did. I'm sure it was meant complimentary, said Carlson."

"If you're all right," she stammered, as she glanced at her empty sheet music.

Carlson beckoned her on. He could tell what she was feeling.

Flushed with adrenalin and surprise Nikki was near to bursting with the great urge to write her own song.

## GODS IN DARKNESS

*I can calculate the motion of heavenly bodies, but not the madness of men. - Isaac Newton*

They felt a brief hard drop before the Promethean Titan snatched the three men from the grip of Gaia's pull and hurled them blindingly aloft.

The static voice of ground control crackled one last time. "Owl Eight, you are a go. This final transmission is coming to you. And fade to black."

"You got it," answered Captain Cormac 'Jack-Hammer' Ross.

The B-52 Stratofortress that had carried them seven and a half miles up, disappeared in an unfamiliar haze, far below and behind. They would continue the two hundred odd miles up on their own, in an experimental vomit comet; a modified three seater X-20 DynaSoar space plane that did not officially exist. Despite the sound dampening insulation, the roar of the second stage Titan booster rattled teeth for another two minutes as they blasted higher into the east to gain orbital push.

Azure skies bruised quickly to navy then fathomless black, as stars were suddenly kindled as if from a million pilgrim's candles as silence took them.

"We won't hear anything outside of this cockpit again until re-entry," said Captain Ross over their private intercom. His voice was grim and deep as belied a hulking man who barely dodged the maximum height requirements of the Air Force test pilots. He had piercing gray eyes and a face that seemed incapable of smiling. A scar from Korea arced down his forehead, across his right eye and ended on his lantern jaw. No amount of medals could take away the sinister look and make him presentable for the polished public expectations, and as such he was never invited to be a part of the standard astronaut program. He wasn't promotional material the colonel had said; but there was still a place with the classified and secret side of the space race, the Crypto-Cosmic side.

"Take us to the appointed Lagrange point," ordered the

mysterious passenger. A slight man with dark deep set eyes, he had a confident air enshrouding him and though clearly not military, he commanded like a Field Marshal.

"You got it."

"How many times have you been in orbit Captain Ross?" asked the passenger with an air of indifference. What looked like three strangely colored and ornately engraved medals clanked together over his tight fitting space suit.

Cormac shrugged, careless if the rear passenger could even see his response at the helm. The very notion that a relatively untrained person could tag along, flaunting what appeared to be contraband weight blatantly around his neck, grated at him. But the sole order of the mission did specify following the directions of the as yet unnamed person.

"Captain 'Jack-Hammer' Ross! He has been up, what seven times now?" answered the Co-pilot Major James Driscoll.

A blue-eyed California native, Driscoll was a respected test pilot in his own right. He had been too young for Korea but there was no good reason he had not been a part of the officially recognized space program. In contrast to Cormac, Driscoll would have been a NASA publicist's dream candidate, but now that both he and Cormac were on the Crypto-Cosmic side, all histories and records had been sanitized and sterilized.

For this "lost" aspect, each were perfect for the Crypto-Cosmic program in that neither had families. The successful and handsome Driscoll, an Irish-Catholic teetotaler, had climbed through the ranks very well for his age but he was unmarried as well as being an orphan.

No one in the program knew of any family for Cormac either, rumor said he was from Montana, but he was certainly no teetotaler.

"Eight times. He has been in orbit eight times," corrected the passenger.

"Then why'd you ask?" rumbled Cormac.

"I am making conversation. I know a good deal about both of you already, yet you know nothing of me."

Driscoll asked, "What do you know? Sir?"

"I am not a sir Major Driscoll. I am not military. But understand that I know enough classified material to have specifically requested both of you for this most unusual, yet supremely important mission."

"You can tell us your name," said Cormac, as he adjusted the yaw control of the X-20. "You have sway enough to make this operation happen, whoever you are."

"And with full-black radio silence, no less. Somebody trusts you," added Driscoll.

"I hope that does not make you nervous, but we cannot afford to have anyone overhear us. And someone is always listening."

"The Cordiglia brothers?"

"Possibly, but more importantly the Soviet's and what is left of Das Reich."

Cormac grunted at that.

"My name for now is A. H. Ryman. And I do have extreme influence at the J.P.L. and with General Manning. We would not be having this conversation otherwise."

"So do we call you A. H. or Ryman?"

"Ryman is fine. How much farther to the Lagrange point?"

Cormac glanced over the controls and calculated. "We're around halfway, but I can't promise a time frame just yet. Have some debris I need to get around. The lower Detritosphere is getting especially bad."

"Is that the official Crypto-Cosmic term for the low earth orbit region?"

"It is."

Letting the aft winglet give a tiny burst, the X-20 rolled around the oncoming twisted carcass of a shredded capsule. A portion of the booster held together by the barest skin of metal lingered alongside. A single insulated wire, like an umbilicus linked the dead ships together in cruel mockery of life.

"One of ours?" asked Driscoll.

"You could say it was mine," said Cormac.

A red star resembling nothing so much as a cheese grater identified the victim.

Ryman chuckled. "Why would you say that?"

"I made that. At this orbit, it's gotta be one of the Voskhod's I dumped a load of ball bearings on last month."

"Only one?"

"If you've read the classified reports Ryman, you know how many I've encountered."

"Encountered is not really the right word is it? Perhaps annihilated is better."

"It's my job."

"Of course it is. That is why I selected both of you. You follow orders."

Driscoll responded, "Be that as it may Mr. Ryman, I haven't fought the Red's like the 'Jack-Hammer' has."

"No one has. But we all have our talents. Mark my words, you have an important future before you, Major Driscoll. But I must admit I would like to hear more from Captain Ross about encountering Cosmonaut's."

Cormac grumbled. "You said you've read the files. We would like to know what the mission is. General Manning said we would be debriefed in orbit. You just want to look around up here? It's no Sunday in the park."

"I am quite aware that space is an intrinsically hostile environment."

"Are you?" pressed Cormac, unstrapping his shoulder harness and turning in his seat to look Ryman in the eye. "This isn't some pleasure cruise favor for a—whatever the hell you are."

"I am a senior jet propulsion engineer, an Advanced-Laboratory chemist, and most importantly, a Meta-physicist or Mancer if you will, at the absolute peak of my field."

"Whatever. It is burning cold out there and the universe doesn't care that you have dirt on Manning or that the J.P.L. owes you a real big favor, the universe will kill you in an instant all the same. So let's cut the chit chat and do the work. Tell me why I'm up here."

Driscoll gulped. "You have dirt on Manning?"

Ryman laughed without mirth before answering. "Quite. General Manning has a penchant for the asphyxiation of young homeless prostitutes. All the pretty young things that have taken Kerouac, Cassady and Ginsberg into their naive little hearts."

"Who?"

"I would not expect you to know Major Driscoll."

"Damn beatniks," muttered Cormac.

Again Driscoll balked at Ryman's revelations. "How could General Manning do that? How do you know all this?"

"Let us just say that I am not without sin. And if you had any idea of the former gatherings at 'the Parsonage' which was the Agape Lodge, you would not need to ask."

"Lodge? Like the Freemason's?"

"You delight me Major Driscoll. Your fraternal order is similar yet different. I am the current, yet disputed, Outer Head of the Order of the O.T.O. Lodge. Which is centered around Thelema or more plainly, following the Whole of the Law."

"Whole of the law? Good, I was afraid you might be weirdoes."

Cormac looked at Driscoll and rolled his eyes.

"And as far as you need to be concerned Major Driscoll, I am the J.P.L. these days, if only from the shadows."

"You?" said Driscoll, shaking his head within his stationary helm. "Jet Propulsion Labs are a conglomeration beyond any one man."

Ryman answered, "And you forget that the J.P.L. was Jack Parson's Lab before that. I should know, I was his unspoken right hand. I was there when the mercury fulminate explosion took his life. You remember that, do you not Captain?"

Cormac shook his head. "Nope. I was in Korea, shooting down Chi-Com's."

"Your services were greatly appreciated then, as they are now."

Driscoll broke in, "What does Jack Parsons have to do with anything now?"

"Not a thing, I simply walk the same path he did."

"Will someone just tell me what the hell I'm doing here," said Cormac. "What is the mission?"

"Patience. Get us to the Lagrange point and all will be revealed."

The curtain of darkness flexed larger as the earth shrunk. The stars cast cold light from the distant reaches as Cormac continued his hawk-like ascent to a higher orbit. He occasionally swung the X-20 wide of various cascading jetsam. Some of the floating debris was ice covered and alien; catching light like a swarm of fireflies, it went in every possible direction contrasting to the usual human expectation of earthbound flotsam caught in a single flowing current.

"This is my third mission," said Driscoll, "and you never get used to it."

"To what?" asked Ryman.

"The sheer beauty of the earth. Right down there, the Bahama's. Turquoise perfection. Clouds sprinkled like newly fallen snow. And in a few minutes, the Straits of Gibraltar like only God can see them."

"A god. Indeed."

"Just wait until we get to the night side," said Driscoll. "All the city lights almost make it seem like it's all a kingdom in some fairy tale."

Both astronauts noticed that Ryman displayed no interest in seeing the truly rare vista. It was as if the very idea were beneath him and somehow vulgar. He instead watched them piloting the X-20 over and under the clouds of stardust.

Farther on, they saw a gray suited body rolling toward them in the ether. CCCP was emblazoned across the top of the figures helmet. The mirror like faceplate hid the certain death mask behind. A six foot tether dangled uselessly from the body harness.

"Friend of yours?" asked Ryman, with an edge begging for something more.

"Probably," said Driscoll, "the Ruskies started calling Captain Ross the Rezuhin, on their private channels."

"I do not speak Russian."

"It means 'Cutter'. There is no one they fear more."

"What do they do when you cut them loose?"

"Well they don't take it kindly," snarled Cormac.

"I mean what is the reaction when they have lost the encounter?"

"Every single time, the stupid bastards start flapping their arms trying to swim through space. It's pathetic," said Cormac, stifling a chuckle. "Fear makes everyone forget their training."

"This is what I hoped we could talk about. Hearing it firsthand is so much better than reading a sterile military report. Tell me more."

Composing himself back to the humorless edge, Cormac said, "It's simple. Once they are out of reach of their own ship with a cut line, that's it. Ten feet away from your capsule, might as well be ten miles. You can't swim through space and you can't get back with nothing in the vacuum of space to push against."

"What do they do when they realize it is hopeless?"

"They die." Cormac furrowed his brow, answering, "I once saw a cosmonaut accept his fate and cut his own airline, rather than drift for hours in hopeless despair."

"Brutal work. Yet you never used a gun?"

"Not up here with the weight requirements. In theory, I was never supposed to get out and space walk. Offensively we are only supposed to outmaneuver the Red's and drop ball bearings in their path. Their capsules can't turn and get out of the way. They become what you saw back there. That was actually the biggest piece of one I've ever seen. Must have only winged him."

Cormac went to rub his chin out of habit and hit the smooth face plate and put his hand down before continuing. "But the Soviets send more men up on virtual suicide missions than you could ever shake a stick at. I had to get out and start cutting tethers when they got outside first and started messing with our satellites."

"How many cosmonauts have you killed?"

"I couldn't say. I don't always know how many they have inside their capsules."

"But outside, face to face, cutting them loose?"

Cormac paused a moment. He considered himself a soldier, perhaps even a knight errant, doing what needed to be done as he understood it, but Ryman's prying bordered on sick fascination, too eager even for scholarly interest. Besides after being debriefed a dozen times, the egg-heads had put together an Ultra-classified space combat manual, why didn't Ryman just read that? Unless he wanted to hear about death from the dealer himself. "Twelve."

"A noble lot indeed," said Ryman.

"But you asked about guns and I told you about weight

requirements, so I have to ask about yours."

Driscoll nudged Cormac for asking, but Ryman grinned.

"You noticed these," he said, jingling the three talismans.

Driscoll scrutinized them. "They don't look like anything I've ever seen before. I almost wondered if you received the Bronze in the Olympics, but those aren't bronze."

"No. They are most certainly not medals," Ryman sneered. "Do not trouble yourself over our weight requirements Captain Ross. We still have your standard offensive cargo should the need arise, though it is a good twenty pounds lighter."

"Twenty pounds?"

"I assure you Captain Ross, my contraband, as you so colorfully refer to it, is not more than twenty pounds. Perhaps no more than ten."

"What else you got?"

"Reading material. A training manual you might say."

"You are two hundred miles above the earth for a very limited time frame. What the hell are you gonna read?"

"As I said, do not trouble yourself with worry over this minor change in your standard operating procedure. We are indeed under your weight ratios for our fuel and mission parameters. Besides," he paused a good long while, "I know very well that despite your self-righteous indignation, you personally eliminated three ball bearings to effectively counter your own contraband."

Driscoll turned to Cormac in disbelief. "What is he talking about? Tell me you didn't bring anything you weren't supposed to."

"All right, ya got me on that one, prick."

"What was that Captain Ross?"

"I said you're a prick."

"What did you bring?" demanded Driscoll.

"Just my Arkansas toothpick."

No words came from Driscoll's mouth for a moment. "You brought a knife to space? We have tools, we have—."

"You never asked how I took care of those Red's did you? You were just glad I did. So let's leave it at that." Cormac gave sharp glances to his two companions. "I've used wrenches too. This is quicker."

"This is highly irregular."

"Least I didn't bring a damn book."

Ryman spoke soothingly. "I assure you both. No one will be reported for any of this. General Manning is well aware of Captain Ross's barbaric implements and if there is one thing neither one of us will do, it is punish results."

Unwilling to let it go Driscoll muttered, "You broke protocol."

"Shut up."

There was a tense silence for a few moments until Driscoll piped up. "What are those not-medals then Mr. Ryman?"

"They are pentacles. These for the Moon, these Jupiter and these is for Saturn. They are vital for dealing with my mission."

"Your mission?"

"Quite. Your mission is to specifically get me to the Lagrange point and deal with any troubles therein. My mission begins and should in short time finish, afterward you are to bring me back to earth Captain Ross."

Driscoll looked puzzled.

"Do not trouble yourself Major Driscoll. I simply expect Captain Ross to be more capable at eliminating the threat posed by anything we encounter. I have no doubts that you will do your best in the coming exchange."

"Do you really expect a threat?"

"Certainly. The Soviets will not simply hand me control of their secret space station!"

Dead silence reigned for a cosmic moment as each man took that revelation to task.

"Soviet's don't have a space station yet," said Cormac, breaking the stillness.

Ryman gave a venomous chortle. "Do not be offended that they seem to have made it past you and the rest of the Crypto-Cosmic Command. They have done so a handful of times already Captain Ross. Not that it really matters. We have known for some time what it is they were building and have allowed them to do the dirty work of constructing and putting it into orbit. We are going to take their weapon, called a Salyut, and turn it against them."

"If you don't mind my asking Mr. Ryman, but how could you know that? My understanding is that all the best spies were caught inside Star City and horribly tortured and killed. There's no way you could know what a secret Soviet space station is being outfitted with. I've heard they don't even tell the Politburo the half of it," said Driscoll.

"What do they have?"

"Patience Captain Ross, all will be revealed soon enough. My talents have granted some insight into the Soviets capabilities. Suffice to say, I have seen for myself what the Soviets intend to do."

"Not good enough."

"You were told to follow orders. That you would be debriefed in orbit. What part of that do you not understand?"

"We have a right to know," said Driscoll. "Why not tell us? It can't be that much farther."

"You ought to grace us with your master plan." Cormac agreed, "I'll have us at the Lagrange point in twenty minutes."

Ryman grimaced before answering. "Very well, since you both are my most trusted liaisons, I can reveal some of my knowledge. I use the will of the Universe, the very ether to learn all. Some have taken to referring to it as a sixth sense, some remote viewing, others sorcery and Magick."

"What do you call it?"

"Sorcery."

"That sounds like you believe in the occult," spat Driscoll.

"I do not believe in the occult," said Ryman. "I participate in it. Mere belief is quite different."

"How?"

"Magick is the result of willful intent."

"So a workable faith then?"

"*You* could say that," said Ryman, sneering.

"What does any of this—magic do for you? What did you learn?"

"Astute as ever Captain Ross. I learned that there are forces within the Soviet machine, specifically the paranormal branch of the

NKVD, the GUMOD, that have their own dark agenda and are working against me."

"Who with the what?"

"Professor Andreiev, head of GUMOD, the Soviet Administration of Occultic and Magical Affairs."

"I don't follow. What's this got to do with the here and now?"

"True men of power have always controlled the people through the gods, whether black or white, light or dark, real or unreal."

"What?"

"I have said far too much to the uninitiated. How far to the Lagrange point?"

"Is that where the Red's are?"

"No, it is not. It should be the high ground above the Salyut's orbit so that we can swoop down on them."

"There is no high ground in space, unless we are at the top of the gravity well—which we aren't. They'll see us coming."

"Are you telling me that you cannot accomplish this mission? Are you telling me that you, the 'Jack-Hammer', are not capable of dealing with perhaps three cosmonauts?"

"I want to hear you say it."

"Gladly. They are to be eliminated with extreme prejudice."

"What is their secret weapon?" asked Driscoll.

"They have a nuclear reactor aboard their new Salyut space station. It is attached to a Soyuz module and paired with some minor communication relays. This station will be turned against us as soon as it is fully operational. We must destroy it. I brought forth a plan to take over the thing and give us an ultimate weapon that will dominate and reinvent the world. Any who stand against us, will taste an entropic bomb, especially Moscow."

Cormac said nothing, but went to rub his chin again, but for the faceplate.

Driscoll shook his head. "This isn't right. We could disable and destroy it. We don't have to be instrumental in killing thousands of innocent people and starting a war. I did understand you didn't I, Mr. Ryman? You are suggesting mass murder!"

Ryman answered in a quick jerking succession of syllables, "Of course not, you stupid man. I will perform the Oath of the Abyss and open a gate, a dimensional window if you will; afterward I shall summon an ancient power undreamed of—I will control the dark matter entities and make an entropic bomb that will grant me passage and control of the Qliphothic realm."

Cormac raised an eyebrow at Driscoll.

"Seems awful complicated, Mr. Ryman," said Driscoll.

"It is the simplest plan possible. It will enable a new age, born in darkness to return through the veil, a link of materia to ultrateria. A union of the void and its dark disciples. Ultimately, I will eliminate the outdated uselessness of the nuclear bomb."

Cormac scoffed, "What the hell are you talking about?"

Ryman went quiet, staring daggers at them.

"Maybe he has space dementia," suggested Driscoll. "Take a drink from your line Mr. Ryman."

"I don't know," said Cormac, "but that Red space station is just ahead and above."

"I thought we were supposed to have the high ground?"

"The gyroscopes might be off. I put the star tracker in sync with Canopus, but with our attitude and climb we've probably gone off course a titch. Not unusual, especially with this kinda' ramrod mission thrown together at the last minute before any of the regular tech's could check us out."

"What's that hum?"

A pervasive yet undulating buzz violated the tranquility of their headsets.

Cormac and Driscoll exchanged raised eyebrows, and looked behind at Ryman reading his book. The massive dark tome was held together by a thick leather cover, bronze clasps at the edges were green with age, while yellowed parchment made up its myriad pages. The lettering appeared to be hand written ink of various shades from cobalt blue to ghostly black and finally blood red.

The hum was Ryman.

He muttered archaic sounding phrases repeatedly under his breath, the words hardly captured by the two way radio. "In the beginning there was naught but darkness, untainted by shape or form. Then came the light. It scorched its way into the darkness, marring the smooth beauty of nullity with its unnatural essence, cauterizing the wounds it had caused by its mere presence." His chant broke in varied pitches of primeval verse, emphasizing the eldritch and unholy rhyme.

"Ryman!" Cormac barked. "Snap out of it. If this mission is your operation, you'd better tell the doctor where it hurts."

"I am preparing for this confrontation Captain Ross. You know what needs to be done! You will dock us beside the station, dispatch the crew and I will do what is truly the important work of ages."

Ryman turned his radio off, but they could still see his lips moving as he continued his mantra of the diabolic book.

"You haven't fought them hand to hand before. You ready for it?"

"As I'll ever be."

"Remember, if your suit gets cut, or your faceplate is ruptured, exhale immediately. Get all the breath out of your lungs. You will feel tension on exposed skin, you will have swelling. But you have some time to make it to an airlock, ours or theirs, doesn't matter. Then it's just animal savagery."

"What if my line gets cut?"

"Anything that you can use to retain a grip on a solid surface will help. I've chewed gum."

"Gum?"

"Yeah, some wiry little cosmonaut cut my line two missions ago, while his partner smashed my faceplate in with their multi-tool. I lost my wrench doing the same to him as I exhaled."

"Your faceplate was smashed and your line was cut?"

"I'm telling you from experience, so you know it can be done. The wiry cosmonaut shoved me and I went swinging out, grabbed my gum, and used it hold onto the Voskhod's solar vanes. I crawled back and made that bastard pay."

"How did you exhale and keep your gum?"

"Through my nose Driscoll! Didn't you ever go diving?"

"No, I haven't."

"Do it. It's the only reason I'm still alive and they're dead.

Remember that know-it-all idiot Lieutenant Cluff? That dumb bastard didn't exhale. He got the bends and died."

"They said that was a training exercise."

"This is a training exercise—if it fails. Otherwise we are just silent weapons for quiet wars."

As Cormac brought the X-20 in for a final yo-yoing approach, the night side came over them in a sweeping mantle of ebon couched darkness, fracturing the last rays of sunlight.

Driscoll stayed quiet a moment, deep in thought before saying, "I'd like to think I am contributing more than that. Something for the greater good."

"Yeah, me too. But it is what it is."

"Are we going to die?"

"I made peace with that answer a long time ago."

"If not for the greater good then why do it?"

Cormac snorted. "It's the only thing I'm good at."

He brought the X-20 into a violating rendezvous with the bizarre Soviet station. A hybrid made from the Salyut and Soyuz modules, the station seemed almost stationary in the vast deep of space. A pincer-like armature from the X-20's left winglet, grasped a jutting solar panel wing on the side of the station causing the entire unholy union to subtly change its orbital spin as the whole body shook and twisted.

Cormac pulled his Bowie knife from the side of his seat. "If they didn't already know, they sure as hell do now."

"That bad?"

"It's all bad, but maybe if we scared them enough, they'll slip up. You want to hear them bark at us? White found their frequency last week."

The intercom crackled a quick spray of angry Russian.

"What did they say?"

"They said, they were going to kill us if we didn't leave."

"What if they saw us coming and are ready?"

Cormac growled, shaking his head. "Listen, we've been in our pressurized suits the whole time. They haven't. They'll be sick and easier pickings. You take the wrench. If I'm fast enough, you won't even need to swing it."

"I still don't feel right about this. Not face to face."

Ryman broke in, "Trust me Major Driscoll. This needs to happen. We must break with these melodramatic excuses of moralistic right and wrong. The Soviets are attempting a means to destroy and rule us, we must turn the balance and take back what is ours by dark divine right!"

"Yeah, yeah. You ready for this Ryman? Let's go."

"Captain Ross, I am not a physical combatant. I am not getting out of the space plane until you clear all obstacles."

"Course. Never mind, if Driscoll and I get killed you don't know how to pilot this thing home in one piece."

"I would find a way."

"I'll bet you would try."

"Quite."

"I'm opening the airlock. Hold on to your damned book."

"You have no idea."

Cormac secured his Bowie knife with a strap about his left arm and gave a thumbs up to Driscoll. The radio crackled as the Russian's demands were again ignored. A sudden rush of pressure stole whatever oxygen had stowed away within the X-20.

Twin doors opened a portal to the vacuum of space. Stars set hard against deep black gave cold unfeeling light.

"Unbuckle, we gotta move faster than they do."

Floating in the dark ether, Cormac raised above his seat and floated over the top of Ryman still clutching his book. He secured a fifty-five foot line from an anchored reel to his harness and beckoned the same to the other two men, he then went through the black gate to the outside void.

Driscoll followed suit, looking back once at the gleeful Ryman still seated and perusing his infernal book.

As Driscoll pushed himself up and out the X-20, Cormac grabbed his shoulder and guided him to a short antennae sticking off the side of the Salyut.

Cormac motioned to the stations airlock. "They'll have a second one over on the ass-end of the Soyuz. I imagine they will swarm out of each hatch."

"Why aren't they out already?"

"They're suiting up and pressurizing themselves. Probably think they can take care of us based on sheer numbers."

"Numbers?"

Cormac signaled he was turning off his radio and for Driscoll to do the same.

Driscoll did as the experienced cold warrior asked. Looking behind Cormac, he tried to take in the vast black gulfs beyond.

Cormac leaned his faceplate against Driscoll's, so they clacked together. The sound could only be heard inside the helmets as the vibrations resonated solely through the air in that tiny space. "This is the only way no one can hear us."

"?"

"Listen! Ryman is up to no good, it's like he wants us to fail. There is no way there are only three Red's on a station this big and that is obviously still under construction. Something fishy is going on."

"What do we tell Manning and Crypto-Cosmic Command?"

"Does it matter? They agreed to this whole operation. We're in for the long haul, but I don't buy Ryman's story. He wants something else."

"What if he's right? Maybe they have a bomb or something?"

"I doubt it."

"What then?"

"Don't get me wrong, having a bomb in space is an advantage, but it's not enough on its own. We will always retaliate and give them our own endgame scenario and everybody still loses. Until the advantage is so far in one direction, nobody will ever have the sand to press that button."

"Then why are we really here?"

"Ryman wants the station for something, but none of the logical answers make sense."

"What if he is telling the truth?"

"He's not."

With that, Cormac turned his radio back on and pointed at a

face staring at them through the portal window of the Salyut.

"That was a woman!" Driscoll blurted.

"Yeah, the Red's are real progressive."

The radio crackled again with a stern Russian's accent coming through. "American running dogs of the capitalist pigs. You hears us. You are given your last warnings. You will take your craft and illegal war and leave or we will be forced to bring death to you."

"What do we—?

"Just hold on. They always threaten a few times."

The Russian tried one last time. "Americans you are given your last warnings. We will shoot you!"

Driscoll looked at Cormac then back to the face in the portal window.

Cormac drawled, unconvinced, "They're bluffing."

"And if they're not?"

"The Soviet Command wouldn't let them bring extra weight on one of those capsules. Star City limits what they can bring, down to the fraction of an ounce. Their hypergolic fuel is too heavy. Nobody gave them a gun, more likely they know 'the Cutter' is here and somebody's already evacuated into their suit."

A clear line interrupted from Ryman. "Why do you not have control of that station yet Captain Ross?"

"Red's haven't invited me in yet."

"So get inside and deal with them."

"I didn't want to make a mess."

"The messier the better," snapped Ryman. "Make the Soviet's bleed."

Pointing at the hatch, Cormac said, "Let's try and open that and get inside."

Driscoll threw his weight into it but only succeeded in spinning himself. "It's locked."

"I told you, they were bluffing about having guns. Let me try." The bigger man strained against the hatch but made no progress against it. Cormac ordered, "Bang your wrench on that portal. They'll move."

Driscoll knocked the wrench against the portal window. The

force of the blow threw him back and he had to retain a stronger grip alongside the station. Just holding the wrench with his gloved hand was hard enough, but Driscoll imagined that back on earth he would have easily crushed a car window.

The Russian negotiator barked, "Americans! You will cease this unlawful disruptions of Soviet space!"

There was little chance of Driscoll being able to smash in the portal window. But this was an unnerving feeling that if the portal window failed and cracked, everyone inside would be dead in seconds. Fear made them leave their true and relative safety.

"You leave us no choice Americans!" crackled the reply.

"You got it," Cormac said over the com-link to the Russians. It was the only response he had given their channel yet.

"Watch for that lower airlock on the Soyuz below us."

Driscoll struck the portal window again, leaving a tiny white scrape but no real damage. He looked at what from his perspective seemed to be down at the Soyuz module.

"Poyekhali!" snapped the radio.

"What did that Russian say?"

"He said, 'Let's go'."

What had been dark below, gave a shaft of light. The lower hatch had been opened.

"They're coming out!"

"Keep steady. They're cold bastards when they want to be."

The hatch beside Cormac suddenly popped open.

Oxygen and water vapor blasted out into space.

Cormac moved in to slash the Russian.

A cosmonaut in an orange space suit stood just inside the airlock, a strange triple-barreled pistol in hand.

Shocked that his opponent had a gun, Cormac lunged left.

A mute projectile erupted from the gun barrel. Smoke and phantom blue flame leapt out.

The bullet narrowly missed Cormac beside the hatch, only because the gunman had not been prepared to swing his weapon fast enough, nor had he braced himself for the impact it gave in zero gravity. The gun flung him backward against the airlock wall.

Cormac maneuvered himself around and above the hatch, ready to strike like an asp when the gunman emerged.

"Help!" Driscoll cried.

Three cosmonaut's came at him from all sides, wielding strange dual-use Soviet tools. One had a hammer with a crude spike on the backside. Doubtless a utilitarian instrument but deadly none the less.

"There's too many!"

Driscoll batted away their strikes, barely fending off the attack, never capable of taking the real fight to them.

"I can't hold them off!"

Waiting what seemed an eternity, Cormac tensed ready to strike the gunman.

"Arrgh!"

The gunman didn't or wouldn't exit the airlock.

"Cormac! Help!"

Cormac watched Driscoll take several more hits, though the labored presence of his voice over the radio said his suit had not been ruptured, yet.

Fearful the gunman would appear the moment he moved, Cormac launched himself off the Salyut at full force and all possible speed. He kept one hand on his line and at the right moment tugged on the secure tether bringing his bulk as close to where he needed to be as possible.

A painful grunt spat over the radio.

Cormac raced not to aid Driscoll directly but to where the Russian's tethers came across the bow of the Salyut.

Stout refined rope, strong enough for mountain climbers and wrapped in a protective film held the cosmonaut's in trusted thrall but it was no match for sharp meteoric steel.

Rather than fight the cosmonaut's, Cormac cut their lines before they realized he was there.

Loose, the first cosmonaut struggled to grab a comrade. The other panicked and yanked on the line, only granting enough tension to ease Cormac's slice through the tether. The cosmonaut's line went slack and he floated mere inches beyond reach of the safety of the ship. He flapped his arms and legs wildly in futility.

With a companion grasping onto his shoulder, the last of the three cosmonaut's halted his attack on Driscoll to focus on Cormac.

Cormac missed cutting the thirds tether, his gut told him to move.

An arc light of blue flame and smoke erupted, narrowly missing Cormac.

The 'Jack-Hammer' wheeled to see the gunman preparing for another shot.

Griping his own tether, Cormac wrenched mightily and sweeping hard right, he clothes-lined the gunman.

His finger on the trigger, the gunman shot again forcing himself back against the ship.

Racing toward this most dangerous assailant, Cormac brought his knife to bear.

The gun toting cosmonaut struggled for balance, tripping backward against the solar vanes of the Salyut. He prepared to shoot again and realized his mistake.

Cormac cut his tether.

The cosmonaut's momentum kept him going backward, off and away from the capsule. Floating freely away and off balance he attempted one more shot.

The explosive gas rocketed from the triple-barreled gun sending the cosmonaut away at greater speed, while the bullet went past Cormac and was lost in the far-flung cosmos. The shooters body spun end over end until it too vanished in the void of darkness.

The last cosmonaut still fighting, battered away at Driscoll. The Californian fended off the attack as best he could with an oversized wrench. But clearly dominating the confrontation, the Soviet loomed over the American, trying to smash his faceplate in.

The second cosmonaut clung to the solar panel of the Soyuz like a man hanging on to a life raft in a raging storm. He seemed incapable of action, likely in shock from his near death in the emptiness of the infinite black sea behind him.

"Captain Ross, you need to assist Major Driscoll," crackled Ryman through the radio.

"What do you think I've been doing?"

"I cannot allow the Russian's to sacrifice him."

"Sacrifice?" The 'Jack-Hammer' sped toward Driscoll and the cosmonaut's.

Turning to face him, the cosmonaut swung his hammer in swift yet exaggerated round-houses. "Stay back or will kill your comrade most brutal."

Cormac edged closer.

"Think will you to leave this place ever? Murderer!" said the Russian. "Your bones never to orbit leave!"

"You first Ivan."

"Warmongering dog! I fix you!"

Cormac leaned back just out of impact of the hammers swing.

Three times the cosmonaut attempted to strike, on the last swing Cormac rushed inside the extended reach and jammed his knife to the hilt into the cosmonaut's ribs. He twisted and tore the blade out.

Blood boiled, pluming swiftly through the puncture in a cloud of crimson steam.

The cosmonaut screamed as even the saliva on his tongue boiled, returning to a gaseous state. His cries abruptly went silent though he remained alive a few more seconds as the oxygen fled from his suit. Eyelids sunk as eyeballs swelled outward, the face stretched and warped into a fearful mask of horror.

Cormac sliced the tether and pushed the corpse away to drift in the eternal night.

The first cosmonaut cut loose, slowly drifted farther away, kicking and screaming while the frightfully paralyzed one clung tenaciously to the solar vane.

Cormac helped Driscoll stand as upright as they could comprehend. "You all right?"

"Bruised but I'm not broken. What do we do about that one?"

The cosmonaut shivered in fear, not even looking up at his captor's.

"Don't know. I never killed one who wasn't trying to kill me before. You want too?" He held his Bowie out, handle first.

"No."

"You sure?"

Ryman's voice broke the predicament. "Captain Ross. Major Driscoll. Is the station contained?"

"No, sit tight. We have taken out the four cosmonauts who greeted us, but there is at least one more inside. We also have one, hanging on to the solar panel."

"Excellent, bind him and take him back inside the station once you have secured it."

"Yes sir...I mean Mr. Ryman."

Using the shaking cosmonaut's own cut tether, Cormac and Driscoll bound up his arms tight enough that he could not use them. They tugged him toward the airlock and looked in.

"Get in precious," said Cormac, as he pushed the cosmonaut through the opening. They attached their own tether lines to a bar near the airlock so that they could easily retrieve them upon leaving the station.

\* \* \*

Inside the cramped airlock, they waited while the pressure equalized to a bare minimum.

"What or who is inside waiting for us?"

This particular cosmonaut apparently spoke no English and only watched their questions and nodded with a false sense of understanding.

"No idea. But since they actually had a gun this time, let's keep Brezhnev here, in front of us as we open the hatch."

"How did you learn to move so well in space?"

"I treat it like diving without the water. I use all the momentum I can to go where I want. I don't do anything I don't need to. Plus the tether can be manipulated more than anyone ever understands. Kinda like a pendulum. The Red's would be getting better at it, if I wasn't killing them first."

"Things will change. They bring guns because of you and your knife."

Cormac shrugged, and turned to watch the gauges. "It's finished. We can remove our helmets while we are inside. I hate having these things on this long. Too hot."

"It's only been two hours."

Cormac shrugged again before unclasping the seal and pulling off the cumbersome apparatus.

Driscoll spun the handle opening the airlock to the inside of the station.

On the other side, a pale surprised face greeted them. It was the woman they had seen earlier. It took her a splintered moment to realize her comrade was not alone.

"Sergei! What have you done to him?" she asked, brushing a lock of red hair out of her face.

"Back off sister," said Cormac, with a hand upraised. "Against the wall."

She looked to flee but knew as well as they did that it would be futile in the tight quarters of the station.

"Is anyone else aboard the station?"

"Nyet."

Her green eyes contained an angry defiant fire. Even with the space suit on, anyone would have known from the curves that it was a woman inside.

Cormac paused a bit long before answering, "There better not be. Check it out Driscoll, real careful like. Make your way down and secure and lock that lower hatch. No surprises before his satanic majesty comes aboard."

"I heard that," crackled Ryman.

Driscoll gave a salute and went to an adjoining passage that would take him down into the rest of the station.

The shivering cosmonaut Sergei mumbled, "Skazheete pozhluista...?"

Cormac looked to the woman saying, "Tell him to shut up. And for the sake of my companions, only speak English from now on. Understand?"

She nodded and whispered a hush to Sergei who seemed content to hang his head in shame and say nothing more. "He fears they will send him to the gulag for this failure."

"That's tomorrows worry."

"Da."

"We have your station. I took care of your other men outside so there is nothing left for you to do except cooperate. Got that?" He made sure she could see the Bowie knife. On Earth, blood would still have been dripping off the blade, but here it had all boiled off. "I'm Captain Cormac Ross. What's your name?"

"You are only a Captain? I am *Major* Ludmilla Serakovna."

"Don't get any ideas sister, I'm already taking orders from a civilian."

"Captain Cormac Ross? You are the 'Rezuhin', yes?"

"You got it."

"You have killed many of my comrades, my friends."

"Yeah, so?"

"You are here to take our station, to take our lives?"

"If I was going to do that I wouldn't still be talking to you."

"Did you say that to the men outside? The ones you cut loose to die?"

"Orders. A fight is a fight. Can't do any less."

"Any less? What you did is the worst fate possible."

"Not hardly."

"Your American pride makes you a cruel and unkind people."

Cormac stifled a laugh. "Nails aren't made from good iron, nor are soldiers made from kind men. You're a major, you should know that."

Driscoll's voice crackled, "Station—station is all clear. Ryman can come aboard."

Cormac looked Ludmilla and Sergei over before responding. "You got that Ryman? You should be able to follow our tethers right to the airlock, decompress and come in."

"Roger that Captain Ross. I am coming over to the station."

Driscoll came floating up from a passage leading to the Soyuz, pulling himself along. His face was flushed and pale, sweat beaded across his forehead despite the overall cool inside temperature. "I looked out the window, thought at first I was seeing things. I am sure—I saw it.

"What?"

Driscoll rubbed his eyes. "We are moving at seventeen thousand miles an hour and the horizontal outlook is constantly changing but—"

"But what?"

"I thought I saw the stars blot out and then this 'Leviathan' moved toward us."

"Did you get hit in the head by those Red's? Any broken bones?"

"No, just bruises. I'm serious, I saw something. Something huge, yet almost intangible."

"Dementia?"

"Knock it off. I know what I saw."

"Do you?"

"No." Driscoll looked out the portal, scanning for anything beyond the stars. "It's gone. But it was something real."

Cormac rolled his eyes and made a face. "Probably just one of the Ivan's doing the backstroke through the Detritosphere." He rummaged through the cosmonaut's supply cabinet, tossing things he was not interested in into the air where they floated haphazardly.

Ludmilla, listening intently to Driscoll asked, "Was it toward the Gagarin quadrant?"

Driscoll shook his head. "I don't know where that is, but it was that way." He pointed up above the Earth and toward the left of the station.

She nodded. "We have been taking readings on strange energy above the poles. I have wondered what could be causing the radical fluctuations."

Cormac laughed. "They brought a bottle of vodka and some Cubans. I'm keeping 'em."

"It was big, black as tar. I didn't like how I felt seeing it," said Driscoll, before turning to watch the deep gloom. "It was soul crushing. Made me question my faith."

"My father spoke of elder things when I was a girl. Malevolent beings that watch our world. They hunger and look with disdain upon mere mortals who dwell in the light."

"Why would God allow such a thing?"

Ludmilla looked as if she wanted to respond, but couldn't.

"You sap."

Cormac lit one of the Cuban's. The zero-G flame hung low and close on the match head like a blue swimmers cap instead of flaring orange as it would have on Earth. "You are playing right into her Commie hands. Of course Moscow Milla is gonna tell you there is a bogey man out there. Act like the operator you are and don't fall for her tricks."

"Why are you smoking?"

"For science? Why else do you think they brought them up here?"

"Ryman hasn't given us the go ahead to do whatever we want. There could be sensitive equipment and what about our air supply?"

"Not my air. Besides the Red's brought it. It shouldn't be wasted," he said, opening the vodka.

"Keep your wits about you. I am sure I saw something out there."

"Muh-huh," gurgled Cormac, as he guzzled a large burning mouthful.

Ludmilla gave an audible sigh. "That was for celebration of successful station completion."

"Then why isn't it gone?"

"We were not yet complete."

"And the Cuban's?"

"Commander Arkady had them. I do not think he intended to use them. I think he was to give them as gifts that have been to space."

"Yeah, that's rich," said Cormac, blowing plumes throughout the cabin.

Driscoll intervened, "We still have a mission to do. I'd rather not have to put my helmet and air back on. Not to mention whatever is out there."

"Drop it will ya?" Cormac took another pull on the Kalishnakov vodka before putting the cap back on. "We all see weird things out there. Ice, rocks, capsule fragments. It doesn't mean anything."

Ludmilla took the vodka from a surprised Cormac saying, "It is true. Something is out there. You may check the data yourselves."

She took a swift swallow herself.

"I may?" Though Cormac could speak and read Russian, he could not fathom the Soviet scientific equipment Ludmilla directed him toward. "No thanks, I didn't bring my decoder ring."

"You are a very bitter man. Who did this to you? A woman, yes?" she said taking a second pull.

Cormac ignored her and clicked his radio. "Ryman, you in the airlock yet?"

A long static crackle materialized into Ryman's voice. "I am just taking in the majesty of night. This is as close as I have ever been to the True Greater Dark. I can almost touch the void."

"Yeah. You'd better get in here, Driscoll is having as many flights of fancy as you are."

"You have no conception of the very gravity of the situation Captain Ross."

"Gravity? It's Zero-G, Ryman. Get in here and maybe we can sort things out and get going on the mission."

"Patient as ever Captain Ross, always the dutiful soldier. I am reaching the airlock."

"Good. Make sure you have that outer hatch fully locked. Then press the button with the Cyrillic flat-topped A."

"Yes, I am about to climb in. It is more difficult than I would have thought. My hands are sore—I—Damn you! No!"

"What is it? Ryman?"

Unintelligible groaning echoed over the intercom.

"What do we do?" asked Driscoll.

"Is he inside the airlock?" Cormac directed the question at Ludmilla.

She shook her head. "He has not opened the hatch. It is safe. When you open one side, the other cannot be opened."

To Driscoll, Cormac ordered, "You stay here, I'll go get him."

"What if—what I saw grabbed him?"

"You didn't see anything." Cormac said. "Get a hold of yourself. You have space dementia. There isn't anything out there. He probably dropped his book." Cormac looked at Ludmilla as he spoke. She had a coy expression on her face. Oh she is good he thought, playing up any slight advantage to benefit her fight against us.

"Don't lose this," Cormac ordered, as he extinguished his cigar.

Driscoll rubbed his eyes and looked out the portal window. "I saw something. I have a bad feeling about this."

Cormac strapped his helmet on and adjusted the sealant. "Keep your head on." He climbed into the airlock. "Ryman, hold tight. I'm coming to get you."

A panic ridden cry came from Ryman's radio but there were no words.

\* \* \*

Mere minutes in the chamber stretched into an eternity for Cormac. Speed was half the reason he became a pilot, waiting only made him angry.

The light flashed and Cormac reached for the handle to open the hatch. He did so carefully and deliberately, prepared for the worst.

He saw nothing behind the door.

Inching out of the capsule, he looked for any sign of Ryman or whatever had made him cry out.

Nothing.

Naught but pin-pricked blackness stretching infinitely beyond.

Cormac pulled himself halfway out of the airlock when a force bludgeoned him. It glanced across his helmet but the brunt went to his right shoulder, knocking him almost all the way back inside.

An orange suited cosmonaut with a Baikonur wrench stood there.

Cormac caught himself and struck back with a left hook; hitting the cosmonaut squarely in the knee. An unsatisfactory and equally useless assault.

Unfazed, the cosmonaut hit Cormac on the helmet with the wrench.

A strangely earthen clang echoed in Cormac's head before being joined by another strike.

Reaching higher, Cormac punched at the unprotected groin with a sterilizing intensity.

This halted the cosmonaut's attack.

Exiting the airlock, Cormac quickly attached himself to a tether and drew his knife and faced the cosmonaut who had recovered somewhat on an even keel. He could not see Ryman anywhere, but focus remained on his opponent.

The Russian had tied one of the much shorter, cut tethers to his own waist harness. That he had survived floating freely in space was in itself a dark miracle.

"How'd you get here? If I wasn't gonna kill you, I'd take you to Vegas."

The cosmonaut gestured as if he still had the gun and held up four fingers.

"You shot yourself back? Lucky bastard. Let's dance."

"Poyekhali," said the cosmonaut, hefting his wrench.

The two men bounded together, crashing blows in a slow dance of brutal menace.

The Russian had to respect Cormac's blade and Cormac in turn had to avoid the skull crushing blows of the Baikonur wrench.

Back and forth they struggled atop the world, champions of east and west, paragons of their lands and very ideals. Seemingly equals in strength and resourcefulness.

Faking a hay-maker with his wrench, the Russian lured Cormac in for a strike with his knife. Like a Venus flytrap, he caught Cormac and immobilized the knife in an arm-bar. Pressing ever harder, he was almost ready to break an arm.

But as he raised the wrench, Cormac ripped away from the Russian's death-grip and tumbled backward.

The knife fell away, lost in the gloom.

Charging with wrench upraised, the Russian was halted by his very own shortened tether. It yanked him backward just before he might have done a faceplate smashing blow.

Regaining his sense of balance, Cormac waited just out of reach of the Russian's strike.

Stalking like a caged animal, the Russian beckoned for Cormac to attack, to let loose the beast and join him in death.

With no other weapon but his longer tether, Cormac went wide around the Russian who initially believed the American was fleeing from him.

But hooking back, hard and fast by bouncing and pushing off the Salyut hull like a swimmer kicking off a pools walls, Cormac wrapped the tether about the Russian.

Undaunted, the Russian pulled Cormac in and readied to brain him with the wrench. Cormac yanked back to resist the hit. Neither could gain traction over the other, too close in strength and skill, too close in raw brutality and savage cunning.

But there is no cosmic balance, no level to which all can hope to attain in equal measure. No matter what anyone tells you, no matter how small the difference, someone comes out a little farther ahead in every competition.

There is no such word as fair in the universe.

Cormac raised his feet from the tension he had upon the hull and let the Russian pull him in again.

Cormac swiftly kicked the wrench away. Having lost the wrench, the Russian decided to use his own skills to wrestle the American into death.

The big cosmonaut caught Cormac in a bear hug with each facing each other. He squeezed, hoping to pop something. He would assuredly win in a wrestling match, of that Cormac had no doubt.

But there is no fair in the universe.

Beyond indomitable, Cormac beat his own faceplate repeatedly into the cosmonaut's.

Each cracked.

The Russian let go and tried to extricate himself from the insane American.

Cormac charged in again, slamming his own cracked faceplate into the panicked Russians.

"Nyet! Nyet! Nyet!"

"Das-Vee-Dan-Ya!" Cormac caught the Russian by the shoulders and brought the face plates together in one last shattering embrace.

Each spider-webbed crack grew, popped and the air was gone. The broken helmets were instantly jagged glass caskets.

The Russian splayed out in a reverse fetal position, clutching vainly at his throat as the vacuum took his life.

Cormac exhaled everything from his lungs and pushed himself to reach the airlock.

It wouldn't open.

Knowing that it could only be locked because one side of the airlock was open from the other side, Cormac gripped the hull, and crab walked himself to the Soyuz capsule airlock, fighting to remain conscious the entire way.

He was blacking out.

Puffy eyes struggled to remain focused on the next handhold.

Twice he missed, as his fingers felt like hams and he nearly drifted away into deep space.

At the Soyuz hatch, he struggled to just hang on let alone open it.

It would not budge, locked by an open hatch on the other side no doubt. He dimly remembered having Driscoll secure it so that it couldn't be opened.

He won but he had lost.

The universe is not fair.

He dazedly put an arm through the airlock entrance bar to hold his body to the station and consciousness slipped away.

Darkness returned as light was banished from the universe and all were one within the void once again. And with the departure of life, so too did death abandon the horror of existence. A symmetry of bare equal nullity reigned and the darkness was pleased.

Then came the light.

A hand reached forth scorching its way into the gloom and broke the emptiness of the void.

\* \* \*

Driscoll grabbed Cormac's body and brought him to the airlock. He stomped the big Cyrillic flat-topped A.

"Don't you die on me! Live 'Jack-Hammer'!" shouted Driscoll, beating upon Cormac's chest. "Lord, help this wicked man!"

Fresh oxygen pumped into the chamber and Cormac's lungs refilled. He coughed and his swollen bloodshot eyes blinked as he heard Driscoll's prayer of thanks.

"What happened?"

"I came out to help and saw you crawling to the other hatch. I've never been so scared in my life."

"Didn't," cough, "know you cared that much."

"No, that thing is out there. It was hovering over us the entire time I pulled you inside. I was afraid it was going to grab us and eat us. It was watching like, like a lazy shark."

"Now who is delusional? Let me up."

Cormac attempted to get what seemed like upright, but he only twisted in the chamber like a writhing eel.

"You should be dead. Take it easy."

"Where is Ryman?"

"You never saw him?"

"No, maybe the Russian killed him."

"Which Russian?"

"The lucky bastard with the gun."

"I thought he shot himself into deep space."

"He did," coughed Cormac. "But he shot his way back. We're lucky he was out of ammo by then, killer wrestler too. I had to do this to beat him." He waved his hand about his shattered helmet, which he removed.

"That was risky."

"You think?"

The light blinked complete and the hatch opened.

"Did he see it," asked Ludmilla.

"No, he didn't."

"I saw it from the viewing portal," said Ludmilla. "Where is your comrade? Did it get him?"

"Knock it off, it didn't get him and you didn't see anything," growled Cormac. "There is nothing out there. There is no big black space monster."

Driscoll and Ludmilla were quiet, staring at Cormac.

Cormac frowned and looked about the cabin.

Sergei was no longer tied up, but gibbered softly in the corner.

"What the hell? Why isn't he tied up?"

Driscoll took Cormac by the shoulders. "Relax we have bigger problems than what is between our two countries."

"Tell that to the Commie I just killed."

"Arkady?" asked Ludmilla.

"Wrestler? Yeah."

She hung her head a moment, composed herself as if nothing had been said.

"Sorry, Red."

"I am Major Ludmilla Serakovna, please address me as such."

"Whatever Red."

"Cormac, don't. We need to work together to sort this out."

"Sort what out? We do our mission, we go home. If we lost Ryman, we go home."

Driscoll shook his head, "Regardless of Ryman, I don't think we should go back out there. I only dared to save your life. I told you, I've never been so afraid before."

Cormac shrugged him off. "This has gone far enough. Stop talking about this space monster. Stop thinking you see something that isn't there."

"You are half right," broke in Ludmilla.

"Quiet Red!" Cormac rubbed his swollen face. "How can I only be half right? I'm all right. You're both delusional."

She frowned at his dismissal, insisting, "Sergei can see it too. He is terrified."

"What do you mean see?"

Ludmilla nodded.

Driscoll pointed at the viewing window. "It's been at least partially visible since just after you went into the airlock to look for Ryman."

Cormac cocked his head, disbelieving the pair of them. Sergei was tucked away in a corner sobbing. "You're having a laugh," grumbled Cormac, as he turned to look out the window.

He went silent, staring in disbelief at the refutation of all his accepted knowledge.

A vast blue-black shape writhed and moved its great paddles or perhaps feet one after another not unlike a caterpillar, if there were even solid ground out the window. Stars winked randomly through the monstrosity, sometimes clouded sometimes piercing the mottled hide as if invisibility were a fluctuating rhythm. Only a score of glowing green eyes at the forefront remained constant.

Cormac rubbed his eyes and looked again at the gigantic behemoth.

"It almost looks like a tardigrade," said Ludmilla. "A water-bear."

Cormac furrowed his brow at that remark and returned to staring at the colossal monstrosity outside their window. "Never heard of 'em."

"But they are less than six millimeters. This looks to be at least a two kilometers long, maybe more."

Cormac watched intently, asking, "Why does it flicker?"

Ludmilla agreed. "Like it is phasing in and out."

"I think it is only partially here."

"Partially? You were the first one to argue it was here. Now you're telling me it's not?"

Driscoll nodded, "Ryman said something about opening a gate, a dimensional window. Maybe we are only seeing a shade of the creature."

"Entity. I remember. Ryman called it an entity."

"A dark entity."

"What the hell did Ryman get us into?"

The radio crackled alive through Cormac and Driscoll's headsets. "I am still here."

"Ryman, you son of a bitch! Where are you?"

"I appreciate your concern. I was about to open the airlock when a cosmonaut that you failed to take care of, hit me repeatedly. I lost my grip on your tethers and in trying to escape his brutality, I went free-falling below the station and the X-20. Striking something in the process I was rendered unconsciousness for however long that has been. I awoke to your inane use of my name in vain."

"Are you hurt?" grumbled Cormac, who shrugged at Driscoll.

"Ah, yes. I am very sore and do not know that I can climb back up my line. This is much harder than I ever gave you both credit for."

Driscoll spoke up. "I can pull you in, but before I do, we want an explanation on that thing out there. Is it dangerous?"

"Ah, very. But not to you. Not yet." Ryman's breathing was

labored and he exhaled roughly several times between his stunted phrases. "Please, Major Driscoll, Captain Ross is injured, will you pull me inside?"

Cormac put his shattered helmet into a cabinet. "You want to give me yours and I'll go do it?"

"No, you're still recovering yourself. I'll do it. I am coming Mr. Ryman."

"Good. I await your assistance."

Driscoll put on his helmet, climbed into the airlock and shut the inner hatch.

"That should have been you," said Ludmilla. "He is brave man. Not just a killer."

Cormac shrugged. "We all have our failings, and our talents."

"You may be talented at what you do, but do not think it makes you hero or even valuable. Anyone can kill."

Cormac smirked, "I've heard Russian's say laughing bride weeping wife, weeping bride laughing wife. Which are you?"

"I am not married," she said, licking her lips.

Cormac flipped a switch and took off his suit.

\* \* \*

Driscoll opened the outer airlock hatch. "Cormac. Did you turn your radio off? Cormac?"

There was no response.

"He must have," grunted Ryman. "Can you see me?"

Driscoll scanned past the X-20 and saw the dangling tether going underneath. He looked toward the earth and the behemoth that still loomed overheard, its strange image coalescing in and out of reality. "No, Ryman. I can't see you yet."

"My line is from the X-20, but I am beneath the Salyut. Dragged like a dog through space. Weak as an infant. Help me."

"I'm coming, hold on." Driscoll held Cormac's secured tether from the airlock back to the X-20 where he could see a line running from the cargo-hold down beneath the space plane.

Ryman's radio crackled, "Where are you?"

"I just reached the X-20. I almost have your line and I'll pull you in."

"Thank you."

Driscoll took firm hold on the tether and planted his feet firmly against the X-20. It was hard work straining against his suit and keeping balance. All movement wished to betray him to become his own satellite orbiting the earth; and from every perspective he could still see the bloated phasing creature listing in the ether like a beached whale.

"Cormac, is your radio on? Are you receiving me?"

"We are alone," said Ryman cryptically.

Driscoll wondered at that, as well as feeling no weight attached to the tether, but supposed it was because of the zero-G of space. "Are you all right Mr. Ryman? I can't tell if you're about to come up from beneath the Dyna Soar or not."

"I'm fine!" Ryman leapt up from the X-20's cargo hold and beat Driscoll with a Baikonur wrench.

Ryman mercilessly struck Driscoll's limbs and chest repeatedly. Having been straddling the cargo entrance, Driscoll was in the worst possible position to defend himself. In the melee he lost his grip on the X-20's deck and began to drift away.

Ryman pulled him back and bludgeoned him against the hull of the ship.

"Cry for help and I'll smash your faceplate in! Turn your two-way radio off."

Driscoll groaned but did as his tormentor required.

"If our thug of a captain happens to turn his back on, I alone will do the talking. Even now I am sure that what I predicted is occurring."

Spitting blood, Driscoll mouthed 'Why' at his cruel keeper.

"I read the psychological reports. Our good captain has a thing for redheads and accents and she for brutes. Their union is the positive energy half of the necessary invocation. And you my friend, you and I will be the negative half."

Ryman battered Driscoll's limbs again. "What if it didn't happen this way you ask? I would make it so. I will it!"

But for the vacuum of space forcing his body apart, Driscoll would have been in a weeping fetal position, but the pressure on his suit and broken bones kept him splayed in agony.

Ryman dragged Driscoll from the X-20 toward the Salyut's airlock hatch, following the tethered guideline left by Cormac.

"Soon enough this will all be over. Your broken soul will feed and mark the way for the coming of the Dark Levy and I, Chief of the Apostate's, will rule at the Grand Decreators side!"

Smashing Driscoll's body into the airlock, Ryman delivered several more brutal kicks and beatings before shutting the hatch. He pressed the Cyrillic flat topped A button and waited as the pressurization and oxygen adjusted. He broke the seal on Driscoll's helmet, removed it and his own.

Driscoll stared blankly and gasped.

Ryman returned a wicked smile and slammed Driscoll's head against the steel wall, knocking the broken man unconscious.

\* \* \*

As the airlock's pressurization light went green, Ryman opened the hatch and pushed Driscoll through. "Captain Ross! Where are you?"

"I'm here," said a shirt-less Cormac, as he pulled himself through the docking portal leading to the Soyuz capsule. "What happened to Driscoll?"

"Another cosmonaut that you failed to take care of! That's what! Why was your radio off?"

Ludmilla lurked behind in the Soyuz docking portal, only half dressed herself.

"You people," snarled Ryman. "And your urges."

"Hey, lay off Ryman. I don't have to take anything from you. I was recuperating from almost getting killed out there."

"Yes, recuperating."

Ludmilla saw Driscoll and rushed to his aid. "What happened? Where was he hit?"

"Everywhere I imagine," said Ryman, placing the Baikonur wrench in a form-fitting sheath on the wall.

She opened Driscoll's suit and tried to awaken him.

Cormac took hold of one end of the suit and pulled, letting the bulk of the cumbersome outfit down to Driscoll's waist.

Upon examination, it was readily apparent what instrument had done the damage. Beneath his undergarments, several wrench shaped bruises splashed purple across his pale frame. Broken bones were readily apparent even to the naked eye.

Driscoll groaned.

Ludmilla looked to Cormac and shook her head.

"Maybe if I can get him back in time. What else is there to do Ryman? Did you kill the last," he bit back saying cosmonaut as he looked at Ludmilla.

"Yes, I killed him with his own wrench. He is gone. Drifting away into the void."

Both lovers scrutinized Ryman.

"How did you do that exactly? Thought you said you were too weak to climb back to the station on your own?"

"I was. Driscoll pulled me back and just as I was crawling aboard the vessel and could grab your tether that last cosmonaut, the one that you failed to eliminate, struck and beat poor Driscoll senseless. I was able to surprise the Soviet from behind."

Cormac cocked his head, staring deep into Ryman's eyes. "What now?"

"Watch your tone Captain. You have failed several mission parameters today. Besides the woman do we have yet another prisoner?"

"Woman? I am Major Ludmilla Serakovna."

"Easy," cautioned Cormac. "There is another passenger, Sergei Kurylenko. But he is in shock and hardly aware of his surroundings."

"A Soviet trick no doubt. He probably radioed a warning to Moscow the first time he was left out of sight."

Cormac shook his head. "No, I put him in the head. He's delirious or asleep."

"I radioed Moscow when you latched onto our vessel," said Ludmilla.

"So kinda moot point Ryman. You had to know they would do that."

Ryman smiled cruelly. "Quite. Sometimes I let others think they have the solutions and that it was all their own devising."

Furrowing his brow, Cormac rubbed his hands across his face and asked, "So what are we doing?"

"The behemoth you see outside this ship. That leviathan that appears to be the largest living thing you have ever seen? Yes? It is not truly alive, yet it is a god in darkness. A mistress of the void, its natural state is chaos, hence it's shifting reality between space and time."

"But why is it here?"

"We summoned it."

"We?"

"Not simply you and I. The blood we have spilt this far from the cradle of our existence on terra firma, is a beacon through the void. It comes to feed."

"On what?"

"Souls. Damned souls. All those that have perished in terror and misery, those that cannot let go of their pain, those whose light was snuffed out even before they left the womb, those ravaged with age or even those in simple quiet desperation, in short, nearly every member of humanity. Few can attain a balance to rise above and be translated."

"So you can send it away?"

"I shall bind it to this space station."

"That! How?"

"Think of it as a toe-hold. Simply to keep it in balance. It will feed and I will manipulate its power as I invert the Tree of Death and fully enter, navigate and finally command the Qliphothic realm."

"How?"

"I will fully open the gate allowing its entrance to our world."

"Wrong answer," said Cormac.

Ryman quickly withdrew a small revolver from his pocket and smirked, "I have accounted for everything."

Cormac raised his palms in cautious readiness.

"I do not expect you, a mere soldier to understand half of the gifts I have laid at your very feet. It never ceases to amaze me how people only account for one set of variables. I account for them all."

"Why?" asked Ludmilla.

"The lament of the damned is a 'Why?'. Truly the only thing that surprised me Captain Ross, was that you let Sergei live. Not that it matters."

"Then I'll ask," said Cormac. "Why the deception?"

"Because I can. I enjoy that surprise when the terrible revelation of truth hits people. They cannot handle it. Lies are what people want, what they crave, what they deserve."

"You are the real monster," spat Ludmilla.

"So it would seem. Bring Sergei here, I want him to see this as well."

Cormac watched with a wary eye but went to the head and brought the disturbed babbling man into the cabin.

Still shivering, Sergei saw Ryman's gun and look of cruel intent and crouched beside Driscoll in submission.

"Even in his madness, he knows the order of things," said Ryman. He pulled the trigger and put a deafening shot into Sergei's chest.

Ludmilla screamed.

Sergei crumpled beside Driscoll.

"You bastard!" shouted Cormac.

Ludmilla glanced toward the portal window and saw the Leviathan pulse and flex as Sergei's life force faded.

Ryman held his revolver at the ready, "Hold your tongue Captain and respect your betters. There is nothing so ironic as a killer like yourself, judging me for doing what you yourself do on a regular basis. Remember this sacrament could contain your doom or your salvation."

"I never killed anyone in cold blood."

"Whatever lie you need to tell yourself Captain, the end result betrays the truth. You outmatched every man you ever fought, otherwise you would not still be here and in so doing you knew you would be victorious and thusly what you did was in cold blood."

Cormac shook his head. "I never know what will happen."

Ryman chuckled. "Tell yourself that again, if you like."

Ludmilla focused on the abomination outside. Was it growing larger or moving closer?

"You see it, do you not? How it grows stronger with our very proximity and ruin."

"It's growing?"

"Of course Captain. I learned from the Great Beast personally, when I was but a lad, that it must have tripled in size the day we bombed Dresden."

Cormac tried to fathom the far-reaching history of this vile sorcery.

"Understand, I bear you no malice Captain Ross. I greatly respect your contribution to the cause of destruction and a return to the symmetry of darkness. For you there is a place in the Kohort of Darkness. If you learn subservience and embrace the unknowable wisdom, you might even become one of my Chosen Leftenants."

Cormac concealed his disgust as best he could, but for a man hard as diamond, not wearing such upon his scarred face was difficult. "What do you want?"

"What I have always wanted. You to pilot me back to earth after I perform the ceremony that will bind the Mistress of the Void to this station and thusly our very reality."

"Why could you not do this from the earth?" asked Ludmilla, with a tone daring Ryman to shoot her.

"I needed to be close. To see for myself the marvelous work and wonder. I needed to feel the darkness and know that I did this. And," he paused a long while, "it can be complicated piercing the veil between worlds. It takes joint positive and negative energies. You both supplied the positive and I shall perform the negative."

Cormac and Ludmilla stared in wonder as Ryman produced his grimoire from out of a pouch built into his space suit.

"I recited the opening passages earlier to bring the shadow of the leviathan you see outside, into our realm. It was always there, but fully ineffable and nigh invisible until tonight."

"It was always there?"

"Of course. Nothing spontaneously appeared. Everything has always existed."

Ryman thumbed the thick pages, looking for the correct verse, ever watchful and keeping his revolver trained toward Cormac.

"What more do you want me to do?" asked Cormac, clenching his jaw.

"Nothing. Take Driscoll's helmet to replace your own and go prepare the X-20 for our departure."

"You mean to leave him here?"

"Of course, he is useless, except as a conduit. His fractured form is perfect. If you will serve, you will obey."

"And her?"

"Forget her. She was merely a tool for the positive energies. You may dispose of her if you wish."

Ludmilla's rage flared, staring at both men with a scorn only a woman can muster.

"Look at her, she is dangerous. If you don't take care of her, I will be forced to do so."

"Nyet! Do not touch me," she shouted backing away.

Cormac held his hands up in a supplication of her anger and stepped away from her and toward Ryman.

Still perusing his book, Ryman waved his pistol in an irritated yet idle manner, saying, "Do not tempt fate and make me nervous Captain. Kindly back away and leave me to my work. If you wish to live, you will go out and prepare the X-20. That is all. I am done with this game."

"Tell me Ryman. What will that thing do to the earth?"

"It will change everything you think you know. Move," he ordered, as he put the grimoire down and went to the Salyut's control panel, which relayed where over the earth the station was at any given time. He seemed intimately familiar with the readings despite what he had claimed earlier as an inability to understand Russian. "Yes, I lied about that too. We have less than fifteen minutes. Decide."

Cormac looked to Ludmilla. "Get into the Soyuz and go."

"No!" shouted Ryman in his greatest break of composure. Breathing deep, he calmly said, "If she matters so much to you, both of you may join me in the X-20. She can become one of us."

Cormac took a step, blocking Ryman's line of sight of Ludmilla and the Soyuz docking entrance. "You've played your hand. Everything you say is a lie. I won't let you finish whatever this is."

"There is still a place for you, if you will but obey."

"I don't think so. You couldn't possibly know how to land the X-20 and survive, no matter how many simulator runs you might have done. But a Soyuz capsule? Anybody could ride that. And I won't let you have it."

Ryman frowned and took quick careless aim.

The deafening shot took Cormac in the left arm.

"Get out of here Red!"

Ludmilla disappeared through the docking bay and slammed the hatch shut.

"No! Damn you by all the devils in the nine hells!" screeched Ryman, as he took a reckless shot at the docking hatch. The bullet ricocheted from the heavy steel door and thudded into the padded inside walls of the Salyut.

"You! You have ruined decades of planning! Years of work," cried Ryman, as he wheeled and brought his snub-nosed pistol into Cormac's face.

The Soyuz capsule groaned as Ludmilla broke the connection and it jettisoned away from the Salyut.

The cold warrior held his wound as droplets of blood left his arm and floated freely about the cabin. "You got me weeping, but this ensures you don't kill me and leave me here."

Ryman backed away, putting the pistol down. "Well played you barbaric savage. Allow me to finish my work and take us both back to earth and this can still be the beginning a fortuitous alliance. Bygones can be bygones and all that."

It was Cormac's turn for lop-sided grin. "Sure. What do you have left to do?"

"I have but to read some few more passages from the Lex Libre Hereticus and take a virtuous life, definitely not yours—Driscoll's. Why do you think I chose him? Then the piercing of the veil and binding of the darkness to this station, when it crashes to earth will make me a god in darkness as well. I will burn the light and take back our dominions."

"And to do that you need to kill Driscoll and what else?"

Ryman gave a grimace. "Do not interrupt or mock my life's work. Simply because you fail to comprehend what I do, does not mean it is not real!"

"I'm not mocking, I'm asking. Mind if I get ready?"

"Of course not, just keep your distance, I am unnerved."

"Yeah, me too."

As Ryman began his incantation, Cormac did keep his distance, bandaging his still bleeding wound. He put his space suit back on as well as Driscoll's helmet. He opened the airlock and placed Ryman's helmet inside. He did not close it.

Though Ryman sat across the room and recited from his grimoire, he held his pistol close.

Cormac appeared curious but left a good amount of space between them. He rummaged through the cabinets and took a handful of supplies, the Cubans and vodka. He was weakening from blood-loss and knew that his first instinctual plan of attack would likely fail against a rested, armed antagonist. But there was always a plan B.

Waiting until Ryman seemed as involved as he would ever be, Cormac picked up Driscoll's still breathing body and flung it into the airlock.

"What are you doing!" shouted Ryman, drawing his pistol.

Cormac drew the Baikonur wrench from its wall sheath and threw it with all his might.

Another deafening echo from the revolver rocked the station, the bullet hit the steel hatch and ricocheted.

Ryman's sure shot was thwarted by the careening wrench which missed but struck the wall behind and came hurtling back again.

Cormac dove into the airlock and slammed the door shut. He hit the pressurization control, whispering, "Hang on buddy," to the labored breathing of Driscoll. He placed Ryman's helmet on Driscoll and sealed it.

Ryman's voice crackled over the radio. "You think your escape will avail you anything?"

"Doesn't matter. I got your 'Eye of Newt' right here."

"Yes, perhaps you have him on the other side of this steel door. But if he dies in the next few moments from your manhandling or even if his carcass cannot handle the pressures of the vacuum of space, I will still succeed and draw upon that energy. The behemoth cares not whether you kill Driscoll or I do, it will savor his soul all the same and work dark magick's to my benefit. And oh, the horror for you that I will rain down."

"That's a chance I'm willing to take."

Ryman screamed unintelligible curses through the radio as Cormac popped open the exterior hatch and gently pulled Driscoll through.

There was only a single tether looped through the bar below the hatch and back to the X-20. An irritating trick of Ryman's somehow. Cormac held the tether with his left hand and Driscoll's harness's with his good arm. He took careful gentle steps.

"You were supposed to be the best. You were supposed to be a soldier that followed orders. A killer beyond reproach."

"People change."

"No, they do not," snarled Ryman. "My ceremony is finished. With his death, I conquer."

Cormac looked up at the pulsing leviathan. It loomed larger than ever, phasing in and out of reality. Soon its presence would momentarily blot out the sun.

They were halfway to the X-20, when a rumble shook the entire station and a sudden jerk almost made him lose both his grip on the tether and Driscoll.

"I will not fail, you both will die for this insult."

Cormac instantly knew Ryman was firing the Salyut's booster's. Edging closer, Cormac felt blood soaking his entire left sleeve and shoulder. Moisture began to collect inside his helmet making it difficult to see.

"You will fall," taunted Ryman, as he jerked the controls of the Salyut and randomly fired and extinguished the booster's.

A sudden jolt whipped and hit Cormac in the back.

The tether had snapped, as had the X-20's tentative hold from armature to Salyut.

All four bodies were tumbling through the Detritosphere. Both the tether and Driscoll stolen from his grasp. He was cast loose into outer darkness.

"Your hubris is your undoing."

Cormac reached for Driscoll's lifeless body.

"Doom is coming."

He strained.

"We are foot soldiers of the Dark Levy."

Fingers wet with blood or sweat, slimed against the inside of his glove.

"It will eat your souls."

The tumbling Salyut was below or above them by more than twenty feet.

"The Mistress of the Dark..."

Cormac had never been so far without a tether.

"...and her children are impatient."

He caught Driscoll's limp gloved hand, pulling him closer.

"An eternity in the maw of damnation."

The Salyut was separated from them below by more than fifty feet, but it was moving in a revolution and would soon enough be coming back down upon their heads.

"In the absence of Light, all are one."

The X-20 tumbled a short yet unreachable distance away, the tether still attached, drifting alongside equally unattainable.

"Against the thrice damned light, we shall always fight."

The Salyut cast a shadow finally blocking out the terrible monstrosity.

"Are you dead yet?"

"Not hardly."

Re-orienting himself to the oncoming Salyut, Cormac prepared what would be his only chance.

The Salyut came up fast.

Holding tight as he could to Driscoll, Cormac tensed.

The station hit with a jarring squish in his boots.

Cormac jumped using the Salyut's hit to project himself at the X-

20.

Though the azimuth in Cormac's own mind was close, he missed the X-20 by several feet. His fingers outlined against the sun, cruelly empty.

The Salyut and X-20 drifted by in an awful slow-motion of despair.

The tether flailed behind.

His hand shot out against all the blood and doom and Cormac caught the lifeline.

He never knew how long it took to pull himself and Driscoll aboard the X-20, it seemed agonizing hours.

Inside, he strapped the delirious Major into Ryman's former seat and fired up the Titan booster, shooting himself ahead of the revolving Salyut.

"Hey Ryman. Remember what I do up here."

The radio crackled to life. "You're still alive? I would have thought you would have accepted your fate and embraced the darkness at last."

"Yeah, I don't do that."

"Sergei must have been a suitable enough conduit. Can you see from whatever lost perspective you have, that a tendril from the leviathan now engulfs the station? Accept that I have succeeded and will take the monstrosity back to earth and rule!"

"Yeah about that. What happens if you can't make it back to earth?"

"You cannot stop me. When we reach the atmosphere, my powers shall be complete. I had feared my return without a suitable vehicle, but I feel the power pulsing from the Mistress of the Void, I will survive re-entry and then I shall burn a madness deep into the world."

Cormac turned the X-20 into a rendezvous directly ahead of the Salyut. "Remember what I do up here? I'm the best." He dumped the load of ball bearings directly into the flight path of the Salyut.

There is no possibility of a Salyut changing its course on such an abrupt path. Ryman's screams instantly silenced are testament of such.

For every light, there is a darkness. Repulsed by its loss of a conduit, the Mistress of the Void retreated to await another time and avenue to enter this realm.

There is no fair in the universe, but there is justice.

# I ONCE HEARD THE PIPES OF PAN

I once heard the pipes of Pan, they called me to a distant land

It awoke a feeling in my breast, of chase into the forbidden west

To take my sword and brazen lance, that I might destroy the maker o' the dance

Oh how I burned to chase and set to flight, that song of evil in the crimson night

With my sword running red, that dream I did not dread

A wicked lyric crying a sirens call, but carrying doom and mankind's fall

I stopped as I reached the door, almost forgetting what I was fighting for

My wife and child asleep in bed, I could not leave them to make some devil dead

Here is where the good men fail, when enemies hurt and pass by our trail

To stay instead with those we love and hold, is more precious than all the king's glory I am told

## FISTFUL OF TENGU

A monk with several weeks' worth of beard strode into the village of Baiken. He bore only a short walking staff and the sun bleached robe on his back. His once black hair now looked frosted with the gray of age. He paused at the crossroads, rubbing his scruffy chin and gazed up at the snows upon the mountain pass of Arishikage. The ice gleamed like a crown of stars against slabs of coal black rock. Below in the village, spring winds sent the lotus blossoms coursing through the air amid the curling smoke of cook fires.

He glanced high up the pass and it seemed for a moment that dark features moved against the stark white of the snows. But there was no avalanche or rumble, the mountain remained still and silent as death on the frozen peaks.

For a village in springtime, Baiken was also quiet and only the hammering of the blacksmith shop rang out in the silence like Buddha's gong.

The monk went first to the well for a cool drink of water and approached the blacksmith. He was amused to see it was not an experienced tradesman but a young boy of perhaps seven or eight working the hammer and tongs.

The boy stopped his work and inquired, "Yes? May I help you?"

"I apologize. I didn't mean to disturb you, but your shop was the only sound I heard in town. So I came here first. You're perhaps the youngest smith I've ever seen."

The boy sniffed and said, "It is only because my father has been taken away."

"By the magistrate?"

"No."

"Local shogunate?"

"No."

"Bandits?"

"No. Worse."

"What's worse than bandits in a valley fair as this?"

"Monsters in the mountain passes, Tengu and Oni. They have laid claim upon our lands and take what they wish in the night.

Some say it is a curse put upon us by the sorcerer Yao Hsiang, but I do not know."

"And of your father?"

"He tried to cross the pass while the monsters slept. He sought assistance from the Daimyo. But we heard his screams. He never made it. Most of the folk here have been taken, were slain or hide in their hovels."

"But you still work the forge and hammer."

"I have naught else to do and I accept my fate. Until it comes, I will do as my father and his fathers have since the day the Yellow Emperor did show men the way of the fire and steel. I am a blacksmith."

The monk rubbed his chin, saying, "It is good you have balance. Is there a home where I may get sustenance?" He rubbed his lean belly.

The boy grimaced. "My mother has some rice and a few onions. Perhaps there is even some Saki. But I would have you earn your meal and work the bellows for me."

The monk smiled, "You are a good son."

The boy, Shian-Hu worked the monk all day and by evening allowed a respite when they retired to eat. The mother, a taciturn woman made the meal as her son had promised. They sat by the fire watching the mountain turn purple in the darkness before finally becoming a deeper shade of black against the vaulted night sky.

Here and there upon the mountain were stars just like in the heavens, but these moved across the treacherous snows utterly unlike anything the monk had seen before.

Shian-Hu noticed and commented, "It is the Oni and Tengu. They dance in the passes, likely toying with some poor soul who ventured that way."

"What more can you tell me about them? Do they have a lord?"

The mother gasped, her first audible utterance since Shian-Hu brought the monk inside their humble home. "It is not meet to speak of such things. It but invites them."

Shian-Hu shook his head, "If that is our fate, so be it. There is said to be a Demon Lord of the Tengu. But no one alive has confirmed this."

"Surely some samurai has come to win honor and defeat them."

"Yes," nodded Shian-Hu vigorously, "many have. But it is said no weapon forged by man can hurt the Tengu. All of the heroes that went to the mountain have never returned."

"No weapon forged by man, eh?"

The mother spoke with a biting curt voice, "Monk, you had best return the way you came. There will be only unhappiness in our valley. It is our lot."

The monk shook his head, "No, in the morning I shall go and speak with these monsters and bid them leave you in peace."

"And if they will not?" asked Shian-Hu.

His mother stood and shouted down at the ego-less monk. "How can you go where so many mighty men have failed?" To Shian-Hu she said, "We have wasted the last of our rice upon a fool who will only die tomorrow!"

"Mother! Your manners."

She went into another room and wept. "Forgive me. But we are a poor cursed people."

"No forgiveness is necessary," said the monk. "I will take care of this problem in the morning." With that he sipped the last of his Saki and rolled over to go to sleep.

Shian-Hu, however could not sleep. The ego-less monk knew something he had not yet revealed and obviously was not disturbed over encountering the murderous monsters. The morning would bring a very interesting turn of events.

The monk slept in, well beyond the rising of the red sun. Shian-Hu's mother complained under her breath that it was merely cowardice in his laziness. But when the monk stirred she became silent.

He did his morning prayers, stretching and refreshed himself with cool water from the well. He gazed up at the mountain pass and turned to bid farewell to Shian-Hu and his mother.

"I am going with you."

"If you wish."

"No! I will not have my son journey with you and your assured death." She held her arms across Shian-Hu, holding him back.

"Listen to your mother," said the monk. He turned and walked up the path, never once looking back to see what the boy and his mother did.

It was midday before he reached the high pass where the path disappeared between twin mountain peaks. It was colder here but not so much that the monk concerned himself. The chief danger was the glare of the sun upon the snow and ice, blinding him. He kept a hand over his eyes as he squinted against the dazzling white backdrop.

The wind whipped about him and almost had a malevolent voice, whispering threats. The monk made a gesture of Kujo-kiri with his fingers and the spell of wind ceased.

A gentle crack high above, erupted with a shower of thunder. A rockslide raced down toward the path. The monk more agile than he appeared, side stepped and jumped behind a sheltering overhang hardly big enough for a dog. As the rolling stones settled, he came out and looked above. Something intangible stirred.

And the monk continued up the pass with a spry and wary step.

He heard them before he saw them. Cackling laughter with either mischievous undertones or deep bass rumbles of stifled laughter. The monsters were more easily seen from the corners of his vision than directly. They enjoyed the terror they believed they inflicted upon men, the blood turning to ice as men let fear rule them.

But the monk continued higher up the trail never acknowledging the demonic chuckling or malicious taunts.

When the monsters had enough of being ignored they called out, "Is this one both deaf and dumb? Does the insect not feel the doom that is upon him?" It was then, a dozen of the crow-man-like Tengu and a score of the ogreish Oni, fully revealed themselves from behind fields of glamour. They cloistered about the monk as if about to attack and feed upon his flesh.

Paying them no mind, the monk said, "I would speak with your lord for I have a message for his ears alone."

This caused alarm and concern among the monsters, for what man would dare presume to have a message for their demonic lord?

A towering Oni, roared at the monk, sounding like the hurricane and avalanche combined. But the monk yawned. "Do not waste my time any further. Fetch your lord immediately, for I have a message for him."

The monsters looked to each other and nodded. A black winged Tengu sprang up and flew into the mist shrouded clouds near the frozen peak. He returned a short moment later. "Our lord comes and he will himself feed upon your flesh, for your insolence," spoke the fiend.

The monk said nothing to this, but waited.

The beat of powerful wings, much louder than the other Tengu's, thumped closer. Where the Oni wore but loincloths and carried hammers and naginata's, the Tengu wore robes of fine silk and wielded katana's. The Tengu lord was dressed in even richer apparel. His silken robe bore many devices and patterns of gold and scarlet. His sword handle was wrought with dragon skin and gems, a gold crown perched upon his ebon brow and his beak seemed to quiver with what could only be an insidious and cruel smile. It was hard to tell with a beak.

His voice was like thunder and he said booming, "A mortal dares to demand my presence? You will be especially tortured unless you speak a truly valuable message."

"It is, oh lord of the mountain it is. I ask for you and your servants to depart, never to return," said the monk.

The Tengu's eyes of jet bore into the monk before blinking and laughter erupted from the Tengu lord. "You are the boldest fool I have ever met. And what if I refuse your offer? Then what?"

"It will hurt," spoke the monk placidly.

The Tengu lord raged, "Slay him!"

But remaining almost still as cold stone, the monk raised his hand, "I have insulted your lordship, perhaps we could compose a challenge for us both. So that you might regain your honor."

Incredulous the Tengu lord shot back, "Me? Regain my honor? I have lost nothing. What challenge would you have for us, fool?"

"A challenge of life and death."

"You know no weapons forged by man can hurt me."

"Yes."

"And still you wish to challenge me?"

"Yes."

"Very well. Your doom is upon you."

They rounded on each other, the Tengu lord standing nearly a foot taller than the monk. Quick jabs with sharp talons rained down upon the old monk, to which the monk casually blocked. Raging the Tengu lord attacked all the fiercer, but quick as he was, he could not grasp the monk in his shining talons.

The monk still only blocked the Tengu lord's attacks.

"Tell me who you are monk. To be such a skilled opponent I would know your name," said the Tengu lord.

"Musashi, Miyamoto. I have come seeking the void and to find worthy adversaries. I have found only you."

The monsters all blinked in surprise at facing the famed sword saint, even without his katana.

Bolstering his own failing courage the Tengu lord shouted, "Perhaps you are the greatest human warrior alive, but you have no weapon that can harm me."

"I am the weapon, not forged by man," said Musashi as his hand shot out and took the Tengu lords beak in his left hand.

The Tengu's eyes grew wide with fear, never before had anyone been able to lay their hands upon him. He pulled back but Musashi's grip tightened, even to the point of placing two fingers into the nostrils. Horror filled the monsters black soul as he watched Musashi's right hammer-like fist raise.

The fist came down at the base of the beak and smote it free. Holding the beak in his fist Musashi said, "You had the choice between blessing and curse. I grant your wish."

Screaming and in painful shock, the Tengu lord suddenly went silent as Musashi slammed the broken beak into his feather covered heart. The monstrous lord fell in the snow, his crimson blood staining the whiteness.

Facing the rest of them with his bloody fist, Musashi spoke softly, "Weapons need to be constantly sharpened and used. Sometimes they break." He cast the beak at their feet. "Who is next?"

The monsters turned and fled, some melting away into the fog and others taking wing heading south.

The Tengu lords body shifted, cracked and fell apart in the snows as if it were thousands of years old. The beak on the snows turned to dust and blew away on the wind.

Musashi continued on his journey.

## A GOOD HOME FOR THE SPOON

I was teaching Ezra Pound to box and gaining no traction. His moves brought to mind the scuttling of a sleepwalker with lockjaw. I decided the best thing to do was take him to the *Circque d'Hiver* over on 110 *rue Amelot.* There, I could show him the difference between the palookas and the boxers.

It was a brisk walk in the cool evening air. My old waterproof still smelled of the rum I'd spilled on it at the café on *Place St.-Michel* earlier where one of the *poivrottes,* had bumped into me earlier. She stunk of gin and garlic, and growled at me like a bear cat. I offered her my apologies, only to be met with profanity, rude gestures and something about her bohemian gypsy boyfriend "taking care" of me if I didn't leave. I wasn't afraid of any would be hero, but I also had better things to do. This was a few hours before I met with Ezra.

Ezra was excited, asking if the waiters really boxed at *Stade Anastasie.* I told him they did. They were some of the best boxers I had ever seen; always struggling for recognition and standing. There were always beautiful ladies at the boxing matches. The stands always reeked of sweat and expensive perfumes.

The wind barreled down the boulevard as Ezra ad I crossed over the Seine. I thumbed the worn rabbit's foot in my pocket. It was good to keep luck so close. The worn sinews contrasted with the cold silver spoon Gertrude Stein had given me earlier that afternoon, previous to the *poivrotte* incident. Stein and I spoke of art as we usually did. A painting she had recently purchased of a child eating, made me mentioned offhand that my son, Bumby, had started on solid food. She gave me a scolding, as per usual, then handed me a silver spoon, adding that it would be fine for Hadley to use as a gift, and that it didn't match any of her other silverware anyway. I accepted, if only for the sake of pleasing her. The thought of trading it to the old man with his stalls of books beside the Seine passed through my mind more than I cared for. If you were lucky, you could barter for two or three English novels, since the French counted them of little to no value. Back then, books always won against the lesser essentials.

Ezra interrupted my thoughts: "Hem, will you look at the moon . . . its beautiful tonight."

I saw, but didn't care; still bothered by Miss Stein's curious and unwanted gift. "Looks much the same as last night. The city of light dulls the moon."

"I don't think it looks as good anywhere as it does here."

"No, it doesn't."

Ezra stopped short, looking at me. "What's gotten in to you tonight?"

"I'm just tired. The moon does look beautiful."

He kept staring. We continued on to the *Circque d'Hiver*. Not far to my right down the boulevard was the *Vincennes* race-course where Hadley and I had lost again. I hoped the boxing would prove better entertainment tonight. Even when you were punched in the face and lost, a good fight made you feel alive. Losing a bet with the horses only made you feel you had a foot in the grave; helpless and ashamed.

A modern-day coliseum, the *Circque d'Hiver* is a great oval with ample seating and beautiful Corinthian columns to help project a historical flavor. Despite the wonderful lights and exotic scent of a thousand perfumed patrons, the fights were poor this evening; only boxers of juvenile skill or great ones whose form I knew Ezra could never hope to attain. Still, he had an enjoyable evening. We drank beer during the fights. Afterward, we talked more about Bel Esprit over *café crème* until it cooled enough to think about drinking something else. When we stopped at a café and ordered some dry white wine. I was hungry and Ezra bought me a plateful of *goujon*. They were better than sardines, especially when I was famished. We finished the wine and went home under the full moon.

It seemed a long walk to Ezra's at 70 *bis rue de Notre Dame des Champs* in *Montparnasse*. We stopped for drinks again, discussing those subjects writers are wont to discuss: secret inspirations; jabs at former acquaintances and lovers, the scent of something sweet from childhood and the reek of becoming a man. But again, we turned to the fine liquor.

"I hear the absinthe is especially good here," said Ezra. "At least Olga said it was."

I smiled at that. Olga Rudge, Pound's mistress, always had good taste. Between Olga and his wife, Ezra had quite the marriage; all bases covered, as it were.

We drank the pale jade liquor, laughed and told stories about forgotten friends and remembered enemies until it was very late. I said my good-nights and stumbled toward the Luxembourg gardens; a shortcut home. My head throbbed in a good way and even with the wind I didn't feel the chill so much as I had an hour earlier.

Night can be graceful; tonight, the well of inspiration would fill again so I could write tomorrow. Gossamer shadows danced and flitted on the edge of vision. I wondered who they were and where they were going. I did not feel ready to go home just yet. I heard an odd sound; a sick dog barking or coughing somewhere in the darkness. Turning, I bumped into that same *poivrotte* from earlier. She was in no better mood. Her androgynous raven hair was a mess, and she stank. She greeted me with a slew of coarse language that only made me laugh. She raised a fist to strike my chin and, even with absinthe flowing in my blood, I easily blocked her clumsy attack. I laughed again, which made her angrier.

"*le Loup!*" she shouted.

I was puzzled now; she must have been even more drunk than I realized. Would someone come running, thinking that she was calling me a wolfish rapist? Surely anyone could see that even the most soiled dove of Paris would be more appealing than this bird, but experience has taught that people will do and believe anything. I had no worries, as the shadow people were all gone; I didn't even hear the low mutter of Paris at night any longer; only the somber fall wind.

She cursed me again.

"You talk a lot of rot. Stay away from me," I said, turning to head home.

Like a good boxer, I kept a peripheral eye on her and knew she was twenty paces back when a silent brawny bulk slammed me to the ground. The wind was knocked from my lungs and I lost a little absinthe right there on the park ground. A strong, hairy hand clutched at my shirt, popping off several buttons. An *ungodly* smell seeped from the man whom I could only assume was the *poivrotte's* gypsy boyfriend. He coughed with what sounded like tuberculosis lung, the moon dipping behind clouds, masking his face in darkness.

I sent an uppercut to his long chin. I felt his body roll away as I kicked at him to gain both footing and time. The woman shrieked, and I wretched again as the man hit me in the gut. His hairy forearm was about my neck, squeezing the life from me. He was strong as any man I have ever fought; I could not release myself from his hold. I did the only thing I could; biting down until I drew blood. He howled like an epileptic dog, letting go.

The woman was laughing insanely, and I have seldom beheld a more wicked countenance than hers.

I turned to face the man, regretting I did not have my knife. It was then I knew the absinthe had struck me harder than I ever would have believed. What I thought stood before me looked more like a wolf than man; a wretched mongrel cross, something out of a pale-jade induced nightmare. The woman shrieking '*le Loup*' must have addled my already ossified wits and birthed this hideous mirage.

The wolf man coughed and howled his bloody rage. I brought my fists up to box him, since I was too soused to think of anything else. I wondered if the ruckus would bring the *gendarmes*. For once, I hoped they would come quickly.

He charged faster than I was prepared for; had me on the ground in an instant. His long nails clawed and tore my clothing while I kicked and punched. I felt ripe gashes open and bleed all over my chest and face.

The son of a bitch enjoyed his masquerade, howling again. A blow to the head caused stars to explode across my sight far more vivid than any decorating the Parisian sky. Was this the end? Would I die here, in the cold Luxembourg gardens with nothing more in my pockets than a rabbit's foot and silver spoon?

Silver—son of a bitch! I yanked the spoon from my jacket,

pressing it against the bastard's face and he howled again, this time in pain. A hard slap sent the spoon from my grasp. Again, he slashed and tore, clamping a hairy hand around my throat.

I tried to escape, but couldn't budge beneath his weight. The moon cast an eerie light over him, revealing a spoon shaped burn upon his cheek.

The wolf man leaned in, exulting in triumph. I fought back, pressing my thumb into the yellow orb of his eye. He reeled back. Twisting on the lawn, I frantically reached for Gertrude's gift.

I felt the blows of the woman's handbag on my back, but ignored them as I traced my fingers through the pale dead grass.

The wolf man howled again, and I sensed his approach.

I touched the cold silver spoon. Never had such a delicate utensil felt so good, so potent in my hand.

He grasped my left shoulder and spun me about like a rag doll. I faced him, plunging the tiny cupped head of the spoon into his right eye. I let go, the spoon standing erect from his face; a tiny arrow with swirled, flowery fletching.

The wolf man's remaining eye flickered. He froze like one of the statues on cobbled *rue Mouffetard*. The woman screamed again, but no longer in joy. The wolf man took a precarious step, crumpled, slumping on his face. As he hit the ground, he curled up in a fetal position, seeming to almost shrink—clearly an illusion of absinthe and frayed nerves. He let out a curious gasp, and I caught a whiff of a foul stench as his bowels loosed.

The woman looked from he to I and ran away into the night, gibbering like so many *poivrottes* that have seen their men go down in a street brawl. In the distant darkness, I heard a *gendarmes* whistle. I wasn't about to wait for them; I had no wish to see the inside of a Bastille while they did their guesswork.

I walked away briskly, never spoke of the incident to another living soul. I still wonder what I saw that night; if the absinthe had proven more potent than that in Spain, because I never did hallucinate like that again. I heard some tales in upper Michigan about wolf men, but it always seemed like so much rot.

I told Hadley and others that a window shattered on me to

explain all the cuts and bruises. I was laid up and sore for a week, but counted myself lucky. The next time I was out with Ezra and Olga, I declined any of their drinking suggestions.

I also made it a point to thank Gertrude for the spoon. I told her it found a good home.

P.S. Ezra still can't box.

**DAVID J. WEST**

## LOVECRAFTIAN HAIKU

*Rise Tentacle Rise*
*Beat Back the Byzantine Lies*
*Sink Tentacle Sink*

## PEACE IN THE NEW WORLD

The armored captain ordered the torches thrown and soon the ships blazed like a dozen suns, fallen to earth. Some of the men grumbled, a precious few brave souls gazed to the unknown west.

"Some of you think me mad to burn the ships! But I have granted you the will to conquer, the very need to survive and overcome. We did not land on these shores to walk away empty handed, nor turn tail and flee. I burned the ships to drive you to become the conquerors that I know you are!" shouted Hernando. "But who is with *them*?" He pointed at the mutineer bodies swinging in the breeze. "And who is with *me*?"

The conquistadors shouted in unison while the ambassadors from Moctezuma looked on in bewilderment. The manners of this savage returned god were both bestial and puzzling. Why would he destroy his ships, unless horror! He meant to stay?

Dona Maria alone spoke both Nauhatl and Spanish, and she was Cortez's woman. "Tell Moctezuma that Quetzalcoatl wishes to meet with him and exchange gifts," she said in a demanding tone never before given to the ambassadors by a woman.

"He should command us himself," answered the boldest.

"You are worms beneath his mighty feet and he will not deign to treat with you. Do as he commands through *me* or you will taste of his fire sticks!"

Word of Quetzalcoatl's fire sticks had reached their ears. Trusted servants spoke of the thunder and smoke belched from the black steel, the awful wounds given by dark spirits to the unlucky. The ambassadors begged forgiveness, fearful also of the stocky deer upon which the gods rode.

"We respect Queztalcoatl. But this is frightening behavior."

Dona Marie rebuked them, as her eyes went black as obsidian, "It is a new cycle. And prophecy foretold that in the new year of One Reed, the gods would return. A new age begins and fear shall be its mother and vengeance its father. Accept and bend the knee to the returned god of *peace*."

And they bent their heads and knees, for all had been told of the prophecy and here it was fulfilled, but they wondered silently as they looked upon the burning ships, the hanging bodies and flogged or maimed victims who had resisted the landing; all these things hung upon that cruel word choice by the dead prophets, the jaded double meaning of the word—'*peace*'.

# MAKE A MONKEY OUTTA ME

The city corner lay both pristine and dirty as the great falling shadow grew larger. The dying beast landed hard upon the unforgiving surface. Concrete fractured in a multitude of lines resembling black lightning, radiating out from the fallen behemoth, who convulsed only briefly and lay still. Foul ichor and offal ran crimson from the myriad bullet wounds and from the terrible gashes that split open upon impact. The smell was enough to knock a stout man down.

The police cordoned off the area, all the while looking fearfully over their shoulders just in case the giant monster rose again.

It didn't.

"So what are we supposed to do with it now, chief?" asked Officer Zeke Taylor, a lanky beat cop from the sticks. He kicked at the massive hairy forearm.

The plainclothes chief scratched his week old beard and also kicked at the titanic corpse, testing, as if the gallons of leaking vital fluids weren't enough to be sure of its demise. Glancing at the score of other policemen keeping the gathering crowds at bay before answering, "Dunno, they blow up whales that get washed up on the beach don't they?"

Zeke shrugged, "Yeah, but on the corner of Seventh and White? We'd have giant ape chunks splashed all over what isn't already demolished."

"I'll ask the commissioner. Maybe we could get the fire department to cut him up and transport the parts outta here and take 'em to the dog food factory."

"I don't think that's very funny," broke in a reporter who had sidled past the barricade. He snapped a picture, the flash momentarily blinding the chief and Zeke. "This was a truly unique animal. It deserves respect. Its remains belong in a museum." He snapped a couple more gruesome photographs as a pair of policemen closed in, batons at the ready.

The chief blinked, "Get him outta here! Beat his candy ass if he comes back! And get that crazy broad away from here too," he

103

shouted, pointing at a voluptuous blonde who had rushed inside the cordon and was caressing the dead beast. "We can't have everyone grabbing souvenirs."

"Maybe if everyone did, we wouldn't have such a big mess to clean up."

"Wise guy huh? Just get me the commissioner," snarled the chief, chewing his cigar and striking a match.

It was mere moments before the lean commissioner, portly mayor and a full bird colonel from the army arrived to inspect the corpse.

"So it is dead?"

"Yes sir," responded the chief. "Hasn't gasped or moved for the last ten minutes. Watch your step there, nothing could live after losing that much blood."

The mayor nodded and stepped gingerly over the pool of blood already as large as if a cloudburst had struck. "What is that green?"

"I will bet it is the spleen sir."

"Yes, of course. The spleen. Didn't know they leaked green like that," he mumbled lighting a cigar.

"Well, we have done our part," said the colonel nodding. "You gentlemen take care."

"Wait! We need you to clean this up," sputtered the mayor, losing the cigar to the green ichor.

The commissioner raised his eyebrows, amused at the exchange, still puffing on his own cigarette.

"That is not our job Mr. Mayor. Might I direct you to call you own sanitation services?"

"But you did this."

Sneering, the colonel retorted, "I did my duty to God and country when there was a damned monster tearing the city apart. Get the side show company that brought this colossal monstrosity here to do it."

The chief spoke up, "I believe the company chairman is deceased. One of the first to get crushed in the melee."

"Exactly," broke in the mayor. "We need you to do it colonel. It's the army's mess too."

Wheeling, the colonel strode to the mayor and leaned into within an inch of his face saying, "*You* asked for *our* help. *You* pleaded. *We* did *our* duty and protected *your* city. *We* are not garbage men. *We* do not clean up messes. Good day." He turned and got into a waiting staff car.

"But this isn't my fault!" The mayor spun looking at the commissioner and chief, "What will we do? This will cost a fortune. I'll lose the re-election. Tell them, it's not my fault!"

The commissioner who had thus far remained silent, threw away his cigarette butt saying, "*If* I could come up with a way. I would want the city's garbage budget for one month put into my Cayman Islands account."

The cigar dropped from the chief's mouth.

The commissioner continued, "This is all based on the *if* I can. *If* I can't then don't worry about it and we never had this conversation." He turned to walk away but paused, "In fact, *if* I can, we never had this conversation either. You got that beanpole?" he directed the last remark at Zeke, who nodded soberly. "I will be in touch with someone I know and if this works I need everyone out of the way and off the streets. No one is to alert the army. You have to trust me. It may take a few hours. So at least by 4 a.m. there shouldn't be too many people in the way. Get rid of these crowds, keep any who linger back at least a few blocks. Do we have a deal?"

The mayor, blinked and nodded. "We have a deal Stewart. *If* you can deliver."

"Is it the mob?" asked Zeke.

"No."

Zeke propped his cap back, "What then? A balloon?"

"No," answered the commissioner with a rolling of the eyes. "Get everyone away, I'll be back in a couple hours." He got into his car and barely let the crowd's part for him to speed away.

The onlookers closed the gap again immediately all gawking and jostling for a glimpse of the huge corpse.

"What's he gonna do chief?" asked Zeke.

"I dunno, but I don't like the sound of it."

The mayor interrupted, "If he can take care of this right quick,

I'll shake the hand of the devil himself."

"Careful what you wish for Mr. Mayor," responded Zeke, tipping his cap and following the chief.

The mayor snorted and went to his waiting car.

\* \* \*

It was less than an hour later and the commissioner raced up to the curb, slamming the brakes and parking with the front right wheel upon the sidewalk. He jumped out of the Cadillac and went directly to the chief.

"Is it done? Is my money transferred?"

"So far as I know. But if your plan don't work, I doubt you'll still have a job in this town. The mayor is—"

"It will work," said the commissioner. He turned and motioned back to a passenger in the back seat of the Caddy.

A swarthy bug-eyed man with a dull orange robe got out. Various pendants and fetishes graced his neck, bright gold rings were bound on his fingers and curiously he was also barefoot. He carried a large fan in one hand and a mysterious ochre jar in the other. Glancing upon the colossal corpse gave him no awe or pause, he simply looked once and went to work pulling potions out of a bag and mixing them in the jar.

The commissioner shouted, "I need everyone back and away by a couple blocks."

"But commish, people wanna see this thing," said a freckle faced cop, likely just out of the academy.

"And I ordered you to move them back. This could be hazardous and we need everyone a safe distance away."

The chief who remained behind, mumbled, "Guy looks like a witch-doctor."

"That's because he is a witch-doctor. His name is Tomabusi. He is from Haiti. I met him years ago when I was looking for lost Spanish treasures."

The chief frowned, "You're pulling my leg."

"Yes, I am. Why don't you get back a few blocks away while we secure the manacles for the corpse. Tell people we are going to use acid or something, I don't care so long as they stay away."

"Alright, alright. What are you gonna do? Float him away on a giant balloon?"

"Yeah, that's it a—balloon, now please get back."

The chief walked away shaking his head. Gradually everyone was pulled back a couple city blocks and between the shelter of the corpse and the skyscraper it fell from, a dark ritual began to take shape.

The witch-doctor blew a powder from the ochre jar across the great ape's face. He beat a drum and danced wildly, reciting a jumble of magical incantations that the commissioner could not hope to follow.

The commissioner thought he heard Swahili, Creole, French and Latin, perhaps even Sumerian but he could never be sure.

Thunder snapped overhead as rain clouds threatened and still Tomabusi beat his drum and danced wilder and wilder. His gyrations grew crazed and became faster and faster. Lightning flared and just as suddenly, he stopped and asked, "Do you have a fresh obedient soul?"

The commissioner nodded, "Yes, I do." He walked to the trunk of his car and glanced about in the filmy darkness until sure that no one could see his shadowy work. Worried but still impatient, he opened the trunk and withdrew his own personal dog, Mazzie.

Mazzie was an obedient animal and the commissioner thought she would be the ideal soul for the reanimation. He carried the beagle back to the witch-doctor, who expressed some trepidation.

"This will be the most obedient servant you can think of?"

"Yes."

Tomabusi shook his head. "This is not how we do it Haiti."

"What would you use?"

"A person of course." Tomabusi answered incredulous. "Someone I wish to dominate. I thought you understand this. All of my powers are centered on this dominion. But we need to do this! Immediately before the sunrise."

"Where will I find a good person to dominate?"

"I am thinking of one right now," snarled Tomabusi.

Stepping back, the commissioner mumbled, "I'll find someone

right away."

The commissioner knew who he wanted. He had but to stride a couple blocks down to where the police cordon was keeping the die-hard curious away from the great apes corpse.

The beat cop, Zeke, was telling jokes to a couple other uniformed policemen.

"You. We need to talk," said the commissioner. "What's your name?"

"Officer Zeke Taylor, sir."

"You don't need to call me sir, just come with me I have a job for you."

Zeke glanced back at his fellow officers, waved and followed after the urgent commissioner. "So what is all this about? I haven't said a word to anyone, honest."

"I know you haven't. You're a man I need. A man who can take orders and follow them to the letter. You have grand place in things to come."

"Things to come?"

Rounding the corner they were back to the huge corpse and Zeke was again almost laid flat by the stench. He heard a clucking and was puzzled. As they went around the colossal forearm, he could see Tomabusi gyrating before a pool of blood.

The witch-doctor had a chicken and was twisting its head off as it flapped wildly. He looked at the astonished Zeke and frowning commissioner. "I know, I should have held it upside down for awhile, but I was in a hurry."

He ran the knife across the chicken's throat and tipping the neck, he gathered the blood into his ochre jar. Tossing the dead birds body aside, he rapidly went to work mixing the contents of the jar, while humming an unidentifiable native tune.

"Commissioner, what is this? That was not legal."

"Don't you worry about it Zeke. We'll have everything worked out very soon." He smiled unconvincingly and as if pondering something far away said, "Say, will you fetch my coat from the car?"

Zeke nodded, while inwardly disgusted with the commissioner and his pet witch-doctor. He heard a quick rushing of footsteps

108

behind, a crack to the skull and all went black.

\* \* \*

Zeke dreamt that dancing throbbing drums played poker between his ears. He felt hot blood coursing down his chest in rivers of gore. He wanted to run and feel the primal thrill of the chase, to combat foes and taste independence. Paranoia washed over him like dark tides. Tentacles reached up from deep below and urged him down. He wanted to be back on the island in the mist shrouded jungle, never mind he knew he had never actually been there. But most of all he wanted to feel freedom. But he only felt the pain racking his entire core. A pain so deep and penetrating he wanted to die, he hoped he died and at the last moment when he could bear no more pain he was sure he was dead.

\* \* \*

He was on the ground. It was cold and wet. Everywhere pain was shooting tears along his coiled body. He wondered briefly if he was covered in maggots or leeches. He opened his eyes and the perspectives were blurry, unreal. A hollowness in his veins cried out for refreshment and a ravenous hunger like a hole bit into his stomach. He felt so terribly dry as if all fluids were gone and only dust remained.

Zeke knew he was lying on the ground but his vision said he was several feet off the ground. He grunted as he went to pick himself up off the ground. Every joint screamed and several bones cried out, threatening to buckle. The he heard malevolent laughter and the words, "It worked, it worked, I can't believe it worked."

Adjusting to the gloom, Zeke turned his head to the sound and blinked.

Below him stood both the commissioner, the witch-doctor and another lanky man. No, the man wasn't standing on his own, he was propped between them.

"Open your eyes, Zeke Taylor and see. You will do as I say and I will set things right again. I can't imagine you will want to stay this way."

Zeke blinked and tried to deny what he saw--himself, slumped between the two grinning devils. He shook his head, thinking it was a daze, a dream, a nightmare. What terrible thing had he drank? What could have been slipped to him? What?

"This is real Zeke. We have transported your soul into the colossal ape's dead body and you will use that body as we command, *if* you ever want to return to *your* old body again. Do you understand?"

Zeke's voice couldn't come but he nodded, though a fire raged within at these two laughing villains. He struggled and got to his feet. He was fifty feet of bloody raw muscle, over a hundred tons of sheer animalistic power. Like the physics professors who argued a bumblebee shouldn't be able to fly, Zeke as a giant zombie ape just did the impossible. He stood and roared mutely.

"Zeke, you will do several jobs for us before sunrise. Do you understand?"

The great ape nodded with eyes unblinking.

"First bring to me that which I desire. Bring me the Phoenix diamond from the Trans-Metropolitan museum. You can reach down from the sky lights and smash the barred security cages open. Obey me, or we will destroy your old body."

Zeke remembered through a charcoal fog that the museum was only a few blocks away.

He lumbered toward the museum. A dozen police cars swarmed behind faster than he expected, they shot at him and without thinking he scooped them up and threw them at one another. He remembered those drivers were his friends, his brothers of the badge and he stopped and turned the smashed vehicles over. He ripped the doors off and looked at the cowering men inside.

He could not speak, could not tell them. Putting them down he continued to the museum, hoping he remained cognizant long enough that he would not harm any of his fellow officers; but an emptiness in the back of his brain ached and crowded at his submission to the fiends. It growled and hungered to rise up and destroy this maddening place.

Gripping the edge of the roof, he hauled his gory bulk up, demolishing the side of the entire edifice. Tearing through the glass and steel he ripped off the barred cage that sat upon the diamonds pedestal as if it wasn't there. Holding the diamond in its tiny case proved the most difficult of the entire task. Returning to the commissioner he dropped the case at his feet.

"We should leave before we are found out in this," said Tomabusi.

The commissioner nodded. "To the airport."

Zeke looked for his body, but didn't see it. He groped at the two men getting into the Cadillac.

The commissioner looked at him and said, "We are keeping your body safe. You have to trust me. Follow us to the airport and we will reunite you with your body. But along the way, I want you to grab the gold bullion truck that I just called the mayor about. I told him for the cities safety it should be moved." He laughed while Zeke did the closest thing an ape could do to scowling.

They roared down the now deserted city streets with the colossal ape close behind. To those who had no idea, it must have seemed that the zombie ape was in pursuit of the Caddy.

Zeke followed them down wide avenues and once down a side street that was almost too narrow for his wide shouldered frame. He saw their brake lights glow, they were waiting.

As he neared he saw the bullion truck pull out of the underground banks garage. He casually hefted the heavy iron truck up and tore the doors off, spilling the men out. They were more afraid than hurt.

They shot at Zeke like the others, but he hardly felt the bullets anymore, just the growing hunger wrestling with his hollowness. He had but to lean in toward them and they scattered away like leaves.

The commissioner honked and was soon speeding away. Cradling the bullion truck in his arms, Zeke followed.

At the airport he set the truck down.

"This cargo plane is ours," said the commissioner, "tear off the useless portions of the truck and place it inside our plane. Do you understand? As gently as possible."

Before Zeke did any of that he looked at the growing tide of advancing police forces. Already the army had planes in the air though they had not yet starting shooting. Black helicopters buzzed in the background, jockeying for position.

"Hurry, beast!"

Zeke signaled that he wanted his body and held the truck back.

"Your body is fine. It is in the trunk of my car. Get the gold on my plane and our deal is at an end. I will tell you how to be exchanged with your former self, understand?"

The witch-doctor stood beside the commissioner and beckoned to the gold then the car.

Zeke bent the cab and fenders of the truck and squeezed it inside the cargo doors. He heard metal scrape but nothing a new coat of paint couldn't fix.

"Take this," said the witch-doctor offering his ochre jar. "Drink a little but save enough for your human body. Dab some upon your bodies sleeping lips and you will shortly be made whole."

Zeke carefully took the jar between his massive fingers and gingerly licked at the contents. It was awful and tasted of blood.

The plane's cargo doors were shut and the engines were fired.

The police were virtually at Zeke's back, though reluctant to engage him closer after events from earlier that night.

Zeke went to the caddy and popped open the trunk with his nail, likely destroying the locking mechanism in the process. Inside was his old body. Why did it seem so old, so wrong? It had been his less a couple hours ago? Or was it even shorter? With every moment the great ape's monstrous body seemed more natural, more real.

The plane turned a sharp corner to approach the runway.

Bullets flew, echoing from a hundred guns. Zeke felt their tugging at his festering corpse. Already some former vitals' threatened to spill out. Cradling his gut he knocked away the foremost squad car. The others quickly hit their reverse to avoid the rampaging behemoth.

Lights blinking, the cargo plane apparently had clearance for takeoff or was doing it anyway. Soon enough the monster men would be away, free with all their riches. It wasn't right and he restrained himself from crushing his own body as a few dozen rounds still prickled at the back of his neck.

The plane started taxiing down the runway.

Zeke picked up his old human body and carefully as he could spread the contents of the jar on his cold lips. He noticed how pale his body was, how cold. This was not like a coma, a deep slumber of the ages. A hint of crimson spread across the deep blue shirt. Peeling back the flimsy cloth he saw that there was a gunshot wound to the chest. His old body was as lifeless as could be.

Dead to the world, alive to the animal.

He raged in primordial silence for but a heartbeat as the taxiing plane sped up on the runway. Zeke could think of nothing else as the animalistic rage took over. Shambling down the runway he struggled to catch the swiftly speeding up plane.

The engines roared as the nose tilted upward.

Tossing aside a parked bus and a wheeled staircase, Zeke roared mutely. Helicopters with Gatling guns blasted, their shells falling like rain. Zeke's skin writhed as if python sized maggots burrowed. He flung a small luggage cart at the helicopter bursting it into a black iron flame. It hit the ground with the suddenness of a stone.

The landing gears danced off the tarmac and took flight.

Maddening desperation took hold and Zeke used the only thing he still had, himself.

He threw his broken old body at the plane as hard as he could. Like a fleshy missile the old Zeke Taylor body slammed into the cab of the plane with incredible velocity. The audible splatter pulped the pilots within.

Zeke smiled grimly at the last fearful seconds of his betrayers. Their evil faces screaming behind the windows of their cursed plane.

Smoke erupted from the cockpit and the plane nose-dived into the ocean. Halfway submerged and a fireball blasted illuminating the night. This also brought more gunfire from the police behind. How could they know he had destroyed evil men and was not simply attacking the city? It didn't matter anymore, he must leave.

Zeke mutely howled and went for the ocean himself. The salt stung his opened hide but he ignored it and slunk into the tepid waters. A fog swelled over the bay and would ease his passage. He knew where he was going; back to the mist shrouded jungles. Even if he had never been there before.

It was going to be a long swim back to his island.

## ECHO FROM THE ABYSS

Ten year old Darius let the tide flow over his toes, recede and come again, burying his feet in warm wet sand. Hypnotized by the constant motion, the gnawing in his belly almost vanished.

Dark shapes of other Zanzibarian beachcombers flitted about in his peripheral vision like flies, their excited buzzing begged attention, but the swirling sandy water beckoned stronger in vivid blue and golden kaleidoscope patterns.

Then it was bathed in pink.

His mother pulled him from the reverie. "Darius! Get out of the water!"

He stepped back, just out of reach of the licking Indian ocean.

Swimmers, their skin glistening wet, raced from the water.

Something massive followed, lolling out of the sea like a gray tongue. Tubular with mottled elephantine skin, it rolled with the tidal waters, oozing blood from a dozen gashes.

A score of waves brought the leviathan to shore. A host of tendrils sprouted from one end while the opposite had a dozen thick tentacles swaying with the tide.

The monstrosity lay still, but the beachcombers kept well away, fearing such a colossal corpse.

"Is it a whale?" asked Darius.

His mother shook her head.

"Squid?"

She didn't answer, shielding her face from the noon day sun watching for Darius's father. They waiting for Darius's father to return, hoping he had found some meager food supplies. Zanzibar, now a part of the Great Caliphate remained forgotten amidst the world war; a lonely rest stop upon a non-strategic route.

A trio of men prodded at the corpse with umbrellas and sticks. The leviathan gave no response. Darius and his mother watched the handful of brave souls poke at the giant corpse, half expecting its tentacles to lash out and bludgeon the fools.

"What is it Mother?"

She shook her head, whispering, "The Old Deep One's return."

"Can I touch it?"

She shook her head again. "No, it would be unclean."

A shadow fell upon them and turning they beheld a tall dark skinned man dressed as a pharaoh of old Egypt. All recognized the lord of the Great Caliphate, he who ruled both Africa and Asia, the Crawling Chaos, Nylarthahotep. "Eat of the bounty I have bestowed upon you," he boomed. "Eat that your hunger be sated and your soul filled of my divine generosity."

He pointed at the leviathan and the men scattered across the beach took their knives and sliced into the beast. Huge strips were cut from the monster and passed about. The whole of Zanzibar came and partook of the flesh as lord Nylarthahotep looked on.

"Eat, eat. This is for you, my children."

Soon thereafter the mysterious lord vanished, leaving those present to wonder at his power saying, "See how he cares for us. Soon the war will be over and his Great Caliphate will rule the entire earth."

Someone returned with a machete and hacked at the great flabby body and brought slices to Darius and his mother.

"I'm so hungry Mother."

She gazed about for her husband, but not sighting him answered, "Eat," she said as tears streamed down her face.

Darius ate the blubbery gray meat and was filled. His swollen belly felt near to bursting. He could not remember the last time he had eaten so much.

"Don't cry Mother, it is good that Lord Nylarthahotep gave us this food."

"His blessings bring a curse."

Darius only smiled and wondered at her words.

His father never returned.

Throughout the night, Darius dreamt strange dreams and felt the sea calling to him.

At dawns early light he and all the other folk of Zanzibar who had eaten the flesh of the leviathan, waded into the sea. As the water went over his head, Darius heard the echoes coming from the deeps, calling him home. He was one of them now. By accepting of their flesh, he was one of them. He dove into the depths, followed by the rest of Zanzibar and joined with the folk of deep R'lyeh.

## ONE THOUSAND ONE NIGHTS UNSEEN

"The desert, sometimes it gives and sometimes it takes," said the Sergeant-Major.

"Yeah, it will take all right," spit Corporal Wilson. "But I haven't seen it give anything."

"Plenty of sunshine, plenty of hot days and freezing nights. Hell, it gives more variety than anyone could possible want. It even gives us an enemy, a purpose."

"It sucks," said Wilson, slinging his rifle. "Nothing to do but sit here, without beer, without girls, without fighting, without porn. This damn place sucks the life out of you."

"You need to appreciate what we have here Wilson. Nobody else ever gets to come to Saudi Arabia, nobody. Time comes and Saddam, the Republican Guard with their Gerald Bull 155mm's; oh we'll fight, we'll get to experience it all soon enough."

"You can fuggin keep it. Damn rag-heads. Look, there's a couple more." He raised his rifle in an aggressive, though poor firing stance.

A pair of Bedouins crested the flowing dunes and came with arms wide open. They held empty canteens and pointed at the water truck.

"Put your gun down Wilson, they're friendlies. Republican Guard has to be miles from here anyway." Greeting them with the customary bow and heel of hand to forehead, the Sergeant-Major said, "Salaam aleikum."

"Aleikum salaam," they returned.

"Salaam, salaam . . . you bastards," muttered Wilson, repeating the benediction with a scowl.

"Sergeant Major! Report!" called the XO, from the flapping tent entrance. "You too Wilson."

Wheeling, they each strode to the command tent and saluted facing the XO.

"At ease. Come inside and take a look at the situation map." He pointed at some indistinct areas with a handful of roads trailing across the open desert. "Seems a whole platoon of Captain Davis's has gone AWOL. We are all to be on the lookout and be extra vigilant in finding them."

"How long have they been missing? Sir."

"They should have reported in by O-five hundred yesterday. More than a good twenty four hours ago. We are to keep it on a need to know basis, we don't want anyone panicking and we especially don't want any trouble with our Saudi hosts. But everyone in this quadrant is supposed to search in shifts. I am sending your team out to the Tango Delta quadrant."

"Any intel on what may have happened sir?"

"I'd sooner believe they found a good spot for some R&R and are hoping they can beg forgiveness instead of asking permission. But the fact is they are AWOL and no eyes in the sky can find them just yet, so it's a ground pounder patrol. You will leave immediately."

"Yes sir!"

\* \* \*

The Sergeant-Major took Wilson and three more members of his fire team in a Humvee and drove out to the north west, Tango Delta quadrant, smack in the middle of nowhere.

Borders were arbitrary out here at best, but as far as U.S. coalition forces were concerned, it was all an uninhabited no-man's land. No one in Operation Desert Shield had even seen the lay of the land except from the air and even then it was just cursory and very quickly, and all simply to be sure Saddam wasn't about to cross the border. But the Sergeant-Major's orders were taking the fire-team farther into Saudi Arabia and away from the border, it didn't make sense that anything could have happened operationally. He kept reminding himself that the simplest answer was the right one, but he couldn't shake the feeling of something darker lurking out in the wilderness.

"Do you think we'll find them?" asked Wilson.

The Sergeant-Major shrugged. "It's the desert. Kind of a we will or we won't. There's things out there that have been swallowed up for centuries or they could just be broken down in plain sight."

Thompson pointed, "What about the radio?"

"Who knows. Stranger things have happened. Good chance they

don't want to answer."

"Any chance they found some girls?" grinned Thompson, hopeful as anything.

Wilson snorted, "That'll be the day. The Saudi's would sooner let you screw a sheep."

The Sergeant-Major chuckled, "That's the truth. No way any Bedouin would let any leather-neck sleep with his daughter, not for any price."

"So what does the map say about where we're going anything?"

"It's Arabic name is Baten al Ghul, the Belly of the Beast."

"That's encouraging."

"Hell yeah it is. I overheard a Bedouin tell the XO that it's haunted."

"Wonderful. What the hell did I sign up for?"

"It sure as hell wasn't to fight for some damn Kuwaiti's oil!"

"Just hold on and for the moment let's take in where we are and focus on finding Captain Davis's lost platoon. The XO's report said it was three Humvee's, a water truck and a cargo flatbed. Odds are on our side that somebody will spot them from the air before we do."

"Yeah, no way they all broke down."

"What the hell, why are we even looking then?"

"You wanted something to do, don't look a gift horse in the mouth."

"This is still a bullshit detail."

They drove for several hours covering miles upon miles but finding no sign other than an occasional abandoned car or wandering shepherd.

"What's with the abandoned cars?"

"It's against the law here to drive a car without air-conditioning. So if the A/C goes out, they leave the whole damn thing and just buy another. I'll bet most of the cars beside the road are just fine by white trash standards, but not with the Saudi's. Besides the make enough on their Dole, that they can afford to just buy an new one, so why not upgrade constantly?"

"Yeah, especially when we are here to cover their butts!"

"It's what we are trained to do."

\* \* \*

By the time twilight crept over the desert they were a hundred miles from base. Red-rimmed light crouched behind stark rocky points designating the borders of the valley. A sliver of a moon hung beside cold stars in the dark night. And where they may have expected night sounds, there naught but unnerving silence.

"I just got off the horn with the XO, he said we can hold up here and continue the search tomorrow in daylight on our way back."

"So he's worried about us?"

"No he isn't. We at least answer the radio."

The men grumbled or laughed, bivouacking out here by themselves was little different than the living conditions back at the base camp.

"We have everything we need, set up the tents, break out your bags, it's gonna be a cold one."

The stark contrast of the desert was something the men were still not used too. Broiling heat by day and freezing temperatures at night created a duality of nature that was ironic for the war-zone.

"We'll keep up a watch in two hour shifts, we'll all get enough sleep."

"Hey Sarge, can we light a fire?"

The Sergeant-Major just looked at the tow-headed Thompson.

"I mean Sergeant-Major, sir."

"No good reason to, but out here, no good reason not to either. But I don't think we have anything to burn either, no trees, no scrub brush, nothing."

"I got a broken crate in the back of the Hummer and I think I see something right over there in that gulch. Driftwood or something."

"Go ahead," said the Sergeant-Major absently gesturing to the defile.

Thompson trotted out to the gulch and reached down picking up what looked like a desiccated branch. He gasped and dropped it back into the welcoming sands.

"What is it? Snake?"

"No sir. Come here."

The Sergeant-Major along with the rest walked over to where Thompson pointed.

Several skeletons were clustered into a haphazard pile and dusted with the ever-present sands. Rib cages stood out and had been the assumed driftwood. Hollow eye-sockets leered back at them.

"Nothing we won't see more of soon enough."

"Who were they?"

"Could have been anyone, I don't see a shred of clothing do you?"

"No."

Wilson blurted, "I don't want to camp here."

"I ain't driving all the way back to base tonight. Sides you wanted an adventure Wilson."

"Yeah, but what did this?"

"Who cares. Could have been anything, gas, cluster bomb, probably just the desert itself. Everyone get some sleep. Since you're so worried Wilson, you get first watch."

"Yes Sergeant-Major. I'm still lighting that fire."

"Go ahead."

* * *

Wilson fed the last shard of the broken crate to the dying flame. The men's snoring kept him as alert as anything. Already the moon was slipping below the hills and he knew his eyes played tricks on him.

Furtive shadows seemed to slither about the crags and gloom and he couldn't help but wonder if he should wake the others.

As the waning moon was fully enveloped by the sucking sands, he was sure something living moved. Taking the night-vision binoculars he scanned the ridge line. Figures shambled across the horizon, dozens of them.

"Sergeant-Major! Wake up! Trouble." Wilson whispered urgently.

The men awoke and prepared their weapons sure that Wilson meant the Republican Guard.

"What is it? What'd you see?"

"Whole lot of people up on the ridge-line. Could be a whole platoon for all I know. Look through the night-vision."

It was more than a quarter mile away but numerous bodies did move about, seeming to dance beneath the stars.

"I don't see any weapons. They almost look naked."

"In this temperature? It's damn cold!"

"It don't make any sense but yeah. No weapons, I could swear I just see bare skin too. They look like they are having a rave or something."

"I don't hear nothing."

"Neither do I. I can't see a thing without the night-vision, how the hell do they see anything either?"

They passed the night-vision back and forth each trying to make sense of the bizarre scene.

"Could it be some kind of rag-head ritual?"

"I don't think so. This goes against anything I have ever read about. It would be taboo."

"I got it figured out," said Wilson. "These dumb bastards get high on the hashish, start raving to the music in their own damn heads, then die in that gully there like we found 'em in. Those bones didn't have any clothes either."

"They all look skinny as hell."

"Of course they do. They're a bunch of fuggin' junkies."

"I hate to say it, but that seems as right as anything," said the Sergeant-Major, before taking a long pull on his canteen. "They don't seem to be causing any harm though, so I'll take watch and the rest of you get some sleep."

The men lay down, but none rested easy, electric-green visions of writhing skinny bodies in darkness permeated their dreams and once, just once, in the night they thought they heard a solitary scream far off in the haunted distance.

\* \* \*

As the sun crept over the dunes, a white jeep approached swiftly, a tail of dust like a comet trailing behind. The driver only eased on the brakes as it was nearly upon them. A star and crescent upon the doors marked this as a vehicle of the local Saudi constabulary though it was definitely different than the usual Saudi Arabian logo and the Sergeant-Major noted it.

A tall mustachioed man in his forties got out. "Salaam aleikum."

"Aleikum, salaam," responded the Sergeant-Major.

"Americans yes? I will be brief, I am Mustafa ibn Sulaiman , I am with the how you say, Special Criminal Police, not the Sharia Police, yes?"

"I think we got it."

"I have been ordered to assist you in finding your lost platoon, that is believed to have gone missing somewhere here in Baten al Ghul, yes?"

"Appreciated but we were about to head back to our base camp, nothing more we can do here," said the Sergeant-Major, poking a thumb back to the northwest.

"Ah, then you do not wish to look upon those missing vehicles?"

"You found them?"

"Yes, I did, though I strongly suspect the ghoul have taken your men."

"Say what? Who's that?"

"Maybe he means those weirdo's we saw last night," offered Wilson.

"Did you see something last night? Very dangerous." asked Mustafa.

"What's the big deal? They a bunch of hashish nut-jobs or what?" asked Thompson.

The Sergeant-Major pressed, "Are our boys in some kind of trouble with the local authorities? What'd they do?"

Mustafa held up his palms, "Please tell me what you saw last night."

"Bunch of naked assholes dancing up on the ridge-line."

"Wilson!" growled the Sergeant-Major, "speak respectfully to our host or you ain't ever getting out of KP."

"I know of what you speak," said Mustafa. "You are among the few that have seen the ghoul dance and lived to speak of it. It has been one thousand one nights they have gone unseen."

"Ghoul? Who?"

"They are the demons of the desert, they feast upon the dead. When I saw your trucks high upon a dune to the southwest I suspected ghoul had done it."

"What? Why are you telling us this?"

"I was directed by my commanders to solve the mystery, find you American's and I have. I will show you the vehicles so that you may confirm their identity with your superiors."

"Appreciated Mustafa, but why don't you think the men are there?"

"It has been nearly three days that those men have been missing in this valley. No one survives more than one night in Baten al Ghul."

"You're saying those dancers were some kind of demon?"

"Oh yes. They are ghoul, they are not like other men. Last night they may have celebrated some dark holiday, perhaps the stars were right for them. You were blessed by Allah to have been left alone."

"I don't think they knew we were there."

Mustafa chuckled for the first time showing any trace of humor. "They assuredly did, but they were not allowed to molest you, so long as you did not offend them. They will not be so kind a second night. Not in this valley."

"Just show us the damn trucks, please."

\* \* \*

High upon the dune and half covered in sand, the vehicles were scratched and torn in chaotic abandon. The tires that could be seen were flat with chunks ripped out. The wind shields were shattered and tatters of canvas flapped in the breeze.

"Is anybody in there?" called the Sergeant-Major to the others that moved higher up the shifting embankment.

"There will be no one," said Mustafa.

"How can you be sure?"

"I am sure. But you shall at least have some closure for your superiors, not that they will believe all you may relate to them."

The Sergeant-Major looked at Mustafa. "You think they got stuck, and ran out of water?"

Thompson, Wilson and the others slogged up the dune, with their weapons ready.

Mustafa shook his head as he and the Sergeant-Major trudged behind. "Your comrades will not be present."

"Have you been up there already? Have you searched the trucks?"

"No, I have not but I recognize the signs and portents easily enough, especially in this valley."

"No one is in the vehicles Sarge!" called Thompson.

"No one?"

"Nope, nobody."

"So they must have gotten stuck and decided to hot foot it back to camp."

"No," insisted Mustafa, "they are surely dead somewhere here in Baten al Ghul. But their bodies will not be with the trucks. Look all the signs are here." He pointed at a horrible four clawed gouge across the foremost Humvee. "The Ghoul have taken them."

No trace of bodies remained in the sun-bleached trucks. But all of the gear, ruck-sacks, canteens, weapons and the like remained.

"Look Sarge, shells everywhere. Like they were shooting in all directions?"

"Water truck is empty, like someone opened it up and let it drain all the way here."

"Big firefight."

"Of course they were," said Mustafa. "The ghoul would have come at them from every direction."

"But why? Why attack such a hard target?"

"Because they are Ghoul, it is what they do."

"Nothing is gone? Why didn't these ghoul take anything?"

Mustafa answered, "None of your equipment has any value to the ghoul."

"Yeah, right," argued Wilson, but his sarcasm faded as he noticed an M-4 left beside the passenger seat in the first hummer, along with a few magazines and grenades.

"Can't they be killed?"

"Probably. I have only heard a handful of tales of noble men fighting back and succeeding, but that would always be against a lone ghoul, never an onslaught like this, especially after dark."

The Sergeant-Major continued poking at the wreckage.

Mustafa continued, "They must have had good reason for attacking the column."

"What's that you say? Who's side are you on?"

"Allahu akbar, assuredly we are on the same side. Ghoul would attack me just as quickly as you if I offended them, as I suspect these men did."

"Say what?"

"They must have found something on their maneuvers. A crypt, or another holy place of the ghoul. It likely held treasure of some kind, something of the dim ages. Many men have trod these roads with gold and silk, these things do not stay lost in the desert. The Ghoul know of these treasures and keep them for their own. But if driving along a dune such as this and these soldiers found such a tomb and looted it, then the Ghoul would come for them and exact revenge."

"So are they prisoner somewhere?"

Mustafa shook his head slowly. "No my friend, no. They are in the belly of the beast."

"You mean somewhere in this valley?"

"No, the literal belly of such Ghoul. They were eaten. Such is how the Ghoul survive, like jackals on carrion, but like jackals they will sometimes kill for sustenance."

"How can I use any of that to explain any of this to my XO?"

"You cannot. But you can report you found the vehicles."

"Will you report this to your commanders?"

"I do not need too. It is known what happens in this valley. We do not speak of it."

"I don't buy it." the Sergeant-Major grumbled, "Then how does anyone know anything about what happens here?"

"It is the mystery of the desert."

"I can't believe this. There has to be another explanation, those men went somewhere, even if *they* are who we saw dancing in the dark from smoking too much hashish."

"Believe whatever you like Sergeant-Major. Believe in a comfortable lie if an absurd truth is too unbearable."

"You really believe this valley is haunted?"

"I do not believe it Sergeant-Major. I know it. Truth does not change, the curse on this place does not evaporate like water but remains hidden, waiting beneath the sands for all time."

\* \* \*

Forty miles back to camp and the Sergeant-Major slammed the brakes on the Humvee.

A path of stark white bones was splashed across the road they had traveled only yesterday.

Mustafa who had followed behind, exited his jeep and stood beside the Sergeant-Major. "I count a full platoon of men, yes?"

The Sergeant-Major wiped his brow and knelt to examine one of the only artifacts still clinging to bone before him. A cheap wristwatch. Its hands frozen on ten hundred hours.

"It is them, yes?"

The Sergeant-Major nodded. "But why here? Why so far away?"

"As I said, I suspect they robbed a tomb or crypt, a holy place of the Ghoul and great vengeance was visited upon them. The Ghoul devoured their flesh leaving naught but bone. They moved the bones here to draw us away from wherever their crypt must lie. Presumably halfway between here and the where the trucks were found."

"This is pure hate, pure evil."

"Perhaps."

"Should we gather them up?" asked Wilson.

The Sergeant-Major looked to Mustafa, who nodded. "It will bring no ill luck to take back your own dead."

"I still don't understand. We must get our revenge."

Mustafa shook his head. "You have seen their works, you have seen them dance and yet you yourself hardly believe, your commanders will not listen."

"This was wrong."

"I do not defend the Ghoul and their ways, but I understand it. They hate men."

"Why?"

"I dare speak of this to you only once, as we are each warrior brothers under the skin. Long ago, before Muhammed brought us the Koran, men and Ghoul worshiped the same elder gods. When man rejected the elder gods to follow Allah, the Ghoul felt we were apostate and deserved punishment. Allah in his wisdom has granted men the dominion of the earth, but not of the whole earth, there are dark places, haunted places like this where the old gods still hold sway and hold council and these places can never be wiped clean. You should leave Baten al Ghoul and never come back. I leave you now. Aleikum Salaam." Mustafa got back into his jeep and turned around and disappeared back into the desert.

The Sergeant-Major oversaw the rest of the bones collection and brought them back to the base camp.

* * *

That evening, the Sergeant-Major filed his report as truthfully as he could and the XO threw it down in disgust. "I can't turn this in. What the hell are you thinking?"

"What am I supposed to report?"

"Whatever you want. Say it was a 'Friendly Fire' training accident. You are not to speak of this incident again. Send Wilson, Thompson and the rest in here so I can remind them too."

"Yes sir." The Sergeant-Major paused at the entrance. "Sir, what about that Saudi police officer that assisted us? He'll know it wasn't a training exercise."

"You weren't directed to have any local assistance. We were in touch with the Saudi's and were assured there was no one within our quadrants. You must be mistaken."

"Yes sir. I'll get the others, sir."

The Sergeant-Major paused trying to remember the badge on the door of Mustafa's jeep. It had seemed odd and now that he thought about it again he sketched the design and logo as best he could on scratch paper.

"Thompson, Wilson, the XO needs to remind you that it was all a training accident. Report immediately."

They each got up and beckoned to the other members of the fire team to follow.

"Wait, Wilson. Are any of those Bedouins around to fill up their canteens?"

"Yeah, one more showed up a minute ago."

The Sergeant-Major strode to the water-truck and glanced about until he saw a white bearded old man adjusting a bundle upon his camel.

"Salaam aleikum."

"Aleikum salaam."

"Do you recognize this?" he asked holding out the sketch of Mustafa's logo.

The old man grinned. "Aye, you met a Jinn. He must have been protecting you."

Furrowing his brow, the Sergeant Major asked, "Protecting me?"

"Aye. You were surely blessed by Allah. They appear sometimes when men most need help and guidance against the dark forces of the deep desert. Without the protection of the benevolent ones, you surely would have been dead men."

## CURSE THE CHILD

*Seven years have passed since Sheba came to Jerusalem town; again the trumps blared and proclaimed welcome to the stygian queen in her ivory gown.*

*King Solomon himself greeted her and extended a hand into her veiled coach; they strode side by side to his gilded court, always without reproach.*

*A staff bearing the image of an elder god thrust up from her hand; by her side a dark boy dressed as a pharaoh in bright silks from a far eastern land.*

* * *

The black vault of night fell and the starry cosmic serpent whirled overhead, tail in mouth, as the Queen of Sheba's retinue entered Jerusalem through the southeastern fountain gates. Solomon kissed her hand as she exited the gossamer-shrouded palanquin. Through the wafting frankincense and myrrh they passed, to speak in the Hall of Pillars.

Nearly alone in the magnificent hall, the king sought to embrace the queen but she withdrew.

"I have missed you, dear Balqis. Did you not miss me as well? What is thy wish? Have I offended thee, my love?"

She stood tall, strong and imperious, speaking in a loud voice like a herald. "I have come to introduce you to our son," she said. "That you may learn at his feet as I have learned at his." She beckoned then for King Solomon to behold the darkling child.

"My son?" Solomon's brow furrowed and he waved away the multitude of eavesdropping concubines who watched from behind inlaid stone.

"My father," said the boy, whose deep bass voice ground defiance to dust. He extended a hand in mocking supplication to his father, the king.

She said, "He is beyond the wisdom of ages; the Mazeroth burns in him and the stars have aligned, releasing all their knowledge."

Solomon twisted his magic ring and wondered. Balqis, the woman, the queen who stood before him, had changed. No longer

131

did her eyes shine; they were now pallid orbs, unblinking. Her voice, once soft and sweet as honey, was hard and firm as the temple stones. The ornate crown she wore shot forth the gaze of a golden-tendriled abomination that seemed to shimmer and writhe in the flickering torchlight.

"It is late dear Queen. Let us retire for the night and discuss these things further in the light of day. Demons and djinn rule the night, and it is not meet to discuss such things during their witching hour."

She looked to the boy who answered, "Why fear the night? There was wisdom in the darkness before there was light."

The boy's black-eyed gaze burned into Solomon and for a moment the king feared he might drop to his knees before the imposing child. Solomon shook off the nausea and muttered an incantation to himself, a prayer for strength, a hope for deliverance. "Send the boy away, Balqis. I would speak with you alone."

She responded coldly, "He is not to be shunned, but obeyed."

"Curse the child!" he shouted. "I care not for how he looks upon me."

Solomon's chief bodyguard, Captain Kenaz, stepped forward, hand on sword hilt. Kenaz, sandy haired and strong, he feared no man or beast, but the pale-eyed queen and lean, dark boy gave even him pause. He wiped a hand over his stubbled chin and cursed at what he must do now.

Looking to the bodyguard, the boy gave a sign of vibrant chaos and opened a gate which warped like a twisting whirlpool turned on its side.

The vortex opened.

The torches blazed momentarily, then the ferocious wind sent them guttering. A tormented sound echoed from the gate, reverberating through the stones. A maddening fear took hold of the folk and animals within the palace. The braying of donkeys echoed across the city and the cocks crowed in terror. Babes whined and pregnant women miscarried.

Sensing the unholy threat the boy posed to his king, Kenaz charged.

A long slender tendril, purple as Phoenician sackcloth, lashed out.

It took Kenaz about the head and shoulders and sucked him through the gate.

With the tentacle spiraling around Kenaz's mouth, Solomon shuddered, wondering how he could hear the man scream.

From behind, two guardsmen broke ranks, swords raised.

"No!" Solomon shouted, expecting their doom.

The iron swords shattered upon the boy's ebon body. Their owners were dumbstruck as the tendrils grasped and brought them to the maw of the beast from beyond.

"You shall heed me," said the boy, with a voice deep as the pit.

Solomon nodded and knelt at his son's feet.

\* \* \*

And so it was that in the following weeks, the new son of Sheba and Solomon instructed the palace upon many things. He constructed brilliant artifices and skillfully showed them the nature of the universe. And Solomon did depart from his God, and even the pagan gods of his wives, and did heed the counsel of Azathoth, Yog-Sothoth and yea, even dreaming Cthulhu.

But not all in the palace were held in thrall of the dark child. Rehoboam, the former heir apparent, sought to renew his position. His was not a noble spirit but an ambitious one that would not be cheated of his destiny. He plotted with the priest Sethur some manner to destroy the dark usurper.

"Nothing of this world can harm the dark child, but we have things from beyond this world," said the priest. He mentioned the sacred Ark and also brought forth the sword of Goliath. "Legend says this was made on another world than ours. It is hallowed and can cut the demon boy."

"How can I know it will work?"

"You have no other choice. Slay and live, or lie and slave."

The prince nodded, and together they prepared their assassination.

\* \* \*

Declaring the stars were right, Solomon, Sheba and the boy

prepared the invocation of the Outer Gods. The world would be reborn, reorganized in their image. In the garden and vineyards of Gehenna, signs were drawn in blood and glyphs carved into stone and wood. The moon hung overhead, uncaring.

At the temple, Sethur prepared the Ark and Rehoboam ran a finger along the edge of Goliath's sword as he joined his father.

The celestial alignment merged with that within the gated world and the boy's voice boomed unutterable incantations into the bleak, starred night. Phantoms swirled and green flames projected like vomit from unknown fissures.

A gelatinous mass threatened to pierce the veil of night and a formless void slowly took shape.

Now the plotters struck.

Sethur and eleven Levites projected the Ark at Gehenna. Light blasted out and wrestled with the void. Time froze and shook.

Rehoboam was there in the darkness, waiting for his chance. Casting dull acolytes aside, he lunged at the darkling child.

The queen reached out to protect her son and Solomon held her back. "This too shall pass," he said.

The boy recognized the otherworldly sword in the prince's hand and fled from its shining wrath. Into the darkness of Gehenna the two ran.

Without the boy's call, the chaos was damned and held back, sucked to whatever gulf had spawned it, to sleep eons more.

Solomon and Sheba could not gaze through the gloom upon the wicked pursuit of their sons, but the cacophony of screams and the thud of bloody chops spoke the harsh truth.

Rehoboam crawled forth, the sword of Goliath in his hand and the dark child lay still. The prince collapsed and it was then Sheba took her son and prepared to depart.

Solomon asked, "Where will you go, what will you do?"

"The child is not dead, but sleeps. Twenty-seven wounds will equal twenty-seven centuries and he will rise again to bring back that which has waited eternities already."

\* \* \*

*Always it is said that with the blessing comes a curse, and it is for both the foolish and the wise to know and understand which is worse.*

*Sheba was beautiful and Solomon was wise. Together they brought a thing into the world which could not love but only despise.*

*Halted in his infancy and pyramidal step, that crawling chaos was brought low only once: the darkling child, Nylarthahotep.*

## FANGS OF THE DRAGON

*Whoever fights monsters should see to it that in the process he does not become a monster. And if you gaze long enough into an abyss, the abyss will gaze back into you.* —Friedrich Nietzsche

1.

The water lapped hungrily at the shore. Waves rippled across shadowy liquid, pushed by something stronger than the moon's dominion. Something splashed far out in the lake as the mournful melody of a flute carried and abruptly went silent.

An eerie green ball of fire raced across the night sky on the far side of the lake. It shot chaotically from side to side down the mountain as if chasing down prey, diving hard, it was gone.

A man driving his wagon approached the lake. "Look at that Ahab, who says there isn't even a lake monster to see around here?" said Phineas Cook, to the dog that sat beside him. "I see lots of things." He cracked the reins and forced the ox, Petunia, down to the lake-shore.

Bringing the wagon to the rim of the ebbing surf, he circled it around next to a massive gnarled stump.

Phineas didn't want to be on Bear Lake at night, but it couldn't be helped. Work at the mill had taken longer than expected and he still had to uphold the bargain with Brother Brigham. The rope was expensive and there wouldn't be a better time than now. Naysayers were asleep, as were curious onlookers.

Bleak stars hung overhead as Phineas removed a rowboat from the wagon and set it upon the lake-shore while Ahab chased his tail.

The ox eyed the water, snorted and threatened to depart.

He ran a hand across her flanks, "Easy, Petunia. I've work to do, nothing to be afraid of."

Ahab whined.

"Same for you. We capture this leviathan and we'll be able to take care of the Church's debts. Think of the good we can do."

Ahab buried his face with his paws.

Icy mist lingered over the lake as Phineas secured a thick hemp rope to the huge stump. He put a pair of buoys in the water, one larger than the other, next to the rowboat. From the buckboard he produced a flag, Old Glory, and attached it to the top of the larger buoy.

It was cold, steam flared from his nostrils as Ahab whined again. "You coward," he said, loading the buffalo gun and setting it within easy reach.

A mournful sound carried across the waters and Phineas watched a moment, discerning nothing in the gloom. He waited a minute longer and whispered a prayer with eyes open. "Lord, walk beside me."

He lanced raw mutton upon a great triangular hook. Ahab whined so he tossed a small piece of meat to Ahab, saying, "You wait here. Watch Petunia. I'll be back shortly." He attached the hook to the smaller of the two buoys by a twenty foot chain.

Phineas pushed the rowboat into the lake, with the tethered buoys floating beside. He kept the baited hook in the boat with the buffalo gun. He waved to the pacing dog and rowed with soft sloshing sounds out into the lake. The rope slowly uncoiled from the stump into the frigid waters. It was fall but already frost danced across the valley.

Three hundred feet out and the larger flagged buoy jerked, held fast by the great stump. Phineas had another three hundred feet for the second buoy but with as late and cold as it was, he decided he needn't row that far. He pushed the smaller buoy to let it drift away. The twenty foot chain dragged from the boat. Phineas picked up the stout barbed hook and let it lightly into the water.

The smaller buoy shook as the weight of the chain pulled it taut. Phineas smiled. Nothing to do now but wait and let blessings come.

A tortured scream shot across the lake.

Phineas couldn't tell if it was human or animal nor from which direction it came. The boat rocked as he looked frantically in all directions. Picking up the buffalo gun, he was momentarily disoriented as the boat spun upon the dark mirrored water.

A horrifying roar echoed over the waters, terrible in its satanic majesty. Beastly divergent from the first cry, this was the sound of a bloodthirsty victor, not a victim.

If he had ever heard a monster, that was it. The sensation of that demonic call sickened him, inducing nausea worse than the time he fell into a swarm of pungent crickets. He'd never thought to feel that horrible again, but this enveloped him in thick dread.

Silhouetted against the hills, the greenish light of a fireball rose and floated across the lake some distance south, writhing worm-like in its flight. The color and speed were too strange for a lantern, the twisting trajectory maddening.

Phineas's eyes and rifle followed the thing as it moved away. He wondered briefly if he saw the eyes of a dragon, its colossal head lumbering back and forth as it swam the lake. If so, the brute would be far larger than he had anticipated, a behemoth for the ages.

The wicked firelight continued south, growing dim until it disappeared behind hills or sinking into the depths. Phineas couldn't be sure where it vanished in the dark. He pondered his predicament when a splash and knock against the rowboat made the blood in his veins freeze in piercing shards.

Something was alive in the water beside him.

Heart thawed and racing, he paused and looked over the side.

A thick wet tongue caressed his hand.

Cursing, he leveled the gun at Ahab's wet black face. "Ahab, you fool, I nearly killed ya." He pulled the dog into the boat and was promptly rewarded with its shaking dry. "As if I'm not cold enough," he growled, before rowing with all possible speed for land.

On shore, Phineas painstakingly loaded the rowboat into the wagon as the wind came down from the north. It whipped and gave him a chill as it cut sharply through his damp clothes.

"Let's go Ahab, we gotta get home."

The dog whined again as a loud creak caught Phineas attention. The rope to the first buoy was stretched rigid to the stump, water droplets catching moonlight before falling.

"The wind must be pulling her tight," said Phineas. "It's fine."

Creaking again, the stump lurched from the bank, exposing a few inches from the sandy shore. Phineas frowned and stepped upon the stump.

"Wind must really be pulling, but this is too heavy to go any further," he said, stamping his foot.

Shuddering, the stump heaved into the lake creating a white wake. Ahab whined as his master was pulled into the dark water.

### 2.

It had been a cold night on the mountain for Porter and he meant to stay indoors tonight if he could, but first he went looking for a drink. He was of medium size but broad shouldered and strong, a fighting man, a gunslinger. Dark hair beginning to pepper erupted from beneath his slouch hat and his beard was long and wild as the north wind. But the most disconcerting thing to the townsfolk that watched him ride in, what made them turn away, was his piercing pale blue eyes. The eyes of a killer.

Riding the full length of the town and back again, he was disappointed. No saloon and no inn. He cursed the luck that broke two bottles of Valley-Tan whiskey on the ride through the mountains.

The most promising sanctuary looked to be a general store. He tied his stallion to the hitching post, knocked grime from his worn duster and went inside. His heavy boots pounding the floorboards as the spurs chimed in.

The air inside was stuffy; sunbeams swirling dust graced through thin windowpanes. A thin clerk paused reading the latest edition of the Utah Magazine and smiled, "Morning sir, what can I help you with today? Name is Thomas."

"Got any whiskey? Valley-Tan?" asked the rider, looking about the sparse room.

Frowning, Thomas put down the paper and grabbed a broom. "No, 'fraid not."

"How about a room then?"

Tightening the broomstick, Thomas said, "No, sir, we don't. You ought to keep moving along if you're looking for such things."

The rider gave a lopsided grin and ran a hand over his long peppered beard. "How's about you direct me to Brother Cook then," he said staring through Thomas.

Thomas repeated, "Brother? You . . . you're Porter Rockwell?"

Port grunted, "You sure you ain't got anything to drink?"

"Yes, sir."

Pounding the counter-top, Port said, "I need a squar' drink!"

"Let me look again. Said you want to see Brother Cook? He's laid up in bed, had an accident last night, he did," said Thomas, as he rummaged through crates behind the counter. "Seems he fell into the lake, near froze to death afore he got home. Heard he blamed it on the lake monster."

"What's that?" replied Port, only half-listening as he squinted at a suspect case in the corner.

Straightening, Thomas proclaimed, "The eighth wonder of the world Brother Rich calls it. Right here in our own valley. You haven't heard of the Bear Lake Monster?"

"No," Port groaned, "What's in that case yonder?"

"It's for tinctures."

"Good enough, hand it over," he said, extending his broad palm.

Thomas paused.

Porter gestured with hands strong enough to break a bull's neck.

Reluctantly handing over a bottle, Thomas said, "You know the Good Lord doesn't want you to drink that."

Porter uncorked the bottle, sniffed it and took a swig. "Well, has *He* ever tried it with raspberries?"

Thomas curled his lips at that. "After last night I imagine Brother Cook needs all the help he can get. Soon enough President Young will have to address things too." He held up the latest issue of the Utah Magazine to emphasize his point.

Porter looked at Thomas. "Don't know anything about that, I just need a place to sleep a couple nights. Give me four bottles."

"But you are here because of the monster?"

"Yup, a monster, sure" said Porter between gulps.

"You don't know much about it then do you?"

"Nope. I understand there's been some killings. Brother Brigham asked me to come take care of it. *If* there was anything to it."

"There is," Thomas said with conviction. "We need true

authority to take care of the problem. You can wait for Brother Cook to be ready to talk, but understand this, he had a hook and chain tied to buoys and roped to a huge stump beside the lake."

"So?" said Port, quaffing another mouthful.

"This morning Brother Rich told me, he saw that stump in the lake heading north."

Port shrugged.

"Something pulled it up the lake, against the wind, the buoys were held down underwater. This thing may be too blessed big...even for you."

"I got my own blessings," responded Port. "Where is Cook?"

"Fine house, above the mill, just up the hill. Talk to Brother Cook, but he'll be no help. If I was you, I'd talk to one of the Lamanites," he said, gesturing south.

Port's gaze hardened at that remark; it didn't seem that long ago he met the Shoshone on the Bear River. Images of frozen blood and thunder washed over him. "Which one?"

"You'll want to find Ligaii-Maiitsoh. We call him Lehi; he likes that. Knows everything about the monster."

"That's no Shoshone name," said Port.

Thomas shook his head, "He's not Shoshone, they avoid him, not sure what tribe he is. But he's been good to us. He's nearly a convert."

"Where can I find him?"

3.

Stepping into the bright sunlight, Port stared eastward across the vast long lake. He stretched his back, which in turn let his brace of pistols leer from his person.

A young mother and her son took one look at the long-haired gunfighter and wheeled around.

Port grinned. Watchdogs are rarely appreciated.

He went down the steps whistling an old tune, but a sixth sense that always rode shotgun with him, whispered, look around.

Three men, dogged his trail. They followed on his right with the rising sun at their backs.

"Hey, Rockwell! Need a word with you," shouted the foremost of the three.

Porter pretended he couldn't hear them while watching them in his peripheral vision. He crossed the muddy street in long strides, so that he was on their right, with the sun and shimmering lake at his back.

"We're talking to you, Danite!"

Porter faced them where the alleyway between buildings flashed sunlight into their faces. He watched as townsfolk scurried off the street. All but a curious white haired old Indian, he just stared.

"Hey, Porter!" called the foremost man. "Heard, you can't be shot or cut."

Port spat, "You pukes need schoolin'?"

The first averted his eyes pulling his revolver saying, "Ain't you the funny man." A second with crooked teeth also drew a pistol, the third a shotgun. They kept their distance with guns trained on Port, who had yet to draw, but they respected the pistol handles sticking out of his coat.

"You want me to feed those to ya?" asked Port with a grin.

The three stood with guns pointed but still nervous. Crooked Teeth shook so that his pistol trembled.

"You boys think I've lasted this long to be gunned down by your sorry hides?"

The leader swaggered, "Maybe. You're getting old. Why not?"

Port prodded, "So why don't ya *try* already?"

Crooked teeth, whined, "Boss said we could just run him out of town."

"Huh-uh. He ain't gonna run. Are you Porter?"

Port shook his head.

The shot-gunner chuckled, "We got him."

Port winked.

Crooked teeth wiped his brow with his free hand, letting his aim go far afield.

Porter lunged sideways, drawing his two navy revolvers. Shots blazed and echoed. Bone shattered as Port's lead was sown scarlet upon dirty white fields.

Bullets whizzed like mercurial hornets past Port's ears, but he was untouched. He was always untouched, but he also respected how close death stood, always over his shoulder.

The three lay upon the ground, alive but wounded, mewling.

"Quit you're caterwauling," Port ordered. He nudged their shattered elbows and forearms with his boot. "You pukes is lucky, I was aiming lower." Glancing about for onlookers, "Where is the Marshall?"

The only soul on the street was the old Indian.

"Chief, I need the Marshall or deputy, where're they?"

The Indian just stared.

The lead gunman stopped crying long enough to ask, "Arrrgh. Why don't ya just kill us?"

Grinding his boot heel into the bleeding arm, Port demanded, "Why'd you come gunning for me? Who put you up to it? How'd you know I'd be here?"

The man screamed as Port's heel pressed. The old Indian still watched impassive as ever.

"Well?"

A new voice called out, "Rockwell! You can't do that, it isn't legal." A smartly dressed man approached, followed by two deputies.

"You the sheriff?" Port extended a handshake.

"I am." The man declined to shake, instead pointing at the three wounded men. "I respect your reputation, but you cannot torture these men."

The deputies picked up the wounded and led them down the road.

Grimacing, Port said, "I suppose its right for them to threaten me on the street?"

"Of course not, but times have changed. You're not the judge, jury and executioner. Not anymore," said the sheriff.

"I never was," answered Port.

The sheriff gave a sarcastic half-grin. "I could run you in for this."

Port glared.

"But I won't, I'll ask that you leave your guns with me while you're in town."

"Ha! *No.*"

Paling, the sheriff blustered, "Fine, but anymore trouble and you'll be locked up."

"Someone put them up to this, I've a right to find out who."

"We'll find out. When it goes before Judge Jenson, next week. They may counter-charge you, so if there were any witnesses, you may need their testimony."

"Got one saw the whole thing." Port looked for the Indian, but the old man had disappeared on the wide open street. "He was just here."

"I didn't see anyone when I walked up. This may turn into a case of your word against theirs," said the sheriff. "Maybe you better leave town before any of that happens, let Brigham protect you again."

Cocking an eyebrow, the old gunfighter spat on the sheriff's polished boots and walked away.

4.

Port rode to the house just up the hill. A black dog lounging on the porch watched him dismount. At the door it licked Port's hand.

"Hey, boy, what's your name," asked Port kneeling. He scratched its exposed neck before knocking.

A short blonde woman opened. "I'm so glad you're here. Come in," she said, beaming. "Ahab, stay outside."

Removing his hat, Port asked, "Really, ma'am?"

"Of course. I recognize you, Brother Rockwell. I'm Amanda Cook."

Realization dawned across his face. "Wheat! You're, Dave Savage's papoose, ain't ya?" Port said with a laugh.

"Mary, see that the eggs are collected." Ushering her daughter out to the hen house, Amanda smiled. "No one has called me my father's papoose in years. Phineas is going to be so glad to see you and get your help."

"My help, ma'am?"

She turned her head, "With the monster," she said, raising her eyebrows. "That is why you're here isn't it?"

"I reckon so," said Port. "But everyone seems to know a trifle more than I do."

Amanda ushered Port into a side room where Phineas lay in bed. She tossed a chunk of kindling into the fire.

Heat made Port uncomfortable. He longed for a cool breeze.

"Sorry if I don't get up," sniffed Phineas, "but I got a terrible chill last night."

"What happened? Heard you fell into the lake because of a monster," said Port.

"I didn't fall, was pulled in. Maybe twenty, thirty feet before I jumped off the stump and made it to shore. I was afraid the monster would get me," added Phineas.

"You think so?"

"Yeah, folks have been seeing the monster for a spell. Lately it's been killing livestock and Indians. Figured if we could capture it, I'd solve some of our local problems and make some money to boot." Phineas paused to blow his nose.

"It's been killing then?"

Phineas looked surprised. "Yeah Porter, I thought that was why you were here. We all heard you were coming. I assumed Brother Brigham was sending you to help us deal. Have you throw down with it!"

Port scratched his beard. "Who told you?"

"That apostate writer Stenhouse. Been shooting his mouth off about how President Young is sending you, his avenging angel, up here to save face. Stenhouse has been up here the last few weeks writing up scandalous material for Godbe's rag. Keeps saying you'll fail, since Joseph's blessing for you weren't against tooth and claw. You read any of that trash?"

"Nope."

"You know how the Godbeites are don't you? The Utah Magazine?"

"Nope. Don't read much."

Phineas wrinkled his brow and Amanda restrained a giggle. "Well, they keep pushing for mining rights, trade with gentiles and abandoning sacred law. They're upset with Church doctrine and are trying to change things. Think because they control the paper and wealth they have a right, I suppose. Things could get bad if they convince the government to seize church property. We're at a crossroads."

Amanda broke in, "They believe they can steady the ark and dictate the Lord's commandments, telling the Prophet *he* is the one out of order. They are Spiritualists, communicating with either ghosts or charlatans through séances."

Phineas nodded, "Personally, I think it's all their high falutin' British sensibilities, but I doubt any of that has to do with the monster itself."

Porter grinned. "Go on."

"This monster has been costing us livestock and even been killing folk on the south end. And Stenhouse is writing up articles, playing both sides, pressing for government regulation while also pleading sympathy from the Saints by saying if Brigham can't control a thing of the devil, how can he control Deseret."

"Brother Brigham," Amanda corrected.

"That's what I said. Now Stenhouse writes if Brother Brigham can't control Deseret, if he's not in touch with the Spirit, how can he lead the Church and be right about everything else," said Phineas. "Monsters should be easy, he says."

"His fault?" Port wrinkled his brow in disbelief.

Phineas shook his head. "It's not. It's ammunition, a distraction for something else. I don't know what yet. But they're sowing seeds of doubt and discontent, while something is murdering folks and livestock."

"Seems convenient," said Port.

Amanda nodded, "That's what I said."

Phineas pointed at the lake, "There is a connection somewhere, but one thing at a time. I already heard this morning from Brother Rich, that bodies were found in the Shoshoni area and I heard screams and saw weird fireballs last night. The monster got 'em."

"I'll go look around," said Port. "Is there anyone trustworthy who speaks Shoshoni to go along with me? I heard about some old

Indian named Lehi?"

Amanda shook her head. "You don't need him. I can go with you and translate. Soon as Sister Ann-Eliza arrives to look after Phineas."

Port raised his eyebrows and looked to Phineas. "This could be ugly," said Port. "I've already got somebody gunning for me."

Looking up at the old gunfighter, Amanda replied, "You need someone trustworthy to go along with you. I can help get to the bottom of this better than anyone, and take a crack shot at the monster too, if need be."

"Not a monster I'm worried about."

Amanda answered. "Have no doubts Brother Rockwell, we do seek a monster. I've seen the slaughtered cattle and sheep. I don't think my Phineas realizes how lucky he is to still be alive."

Port raised his hands, "All right, little sister, we'll head out, soon as the relief arrives. Phineas, why didn't your fishing tackle work?"

Phineas sighed, "It did work. I had stout chains and rope, but my anchor was too weak. Monster tore the stump out. If you find it, I need that rope back, it was Brigham's."

"Brother Brigham's," said Amanda.

"That's what I said. The point is, Porter, this thing is big. I'm not sure anymore what it'll take to rein the beast in."

Port tipped his hat and said, "I'll keep an eye out."

5.

A skin-drum throbbed as Port and Amanda rode into the Shoshoni camp.

Port asked, "Why the drums?"

Amanda said, "They're letting everyone know we are here. Everyone is skittish after the Bear River massacre. The monster only increases the tension."

"I reckon so."

Crowds of people gathered, faces carved with somber expressions, hard and unfriendly. A tall, young man approached Amanda and greeted her in silence. She turned to Porter saying, "This is Many-Buffalo, he is Chief of this clan, Chief Sagwitch's son." She then told Many-Buffalo of Porter.

The Chief glared at Porter and revealed a scar on his breast.

Port intervened, "It doesn't have to be like this, we don't have to be friends, I just want to know about the trouble."

Many-Buffalo, gestured at his tribe and pointed at Porter.

"I'll get to that, but they aren't in a friendly mood," she said. "He says you were there, why should he speak to you?"

Rubbing a hand over his face, Port said, "I was there, but I've never killed an innocent man, tell him that."

"I will in not so many words," said Amanda. She translated to Many-Buffalo and pointed at the lake.

The talk from several of the tribe grew excited pointing at the lake, several made a ward against evil, but Many-Buffalo looked at the sky. He spoke quickly back and forth with Amanda, who pleaded Port's case.

Amanda finally revealed, "He wants proof that you are as good a man as I say you are, before he will discuss the monsters with you."

"Monsters? There's more than one?"

"First things first," said Amanda. "He wants proof."

"Like what?" asked Port, extending his hand to shake.

Many-Buffalo hesitated, and extended his hand to Port's, but with only two fingers out, the rest clenched back.

Port questioned, "What's that?"

"He doesn't trust you."

"Wheat! I knew that. What do I need to do to get him to talk?"

A mountain of a man stepped forward, creating a hush among the tribe. Thick and strong, he looked down on Porter scrutinizing him. "You are Mormonee?" he asked, bringing his bare chest to Port's nose.

Amanda said, "This is Big Bear."

"Yeah, I'm Mormonee," answered Port. "He is probably the second biggest Indian I've ever seen."

"Do you wear the sacred robes?" asked the grinning giant.

"Yes."

"Show me."

Port opened his shirt revealing the garments. "Satisfied?"

"The woman is Mormonee too?"

"Yes."

"She will show me?" He smirked.

Port shoved Big Bear, "That's enough. Can we talk or not, Many-Buffalo? Or do I have to teach some manners to your boy?"

Amanda shook her head.

Big Bear knocked Port's hat off.

"Tell him! I'm here to take care of things and if they don't help me, I can't help them!" shouted Port. "But I'm not here to play games."

Many-Buffalo stood impassive, then nodded to Big Bear.

The giant lunged, grasping Port in a bear hug, trapping his arms and lifting him off the ground. The gathering laughed as Many-Buffalo shouted in triumph.

Struggling to breath, let alone move, Port asked, "What'd he say?"

"He said, if you are the best the Brigham can offer, he doesn't need help," cried Amanda over the din.

Big Bear's laughter boomed into Port's face.

"Wheat! They ain't seen nothing yet."

Big Bear's hug cracked Port's back and grew tighter, forcing air from his lungs and still the big man laughed.

Looking Big Bear square in the eye, Port winked and slammed his thick forehead into Big Bear's nose repeatedly. The huge man blinded and bloodied, dropped Port, who landed on his feet. Porter slammed Big Bear an uppercut to the chin, dropping the man mountain. Rounding on Many-Buffalo, Port snarled, "Was he the best you got?"

Amanda translated.

Many-Buffalo frowned, but motioned for Port and Amanda to follow.

Amanda picked up Port's hat, and handed it to him saying, "You know, might doesn't always make right."

"Didn't *I* just prove that?"

6.

Though it was still afternoon on a warm day, Many-Buffalo kindled the fire inside his tepee. He took a powder and scattered about the perimeter of his dwelling, paying specific attention to the door-flap.

Sitting on buffalo skins, Port and Amanda waited, while Many-Buffalo sang a song of blessing and protection. Taking a seat opposite them, Many-Buffalo spoke quick, harsh-sounding words, staring deep at Port.

Amanda translated, "He said . . . to speak of such things as we ask . . . he must bless and purify his tepee. He will do it again . . . after we've gone. They've had problems . . . but he will not ask for help . . . since he was already denied."

"Tell him this. A proud man won't ask, but a proud man can answer. Tell him, I'm asking to know about these things, so I can help his people."

Many-Buffalo looked at Port as Amanda spoke. He nodded and went into a lengthy round of back and forth with Amanda, as she gave Port snippets.

"He says the lake monster . . . haunted the waters in the time of his ancestors. It has slept for many moons . . . and only awoke when . . . Mormons came. It eats sheep and cattle . . . perhaps even men . . . but it is not to be confused . . . with other curses that have befallen his people. Murders have come . . . the last few weeks . . . only. Sorcery has tainted the people. They fear the witch and skin-walker . . . more than they do . . . the lake monster. The reason . . . they have not moved yet . . . because these evil things follow them."

"What's that?"

Amanda shook her head, "I'm not sure but it has all of them afraid. He is reluctant to tell me more . . . because it invites . . . the evil thing into his tepee. They hoped Brother Brigham could help . . . but the . . . drawing man . . . told them Brigham . . . would not help."

"What's a drawing man?"

Amanda shrugged. "There is no word for it, I translated as best I could."

"What can he say about the lake monster? How big is it? Is there a way to kill it?"

She asked Many-Buffalo and he pondered a moment, before going into a number of hand gestures and excited speaking with a final disgusted look before throwing holy powder into the fire, that made it blaze brilliantly.

"He says they are related . . . that Mormons . . . brought the curse here . . . the monsters are linked to each other . . . yours and ours," said Amanda. "I'm not sure what yours and ours mean."

Port rubbed smoke from his eyes, "I thought we would get some answers here."

"I'm sorry. They're scared. This has touched them deeply," she said.

Many-Buffalo watched them and spoke again.

"He says their burial grounds . . . have been violated. Something steals from the dead. As for your questions . . . the lake monster . . . is long as four wagons . . . and its skin cannot be wounded . . . by a gun or knife."

"Kinda like me," said Port.

"He says . . . works of darkness . . . fill this land. We walk...the path of the . . . skin-walker. May the Great Spirit...protect us . . . on our quest. He will say no more."

Murmuring the drums outside beat again.

Amanda gasped, "Someone is here."

7.

A man on a rickety wagon pulled into the Shoshoni camp. Bearded and slight, he glowered at Port and Amanda as they exited Many-Buffalo's tepee.

"What's the matter Stenhouse? Upset I wasn't chased outta town by your blacklegs?" called Port, chuckling.

Stenhouse dropped off the wagon, tipped his hat to Amanda, "Mrs. Cook," and extended a hand to Port. "My apologies, the uneducated rascal's misunderstood my direction and inclination. I have not levied them out of jail and I directed the sheriff to let the lot of them stay a fortnight therein."

Port declined the handshake, as he tried not to smirk at

Stenhouse's English pretentious accent.

Stenhouse continued, "Forgive my temper, I merely wished to meet with Chief Sagwitch's son myself, and worried that he already had guests, you see."

"Yeah, 'I see'," mocked Port, "you're upset we beat you here before you could spread more lies. How'd you know I was coming up to Bear Lake before I did?"

"Nothing of the sort, I came to speak with the Chief much the same as I imagine you did, as for knowing you would be here...whom else would Brigham send? Understanding his mentality, as I do, it was elementary, my dear Danite."

Port sniffed and spit.

"Regardless of what you may think of me, Porter, I am not the enemy. We may disagree fundamentally on authority, but our core is the same. The New Movement and I seek truth the same as you."

Amanda countered, "What was it Fanny wrote? To doubt one doctrine was to doubt all? Our core is not the same. You abandoned yours."

"Madam, I must protest."

But Amanda wasn't even close to being done, she reared up in the Englishman's face. Port stood back and smiled, this was gonna be good.

"You think we haven't all had hardships? You think we haven't all questioned the tests we have in life? Let me tell you something. You'll be caught in your own traps."

Stenhouse looked to Port for assistance from the feisty young woman, but the old gunfighter raised his hands, cocked his head and smirked.

"Don't you and the other Godbeites fool yourselves. This life isn't where you will be successful. It's in the eternities. Just because Brother Brigham might have given you some bad business advice or won't let you mine our mountains to ruin, doesn't mean you can become a law unto yourselves. If you lost faith in God, it's because you put your faith in the arm of flesh!" shouted Amanda. "Your lies and schemes will snap back upon you."

With that, she mounted her horse and cantered off.

Visibly disturbed at her words, Stenhouse slunk away.

Port followed after Amanda.

Big Bear, still cradling his broken nose, glared at Port.

Tipping his hat to the big man, Port gave his horse heels to catch up to Amanda.

She turned in the saddle, "I'm sorry about that, but I'm so tired of his lies."

"No problem, little sister."

"I did give him what-for, didn't I?"

"Yes, you did," Port laughed, deep and loud.

8.

Dusk rode in with Port, laying red like a mantle across the valley. With no clouds, it would be a cold night.

In the Cook home, Phineas gave his wife a warm hug before grilling Port. "So what'd you find out?"

"Whole lot of nothing. Many-Buffalo didn't have anything I can use and wouldn't tell us much of what's happened to his tribe."

Mary, the Cook's young daughter, offered Port a glass of water and hugged her mother's skirt.

"They're scared," said Amanda. "Something is happening. They feel powerless. And Stenhouse went out there after us."

"Really? What'd he want?" asked Phineas.

Port gulped down the glass of water and made a face, "Said he wanted to talk to Many-Buffalo. Don't know what for. Amanda gave him a good tongue lashing though."

Amanda blushed, "I did, I suppose." Phineas's beamed.

Port took off his hat and slumped into a chair. "Now, I need to find out why Stenhouse tried to get me outta town. He should've known his thugs couldn't do it and why would he wanna talk to the Shoshoni? Can't imagine him getting any farther than I did."

"Nothing to do then but get some rest for the morrow," said Phineas. "Way past your bedtime, Mary."

"Goodnight, Papa," said Mary, hurrying to bed.

9.

The little girl rushed up the steps to the loft. The moon shone in her window like a finger of ice. Nestling in the covers, she said her personal prayers, closing her eyes as the lamp downstairs dimmed. She slept restless, dreaming of drowning.

She awoke with a start as a mystic green light passed her window. It wasn't the rising corn-yellow moon. Whatever it was lay outside her window. Sitting up, she gazed into the darkness and witnessed a pallid form shamble through the trees.

From behind the closest tree, a taloned hand gripped bark and then a white face leered. It was wolf-like, with red eyes glowing like embers which burrowed into Mary's.

Fear petrified her, she couldn't look away from the thing loping closer. So frightened she couldn't speak, only shake. Did the monster smile at that? The hideous wolf-man looked from her to the front door.

It would come inside.

She shivered, too terrified to warn her parents. She heard father downstairs, talking with the strange long-haired man. Her lips trembled but no sound came.

The thing stood directly below her window. It seemed capable of leaping up and through the glass. Those eyes so blood-red and evil. She couldn't look away, what horrors did it have planned for her? Her parents? Her sleeping siblings? It would come inside and devour them.

The monster, with white talons smeared scarlet, motioned for her to come.

Compelled beyond fear and reason, Mary released the latch on the window.

Saliva dripped as its tongue lolled.

Mary pushed the window open.

The monster beckoned her to jump, its eyes hypnotizing.

Too afraid to move, to scream or even look away, Mary did the only thing left her, she cried a prayer deep inside for deliverance.

The wolf-thing beckoned for her to jump into its waiting arms.

Tears streaming, Mary lifted herself to the sill and precariously balanced, halfway in and out.

Licking its lips, it beckoned again as the moon illuminated its awful red matted fur.

Was there no relief? Did those who gave themselves to monsters deserve heaven?

Ahab the dog, bawled out loud in staccato.

The spell broken, Mary snapped back to self-control and dropped to the floor avoiding any possible eye contact. She heard Father and the long-haired stranger startle, each muttering as they stirred. The familiar cocking of guns told her they were prepared.

The wolf-thing snarled at Ahab, who cowered beneath the porch.

Praising the Lord for delivering her family from the evil of this thing Mary shut the window latch.

Raging, the beast summoned a ball of green fire in its left hand and cast it through her window. Flames erupted all about the bedroom as Mary screamed.

10.

"What the devil was that horrible sound?" shouted Port, drawing his pistols. He threw back the front door and looked into the gloom.

Nothing.

Ghostly green-orange firelight blazed upstairs, licking the windowsill and rafters.

Phineas cried, "Porter, help! The house is on fire!"

Somewhere a child screamed an unholy fear.

Port replaced his pistols and stepped back through the doorway only to be grasped by the back of his coat and flung backward off the porch.

Stars reeled overhead as a black wind blew.

The breath knocked from his lungs, senses fled and only the fire above was visible. He struggled to sit up. Reaching for his pistols, his hands found empty holsters.

Forcibly lifted, someone slammed him to the ground. The most disturbing part to the Danite was the low rumbling chuckle the attacker let out. He couldn't see his enemy, but he heard him all right.

Port kicked and connected to thick shin bone.

The midnight assailant didn't chuckle anymore.

Rolling to his feet, Port snatched his Bowie, ready for anything.

As the enemy grabbed him again, Port's blade slashed across its chest. Blood and tufts of a white fur spiraled from the wound. Port trusted his honed senses to guide his hand. Listening intently, to his right a twig snapped. He barreled toward the sound, knife extended.

Port felt steel bite flesh, ripping the blade across what he hoped were vitals.

Howling in pain, an inhumanly strong hand took Port's shoulder, tearing cloth, and threw him to the earth.

Roaring, "Wheat in the mill!" Port launched up, renewed to fight his foe with blood-maddening vigor. He spun about, waving the Bowie, expecting another attack.

None came.

Dark blood along with flecks of white fur trailed into the gulf of night. Port raced back to the house to fight the fire.

Inside Phineas and Amanda held their daughter. The fire was out. Mary was shivering, wiping the last of her tears away. "You did it."

"I've never seen the like," gasped Phineas. "The room blazed like a furnace. You must have slain the thing because the witch-fire up and disappeared. Thank you."

"Yes, thank you," repeated Amanda, her own tears falling. "It's over."

Shaking his head, Port growled, "No, 'tain't. I didn't kill it."


11.

A long night brought morning headaches and breakfast questions.

"So what do you reckon it was?" asked Phineas.

Port chewed his mouthful, saying, "Probably that Shoshoni giant Big Bear. From what Mary said, sounds about the same size. Know I cut him bad, so he's probably gonna hole up in a sweat lodge for a while."

"What about the witch-fire?"

Stabbing another piece of venison, Port answered, "I've seen enough strange things in my time, to say anything is possible. Tricks is key to the sorcerer type. Probably a wolf-skin mask and bear-paw war-club."

"That was no mask," broke in Mary. "That was a monster."

Shaking her head, Amanda said, "That wasn't natural."

"Darkness can play tricks on you."

The little girl shook her head, "No, this was real bad. That thing is of the devil."

"Men can be monsters too," said Port, finishing his last bite. "Much obliged Brother Cook, Sister Cook." He looked to Mary and rubbed his broad hand over her head. "I'm gonna get to the bottom this, an' that's a promise."

Amanda threw down her dishrag, "And just what are you planning to do? Sounds like you're in denial of monsters."

Grinning, Port said, "No need to worry, ma'am. I think Stenhouse, the Godbeites and some of the Shoshoni are in cahoots. I need a few more answers and I'll get 'em."

Blocking the door, Amanda said, "None of that explains the lake monster, what we saw last night was something different, probably the same thing that has the Shoshoni frightened. There has to be more to this than Stenhouse and a few bribed Indians."

"I'm sure there is, but I can't take care of it, jawing 'bout it."

Amanda looked to Phineas, who nodded. "Then I'm coming with you. You need someone's help to translate and watch your back," she said.

Port shook his head, like a black-maned lion. "No, ma'am. I got an instinct about a few things I'd best check out on my own." Before she could protest, he added. "And I won't need a translator this time. Thanks for breakfast. Feel better Phineas." Port tipped his hat, adjusted his gun belt and went out into the cool morning.

As he made for the Cooks' stable, a hint of white moving in the trees caught his eye. It swayed with the light breeze at eye level. Port drew his trusty navy revolver and approached with grim determination.

It looked like a tangled bunch of pale sticks strung in the pines facing the Cook homestead, but closer inspection revealed it was a curious cobble of interlaced bones, calico twine and a couple of dark feathers, about the size of his hand. It was some type of Indian fetish or charm. Then again it looked more like something a white man would make rather than a real Indian charm. The bones looked like chicken as opposed to eagle or crow. That and it smelt of coffee, not the succulent flowers of the field.

Port tore it down and put it in his pocket. He considered telling the Cook's what he found but decided against it, they were spooked enough.

### 12.

In town, a heated commotion carried over the streets. Men shouted at one another and Port could feel the contentious spirit waxing. There appeared to be two opposing camps, one backed by Stenhouse, the sheriff, and their full gang of thugs; the other fronted by tall Joseph Rich, the local newspaperman, who was supported by a good number of townsfolk.

Port couldn't tell what started the argument.

Rich's strong baritone proclaimed, "I lost a horse to the monster. But that doesn't mean it needs to be destroyed!"

Stenhouse countered, "You're the beast's greatest advocate. It clears you of the secret gambling debts, you lost your mount to. It grants sensationalism and lurid stories for your amateur journalism, but you seem to forget the spiritual implications."

Men tried to shout him down, including Rich for the gambling crack, but Stenhouse persisted. "A duel is coming! The hour of struggle is at hand. If *infallible* Brigham," he said sarcastically, "can't cast out the devil, what good is he?"

A man swung at Stenhouse but was instead hit first across the mouth by one of the deputies.

Stenhouse continued, "If a man is to lead this people he has to be open to new revelation. We can change what doesn't belong. We can prosper with what the Lord grants us here in these mountains, there is gold and silver aplenty!"

Stenhouse had Port's full attention.

"My friends, Brigham is a good man but he has lost his way,

don't you lose it alongside him, a new prophet will rise!"

"Yeah? Who?" squawked a man between Stenhouse and Rich.

"Why the very blood of the great prophet himself, Joseph the third."

A number of boos and catcalls came with the mention of Joseph Smith's eldest son. Port just shook his head.

"What about the monster?" shouted a man in the crowd.

Another cried, "It took my sheep."

"What can be done about it? It killed Big Bear and a half dozen braves last night."

Port's eyes grew. He struggled through the throng to get to the man who mentioned Big Bear. The rebuttal from Rich was lost to Port's ears as he pushed and grabbed the man's shoulder.

"You! Who told you Big Bear is dead?"

The man spun trying to escape Port's grasp then breathed a sigh of relief, "It's you. You'll take care of this."

"What about Big Bear?"

"He's dead. Seen him myself yonder. Chief Many-Buffalo brought what's left of his body and the others into town a half hour ago."

"Was he cut up with a Bowie?"

The man blanched, "No! The monster took bites outta him. It's gruesome. Go see."

Port let go of the man's shoulder and drifted out of the crowd.

A familiar voice spoke, "Porter, what do you make of this?" It was Thomas, the shopkeeper. "You ever go talk to Lehi?"

Port shook his head, then spotted Many-Buffalo.

"You should, I'll bet he could explain things."

"Much obliged," said Port abruptly walking away.

13.

Many-Buffalo was surrounded by a dozen wailing women, the remains of his braves lay beneath a broad red blanket. He was speaking with local authority and Apostle Charles C. Rich.

"Brother Rich, can I take a look?" asked Port.

"Go ahead Brother Rockwell. Chief Many-Buffalo has just asked my help in blessing them for their journey."

Port nodded and looked to Many-Buffalo who still gave the unfriendly glare he had from the day before. Lifting the blanket's edge, Port looked upon the terrible visage of Big Bear. He expected to see evidence of his Bowie, but not this—carnage to rival the worst horror he had ever witnessed. Claw and bite wounds from something huge. The same atrocities had been dealt to three more men.

There went Port's personal theory for last night's incident. Big Bear could not possibly have been the enemy he fought in the darkness.

"Many-Buffalo tells me that you and Sister Cook visited him yesterday," said Charles.

"We did. So did Stenhouse."

"He said Stenhouse came wanting to know what could be done about the monster, if there was anything he could do to help. He gave them some of the latest model of guns, repeating rifles and the like and yet, you see here what happened," said Charles.

Port squinted across the way at Stenhouse still fuming his 'New Movement' to the townsfolk. "Why try and get the Indian's to deal with this thing though? Why wouldn't he have that crooked sheriff and his blacklegs deal?"

"I couldn't begin to say."

Port threw back the blanket pointing at vicious wounds, "This gives more questions than answers. Seems worse than a bear attack."

Charles nodded, "These men could have handled a bear."

Narrowing his gaze, Port noticed Big Bear had a small bone fetish on his belt just like the one he found earlier. "Something is sending a message. But I can't read it, yet."

"Some messages can't be read," said the Apostle. "And when words can't cut the evil, it's time to use a sword."

Port grinned as he drew, spun and holstered his navy colts. "I find a six-gun is quicker."

14.

Port had a vague impression of where to find Lehi, the old

Indian that supposedly knew so much about the monster. A whistle drew his attention.

It was Stenhouse, across the street. He beckoned for Port to come and speak with him in front of the sheriff's office.

Flexing his fingers, Port warily eyed the windows and hiding spots behind Stenhouse. He was ready to draw his navy colts like chain lightning if need be.

"What do you want?" he growled.

"Just to speak a moment, without the self-righteous she-cat beside you."

Porter grabbed Stenhouse's tie, yanking him closer, "You'll speak kindly about the lady."

"Hey! You'll keep your hands of Mr. Stenhouse," called the sheriff, from inside the office.

Port shoved the thin man away. "I've heard how you treat *your* women."

Stenhouse rankled at the insinuation. "I beg your pardon. We have had our differences, our run-ins, but I wanted to let you know that a new wind is blowing. Utah is changing, the railroad is here and new revelations come with it. You can be part of the old guard that is swept away and forgotten—or be a part of the reformation."

Port shook his head, "You really know nothing about me."

"I know this," said Stenhouse, his tone turning cruel and superior. "I spoke to Vice-President Colfax only a few short weeks ago, the government is tired of Brigham's unfriendly theocracy, his dictatorship of the territory, his dominion of Deseret."

"You always were too theatrical, Stenhouse."

"Oh no, not this time. This is real. They are going to invade, they are going to take our lands by force and destroy the Church if things aren't changed. We in the New Movement are working toward effecting that change before it's too late. We could use your help."

Port guffawed.

"Laugh," Stenhouse said coldly. "Evidence that Brigham is counterfeiting is being filed."

"That'll never stick," objected Port.

"Oh no? How about this. There are those who will testify that he ordered Mountain Meadows."

Port frowned, "That's a lie and you know it."

"Do I? Does it matter if the government gets hold of the evidence to destroy the Church? Our survival depends on change. Brigham is a fallen prophet. He has lost his way. He can't even repudiate a monster that threatens his own people—what about the monster that is the U.S. Army? The people must abandon Brigham and follow the New Movement."

Narrowing his steely gaze, Port rumbled, "What's your part in this? Who's gonna lose faith in the prophet over a monster?"

Stenhouse's tone changed again, "I'll tell you because I'm afraid. No one has put this together yet. Every night with a waxing moon, the body count doubles. The creature's blood lust cannot be sated. Brigham can't protect anyone. How many deaths have you prevented since you arrived? Yes, even the '*Destroying Angel*' is helpless against this monster."

"Then why doesn't the New Movement take care of it?"

"Things have to get worse before they can get better."

Port said, "Hogwash. You're all using this as an agenda. You make me sick."

"Say what you will, but shame is our only tool. To shame President Young into acknowledging us his spiritual betters. Only then will we step forward and alleviate this threat."

Port shook his head, "So, you will let men die to further gain your political ambitions? Out of my way I got things to do."

"You think so small. Better for a few men to die than for a people to perish in ignorance. We will bring balance to the Church," said Stenhouse. "New revelation has been given, the spirits have granted us release and wisdom. They have given us solution to our predicament."

Port rubbed a hand across his beard as if pondering.

"I offer you a place. Reject us and it will not be offered again and you will be swept away as so much chaff! The field is ripe. Where will you stand?"

Putting his nose inches from Stenhouse's, Port whispered, "That's the name of the game." He lightly patted the Englishman's cheek twice, then strode down the street to fetch his horse.

"What does that mean?"

"Figure it out," Port called.

A few minutes later, Port rode down the hill from the Cook's and came in behind the sheriff's office. He pulled the strange fetish of stick-like bones from his jacket pocket and tossed it upon the roof of the office. Chuckling, he rode on.

15.

Port rode with the wind at his back, watching the long lake and pondering. Why would the Lord allow these things to plague good people? What was the test? The lesson to be learned? What was his own part and responsibility?

All experiences are for our ultimate good, mused Port.

Sheep grazed in large swaths across the rounded landscape, most flocks were tended by young boys.

He trotted his stallion up to a tousle-headed boy and nodded, "Afternoon, son. You out here a lot?"

"Every day, mister."

"Ever see anything strange?"

The boy smiled. "Besides you?"

Port chuckled, "Yeah, besides me. A monster maybe."

The boy went serious. "I thought I saw it once."

Port folded his arms, now he was getting somewhere.

"I was playing by the lake shore when I saw six or seven dark shapes out in the water. A big horse-like head with horns was coming out, right at me. I was so afraid. I couldn't hardly breathe, let alone move."

Port looked out at the lake again. "You saw it? Didn't it try to eat you?"

"No, it wasn't the monster," the boy smirked, "it was a herd of elk crossing the lake. The bull was in front, the cows behind. My fear made a monster."

"You don't believe in the monster?" questioned Port.

"I didn't say that. I'm just saying things aren't always what they seem."

"True," Port said. "Know where to find an old Indian, called Lehi?"

The boy pointed southwest, "Over those hills somewhere. No one lives near him."

"Much obliged," said Port, galloping away.

"No one lives near him," called the boy.

"I heard ya," shouted Port over his shoulder.

16.

Over rolling hillocks and past a few stands of trees Port saw a wisp of rising smoke, thin and gray, curling toward heaven through the light drizzle.

"Hello, the camp! Lehi?" Port called. Experience said you were better off letting folks know you were coming in.

Rounding the bend, a rotted tepee came into view. It looked smaller than the usual ten to twelve buffalo-hide tepees. It was made of perhaps eight skins.

Port's horse nickered at entering the clearing and tried to turn away. Glancing about for a possible predator, Port called again, "Lehi, you out here?"

"I am here," announced a ragged voice as the tepee flap peeled back and the very same elderly Indian from town the day before peered out. "Go away! What you want? Blood?"

Laughing, "You're the old man in town from yesterday!" Port dismounted the skittish horse. "You could've saved me the trip if you would've stuck around."

Exiting the tepee, Lehi frowned. "I have things to do."

"Take it easy. I just wanted to talk to you for a spell 'bout the monster. I'm Porter," he said, extending his hand.

Cocking his head, the old Indian stared with eyes hard and cold as the mountaintop. "I tell you as I told them. Monster comes to eat on clear night when moon grows like swelling belly." He stepped out of the tepee and stood uncomfortably close to Porter.

"They said you could tell me all about the monster."

Smirking, Lehi answered, "You want a story, you got to pay." He opened his hand, expecting.

The horse whinnied and backed away pulling the reins in Port's clenched fist. The ragged voice and unnerved horse put Port's guard up. He considered drawing his sawed-off navy colt.

Lehi grinned. "Forget it. I like you. We are the same, you and I."

Nerves calmed, Port said, "Anytime." He took one of the tincture bottles from his saddle bags and handed it to a pleased Lehi. "About last night, what do you know about the lake monster? What's it look like? Any weaknesses?"

Lehi nodded. "Trust in Great Spirit, but tie up your horse. Let us speak inside," he gestured to his faded buffalo-skin tepee.

A smell that Port attributed to the old man's lifestyle permeated the inside of the tepee, it was similar to wet dog but with a reptilian copper scent. Ratty old furs and skins made up the old man's bed. A handful of tools cluttered the far side of the tepee. A ring of stones held a few glowing coals in the center. Unexpected to Port, was a worn copy of the Book of Mormon.

"You read?"

"I feel it is truth," said Lehi, "but my reading is not yet bountiful."

Port grinned, "Me too."

Lehi sat cross-legged opposite Porter and pushed back his beaded breastwork, revealing massive scars along his chest and shoulder. The trauma displayed was so extensive Port wondered at how the old man survived.

Showing a missing finger and the stub next to it on his left hand, Lehi said, "This is where great serpent bit me, here and here." He pointed to his shoulder, chest and upheld his disfigured hand.

"When was this?"

"To my life . . . not long ago. Was first time I saw great serpent. I sang old songs calling for the Old Ones. But Great Serpent heard me and came. Him very angry with me," chuckled Lehi.

"Why is that?"

"Great Serpent not want to be wakened. He is lost and used."

Wrinkling his forehead Port asked, "Lost? Used? I don't follow you."

Wrapping himself in his cloak, Lehi said, "Great Serpent not meant to be here. He will not listen to me. But there is purpose in all things."

"How big is he? Can he be killed?"

Lehi lit a pipe before answering and stared into the smoldering center a long while. "I will tell you, because you are like me, a hunter of men. No gun of white man can kill Great Serpent. It is long as four wagons. It is a thing from old times."

"But why is it here?"

Lehi shrugged, "Why does sun rise? Moon set? It is."

"Are you saying it can't be killed?"

Lehi smiled, revealing wicked teeth for an old man. "I say, do not even try. Monster will eat you."

Port didn't like his tone. "If it lives, it can be killed."

"You have brave heart. Perhaps is a way.

Port rubbed his chin. "Go on."

"Would be dangerous. We would be risking our lives."

"That's my business. I've got a charmed life."

Lehi nodded and beckoned Port to follow. He stepped out of his tepee, and trotted out of the glade and into the thick brush. The speed of the old man amazed Port.

Lehi gathered a handful of pale roots. "We poison Great Serpent, tonight."

Port looked skeptical, "How come no one has tried this before?"

Lehi chuckled, "Who stupid enough to face Great Serpent?"

"Good point."

17.

Lehi had a wide raft that would take them out into the lake. It was slow going, but allowed for more fighting space in Port's mind. The raft seemed safer than a canoe which could be capsized, leaving them at the mercy of the lake monster.

Port left his stallion on shore with a good bit of tether. Considering Joseph Rich had already lost a horse to the monster, Port left his farther uphill. He brought his blessed Bowie knife, his two sawed-off navy revolvers, and a 45-70 buffalo gun.

Lehi brought a deer-skin sack full of the poisonous roots, Port's gift of a tincture bottle, his flute, a tomahawk pipe, and a bit of firewood that he would use to make a fire on the raft over the top of a stone and mud section he had pre-arranged. A small burnt scar upon the raft denoted where he had done this in the past.

"Tell me again, how we're gonna get the monster to eat these roots," asked Port, regretting not having another bottle of Valley-Tan.

Lehi watched the gunfighter's eyes and gestured to the bottle.

"Much obliged."

Lehi nodded and said, "I will call Great Serpent. When he comes, his mouth wide to eat, throw in roots. But not until he right beside us. Very close."

"Could it sink us?"

"Sure. But I will sing our death song and chant old ways. You can shoot if you like, but it do no good. Roots work fast."

Port wasn't familiar with that many plants, but he never heard of a poisonous root such as this before, but maybe it was Indian magic.

Dusk came quick, casting red twilight over the valley. Somewhere a wolf howled and Port watched the shore. With the sun down, cold wrapped its arms about them. The cold sapphire waters did not look inviting.

Lehi lit his fire with a bow drill. He was amazingly quick. He blew on the shards of spark and they leapt into action as if commanded by the breath of the divine. The orange glow fought and won against the encroaching night. The old man lit his pipe and inhaled deep breaths, puffing them toward the west, to which he bowed.

Port expected him to do something more, perhaps something to the east but he didn't.

"We will let darkness grow a little stronger," said Lehi. "Then I will call Great Serpent out."

"How about another pull on that raspberry tincture then?"

Lehi handed Port the bottle.

An hour or two later their kindling was almost gone and Port dreaded the idea of being on the lake in the dark. "Well, is it time yet?"

Flute in hand, Lehi stood and played a melancholy and

disturbing tune. The notes rose and fell in a jarring dirge that Port theorized was never meant to be heard by a white man. It was primal and savage, a true song of the wilds, full of wonder and midnight.

Something splashed out in the waters, forbidden to Port's sight.

"It comes," said Lehi.

"You sure?"

Lehi didn't answer, but blew a long note from his flute and went silent.

Port dropped the sack of poison roots at his own feet and readied the buffalo gun. If anything could penetrate the monsters hide, he reasoned it would be his 45-70. Glancing about, Port was ready, but no more splashing came.

Lehi broke into song, a sad and painful chant.

Port heard a splash like an oar hitting the water. The bright moon was just coming over Black Mountain to the east and Port thought he could see a canoe heading toward them. "Someone's out there Lehi, it ain't the monster."

The canoe glided closer and regardless of the dying fire, Lehi continued his chant. "Hey-yaw, taw hey-yaw. Zhoo' yea' Zhoo' yea'. Yana Glooshi, hey-yaw, taw hey yaw."

"Who's there?" asked Port of the darkness.

No answer came, or at least none he could hear above Lehi's chanting.

Port threw the last few chunks of fuel into the fire hoping to pierce the darkness a little better, absently wondering if whomever was about to meet them had seen anything up the lake.

The fire briefly flared and hid, perking up and down as it consumed its meager final meal.

Facing the incoming canoe, Port couldn't see anyone paddling it, just the form drifting closer. He strained to hear if anyone had fallen overboard or worse, if there was a struggle from someone becoming a monster's most recent meal.

"Hey-yaw, taw hey-yaw. Zhoo' yea' Zhoo' yea'. Yana Glooshi, hey-yaw, taw hey yaw. Oh yaw-hey! Oh yaw-hey! Yaw!" sang Lehi, powerful and deep.

The canoe was almost to the raft and Port puzzled over its missing pilot. He saw that the canoe was misshapen, strangely wider toward the rear. Was there a body slumped to the rear?

Gazing hard at the canoe, a wisp of flame from the firelight flared up for a fraction of a second and allowed Port to see two black eyes reflecting back the orange fire-light. Two massive eyes each set in the wider portion of what was not a canoe but the monster's head. Like a crocodile it had cruised upon them, drawn by the shaman's song.

The huge multi-fanged mouth sprang open.

Port braced himself, too stunned to shoot or grab the sack of poisoned roots.

Ferocious jaws came down, splintering the raft into kindling, snuffing the weak fire and coals.

Pitched into the air, Port was fell forward into the waiting jaws of the Bear Lake monster. He hit the giant tongue and was aware of a bright green light behind him as the cavernous mouth closed.

18.

Cold moonlight reached through the sheriff's office window, barely warded off by the wood stove. Eight men sat with greasy cards as the lamp guttered low. Stenhouse was the only man sitting out the card game, but his whiskey bottle was emptier than most as he wrote at a furious pace.

"Probably ought to call it a night," said the sheriff. "Just after midnight."

Stenhouse didn't bother looking at him from his crouched position over the desk. "I'm not yet done recording the events of today. I have more."

The sheriff laughed obscenely and dealt the next hand.

A thunder rolled off the lake and even against the hugely waxing moon, a green-hued light approached, casting wicked intentions on the office floor like a dueling gauntlet.

Stenhouse visibly shuddered, saying, "It will keep going, it will keep going."

"You know what that is or something?" asked one of his hired gunmen.

"No . . . no, just unnerving is all."

Another hired gun added, "People been seeing 'em all week. Probably shootin' stars is all, boss."

From that remark the deputy told a crude joke causing riotous laughter.

Stenhouse turned from the desk glaring, "Be quiet, I am trying to work!"

A chorus of off-color laughter was interrupted by a loud thump upon the roof above their heads. Dust shook from the rafters coating the men in pale gray hues.

The card players looked up in wonder then terror as steps bounded across the roof. Stenhouse was halfway under his desk by the first thud.

"What is it?"

"Wha' could be so big?"

Frantic, Stenhouse ordered, "It doesn't matter, kill it, shoot, shoot!"

The sheriff looked unconvinced, "Shoot what? Sounds like whoever it was jumped off the roof. Slim, Roger, check it out." He beckoned toward the door.

Slim and Roger went to the front door, Slim gingerly opened as Roger covered him. With everything still as ice, they stepped out, pointing their guns in every which direction.

"Nothing out here, boss," said Slim.

A massive white hand reached from off the roof picking Slim up by the head, yanking him out of sight.

A chorus of gunfire followed, as Roger hit the deck. "Oh dear Lord, I saw it! Hideous!" As the shooting paused, he slammed the door shut and bolted it.

"Who was it?" demanded the sheriff. "Porter?"

"That was no man," wailed Roger.

A creaking across the roof was met with more lead, but no certainty. Something slammed against the door hard and final. Silence reigned as the sheriff stepped lightly to the side window to look. "Whoever it was threw Slim against the door. That's a strong man."

"I'm telling you that was no man."

"Shuddup Roger, he'll eat lead like anyone else."

Stenhouse beneath the desk looked about fearfully.

The deputy coughed and was glared at for his mistake.

The men waited for another sound. None came for the space of eight heartbeats.

Bursting through the window, a savage white shape roared as it rendered men too slow to defend themselves. Shots echoed from several pistols but the bone-pale attacker cast aside the lamp, blinding the men.

The crunch and splinter of bone and wood tore through the room that lead could not hope to stop.

Brief retorts from the echoing firearms illuminated the room, letting the terrified men see what they faced before the end came on black talons.

Roger ran to the jail cell and shut himself in behind the bars.

Unimpressed, the thing loped to the man cage, gripped the bars and tore the door from its hinges. Roger didn't last as long as the door.

Almost mad with panic, Stenhouse raced for the front door, clutching his notebooks to his chest. Three more shots rang out and the deputy, squealed. Daring to look behind, Stenhouse saw green witch-fire engulf the office.

Stenhouse ran up the street in a panic and threw himself upon the threshold of what he prayed was refuge. He banged on the door crying.

Growling behind him, heavy loping steps drew near, but stopped cold.

Putting his arms over his face Stenhouse screamed.

The door opened.

Joseph Rich looked down at the gibbering mass of Stenhouse. "What the deuce?" Rich held his rifle at the ready and scanned the darkness as the hysterical crying man held fast to his knees.

"Bring him in," said Charles Rich, looking over his son's shoulder into the vacant gloom. "He needs a blessing."

19.

Porter had been baptized by water and by fire, now he was sure where the twain should meet. Hot fetid breath whirled about him like a hurricane as a monstrous tongue lashed, attempting to force him down a bottomless black gullet.

Closed inside the leviathan's mouth, Port gripped the top two rear fangs in the monsters maw, only they allowed purchase without shearing his hands off. The tongue, almost as long as he was tall, proved a formidable opponent. Kicking at the pink monstrosity, Port knew he could not hold out forever.

He despaired thinking of his holy blessing. Not cutting his hair would not help against being digested, no bullets or knives were needed to end his existence here. What of his children and Christine? What would they do without him?

Anger coiled up in him, like a serpent preparing to strike its deadly blow.

The tongue struck again, trying to fling him.

Roaring, Port launched himself at the tongue and grasped it as he would a greased pig. The air pressure changed and he knew there were at the surface. Twisting the tongue, the monsters mouth opened and Port let himself out, still grasping the end.

The monster wouldn't close its mouth for fear of severing itself.

Once outside of the teeth's way, Port noticed something stuck on the lower left jaw-line. A crude contraption of tiny interwoven bones and rawhide, similar to the bizarre fetish he had seen earlier.

The monster struggled, but Port kept a firm grasp with one hand on the slimy tongue. Try as he might he couldn't free the fetish with one hand.

A deep bass inside the monster reverberated out.

He let go of the tongue and yanked the interwoven mess from the bleeding gums.

It let out a rumbling purr, and Port could swear that the great eye went from a dull black to blue. Whatever wicked spirit had held the monster in thrall, was released.

Running a hand back and forth over the thick scaly hide, Port looked the monster in the eye. A thick eyelid closed in rhythm to his strokes.

It let out a rumbling purr yet again.

"What have I got to lose," he said to the monster as much as himself. "Lemme up, Blue."

Port slid over the head of the calmed beast. He found he could grasp the folds of skin where the jaw ended. Port lightly kicked at its neck with his waterlogged boots and the beast started forward. He could even guide the direction of the monster as they cruised over the lake by pulling one way or the other just like a horse and its reins.

"Wheat!" Port called aloud. He had broken the wildest stallion ever.

The Bear Lake monster swam quickly through the water in a way that reminded Port of the seals he had seen in California. It was quick and he had to pull upwards a number of times to keep the creature from diving into the depths. It was exhilarating.

Piloting the monster to shore, Port finally realized how chilled he was. He needed warmth if he was to survive. Thinking of survivors...glancing over the waters there was no sign of Lehi. Old man must have drowned. Port bowed his head for some time.

The beast slumped its way onto shore using its shorter paddle like feet just as a seal would.

Port ran his hand along the monsters snout and ushered it away. He didn't want it getting any ideas about his horse nearby "Go on, Blue. Git. We'll be meeting up soon enough, I promise."

The monster seemed reluctant but finally went into the lake and disappeared beneath moon-stained waters.

It took some time to get a fire going, but once the blaze picked up, Port collapsed beside it. Who would believe it? Revenge could wait, he needed sleep after breaking Jonah's stallion.

Why had he named the monster Blue? He didn't know, but it made him laugh.

"Wheat," he chuckled as he fell asleep.

20.

Climbing off his horse, Port limped on account of his water-logged boots drying by the fire and shrinking to an uncomfortable size. He lost his 45-70 in the lake and one of his pistols and all of his ammunition.

Shuffling into the general store Port could only point at the ammunition.

"Morning Brother Rockwell. You weren't part of that mess last night were you?" asked Thomas the shop keep.

Port shrugged through bleary eyes.

"Did you drink all of those tinctures last night? No wonder you feel so terrible."

Port rubbed his face and responded, "No, just get me some cartridges."

"Anything else?"

"Cartridges!" hollered Port. "Wait, what mess last night? How'd you know?"

Thomas gave a patronizing smile. "Last night right across the street. The sheriff's office burnt down. Everyone who was staying there is dead, burnt up, except for Brother Stenhouse."

"Stenhouse? Where is that polecat?"

Sniffing, Thomas responded, "Brother Stenhouse is among the most respected men we have in the Church, he hardly deserves to be called a polecat."

"Cartridges and where is he?"

Thomas gulped, "I understand he is at Brother Rich's for the moment. He went there last night a crying and a hollering that something was out to get him. No doubt he was distressed about the fire that took so many lives."

Port paid for the ammunition and walked out, figuring he had almost all the pieces to the puzzle. Now to get the last one from the dog's own mouth.

21.

Stenhouse was shivering in the parlor, sipping warm milk. He started at Port's entrance, a dark avenging angel with the brilliance of the sun at his back. Charles Rich calmed him as Joseph shut the door and ushered the other family members out.

Joseph said, "He has been carrying on all night. Not a body in the house got a wink of sleep last night."

Stenhouse was still shaking, though the comfort of the Apostle had soothed him somewhat.

"Come and take a look at this," said Joseph, leading Port back outside.

On the ground in an obvious perimeter all about the Rich home, were big wolf-like tracks, as if a creature met an invisible barrier through which it could not pass.

"What do you make of that?" asked Port.

"What else? Father is here."

Port nodded and the two went back inside. Sitting across from Stenhouse, Port tipped his hat to Charles and said to Stenhouse, "Alright, don't feed me any cow pies. What is that thing? What do you know about it?"

Stenhouse looked at Port and quivered again, "It will find me."

"Are you talking about the Bear Lake monster?" asked Joseph.

"We got bigger fish to fry," said Port.

Confused, Joseph shot back, "No, we don't."

"Hold on son," said Charles. "There is a deeper conspiracy afoot."

Stenhouse stared at the wall and looked far away, remembering. "It was Harrison and Godbe. They started it. Sure, I was right there with them, along with Shearman, Kelsey, Tullidge and Lawrence among others but it was Harrison and Godbe that started it."

He took a sip of his warm milk. "I'm not mad. I have seen things. They discovered the answers when they went to New York and met the medium Charles Foster—he greeted them in Heber C. Kimball's voice! They knew it was Kimball communicating with them from beyond the grave. He told them our path was correct and Brigham was a fallen prophet, then others came and spoke the same; Joseph Smith, Alexander Humboldt, Solomon—even Christ spoke to them."

Joseph Rich snorted.

"Truly, they didn't see him, but he spoke to them and told what we wanted to hear. Our reformation path is correct and Brigham is wrong. He is not infallible."

Charles quieted Joseph. "He is speaking what he believes to be true."

"Of course I am. They brought back their ideas and wisdom. We have communed with spirits. Then Colfax came. The government wants to destroy Brigham and the Church along with it. We couldn't let that happen, we had to do something, reform the Church from within to save it. If we can show how we accept the world, they will accept us."

"What's all this up here then?"

"We tried to talk to Brigham, to make him see, but he was obstinate and cruel. We knew we had to make a stand but time was short. We met at the lodge, with the ferry on Bear River, Godbe's lodge. We held a séance. Harrison directed it. I remember it was cold no matter how we stoked the fire. A powerful force came to our room. It spoke from behind us, strong and vibrant. It surprised us. We all heard it but none of us could see it. It said to use an Indian shaman and the Bear Lake monster, to bring down Brigham. It said, His master wanted to bring down Brigham and would use his earthly servants to do it. We were all so thrilled to know the Lord was on our side."

Port rolled his eyes but remained silent.

"We were validated. I thought it odd to use a heathen for the Lord's work but we did as we were told. I found the shaman. He was staying just upriver from the lodge."

"What's his name?"

"Ligaii-Maiitsoh."

Joseph widened his eyes, "You mean Lehi? He's a friend."

Shaking his head, Stenhouse went on, "He is ancient as the mountains. He said he would call upon the Great Serpent to do our bidding. But something went wrong instead of just scaring people, the monster started killing people. I tried to help the Lamanites watch for the beast but it only made things worse."

"Ever wonder if you aren't on the side of angels, much as you think you are?" asked Port.

Stenhouse looked sharply at the suggestion. "There have been setbacks, but no, we are right."

"Then what was last night?"

Shuddering again Stenhouse said, "That wasn't right, I think it serves Ligaii-Maiitsoh. There has been a mistake. The fiend was supposed to be controllable, but it went blood-mad when it discovered the Shoshoni were in the valley. It has surely slain old Lehi. It will come for me next. I will never see Fanny again."

"That's enough crying. What is it about the Shoshoni?"

"The Shoshoni used to capture Navajo and sell them into slavery. All sorts of horrible things happened. I learned of this from Chief Many-Buffalo. The Navajo retaliated by sending witches out to destroy the Shoshoni, I believe Ligaii-Maiitsoh must be the last one."

Port rocked back in his chair, "I couldn't get him to tell me a darned thing and I even had a translator."

Stenhouse was surprised, "Why? He speaks perfectly good English. Oh yes—you were at the Bear River massacre, he was never going to tell you anything."

Port bristled as Stenhouse continued. "Many-Buffalo said his tribe was in the path of the skin-walker, and were under its doom. I wanted to help him but I knew there was nothing to be done when the crazy old man raved as he did over the Shoshoni enemies?"

"What about them fetish pieces I found? Collection of bones?"

"Some kind of curse is all I know. It lets the bloodthirsty creature focus where the shaman directs it," said Stenhouse trailing off as recognition washed over. "You! You put the fiend upon me!" screamed Stenhouse, rising from his chair for the first time.

"Just like it was put upon the Cooks and I couldn't have that."

"It wasn't for the Cooks—it was for you," snarled Stenhouse.

"I didn't know what it would do. I just followed my gut," answered Port.

Stenhouse still fumed. "You black-hearted murderer." He stood ready to fight bringing his fists up.

Port slammed him against the wall with ease. "This is what I do, boy," said Port before letting him go. "And I never killed anyone

177

who didn't need killing."

Stenhouse collapsed to the floor and wept.

Joseph asked, "What about the Bear Lake monster?"

"Smoke and mirrors," answered Port. "It was a decoy for the old shaman, I don't believe it will give you any more problems."

"You didn't kill it did you?"

"No, I made peace with it. It'll behave itself."

Charles Rich asked a question, "What will you do, Brother Rockwell?"

"We'll throw down with the shaman and his beast. I'll use 'em up."


22.

A posse was organized by mid-afternoon and rode out to old Lehi's camp. It was later than Port meant, but several of the men insisted on getting silver bullets cast. Fancy trays, silverware and jewelry that had crossed the plain as priceless family heirlooms was smelted and molded into balls for precious family insurance.

Port didn't worry about any of that for himself. There were twenty guns riding with him to fire those sacramental rounds. He had his Bowie knife that Brigham had blessed and already knew that it could harm the creature. If he needed to, he would cut the beast asunder.

When they were close, Port had them come in from two directions to triangulate their fire and trap the old man and his creature. He kicked himself for not trusting his, or his horse's instincts. The creature must have been nearby the whole time he visited with the old man. That would explain the wretched smell.

The tattered tepee was there in the glade but Lehi was nowhere to be found.

"There's nothing inside but this copy of the Book of Mormon that father gave him," said Joseph. "I don't understand. He has been here, living amongst us for weeks, he seemed like a good man. He quoted scripture. He said he knew it was true."

Port gave a lopsided grin, "Don'tcha think the devil knows it's true?"

23.

Thundering into town as dusk closed in around them, Port knew something wasn't right. Something whispered on the wind, and the scent of wet dog hung heavy in the air.

Amanda Cook raced her horse up to Port. She had been crying. "I thought you'd never return," she sobbed.

"Calm down, Amanda. What is it?"

"We were in the garden, gathering the last of the harvest, just Mary and I. That witch-fire wolf-man came back. Phineas heard our screams, he tried to shoot it and fight. It hurt him real bad. Apostle Rich is looking after him, but it took Mary. It tore her from my grasp. It spoke, like a demon from hell but it spoke, 'It said you and you alone had to come and get Mary at the lake shore past the camps.' What do we do?"

Port held Amanda close and looked her in the eye. "I will get her back."

"How? It will kill her."

"No, I'll take care of it. Rich, you very good with that Sharps rifle?"

Joseph nodded. "Got a few silver slugs too."

"Keep to the tree line. If the right moment comes, take it. Everyone else stay put."

"I'm coming with you," broke in Amanda.

"No, you're not. Look after Phineas and trust me."

With that Port turned his stallion about and made for the lake shore past the Shoshoni camps, and the full moon glowed down like a dragons face.

24.

The Shoshonis had moved camp, but the markings of where tepees had sat along with cook-fire remnants still dotted the ground. The loss of Big Bear and the others would be a hard tax on the small tribe. He remembered his own people's exodus in the dead of winter. They'll be all right he told himself.

Fingers of ghostly clouds tried to shroud the moon, but still the cold light poked through, casting a long line across the lake. Where it ended upon the shore stood the white-haired old Indian, along with the little girl beside him. She was bound up like a trundle bed with a rag stuffed in her mouth.

Lehi, or Ligaii-Maiitsoh raised his hand in the common greeting, though the smirk on his face was mocking and cold. "I knew you would come Long-hair."

"My motivations aren't hard to understand, what are yours though?"

"I have blood of the Trickster in my veins. I am naked terror. I sow deceit and discord. I am your fatal error."

Port dismounted, "Well I am here. You gonna give me the girl?"

The tall old man smirked, and pointed a long spindly finger "She dies, but only after you."

Port drew his gun, "Where's your creature? Nowhere to hide down here next to the lake."

Lehi cocked his head and laughed inaudibly. "I have no creature."

"You're blood of the trickster, a natural-born liar. I know you have some kind of beast."

"My name is Ligaii-Maiitsoh, it means White Wolf in my people's tongue. If you knew anything about us, you would have known what kind of man wears skins of a predator."

"And I wear a dozen cow skins. Let the girl go."

Lehi didn't move.

Port sent a round nipping past the old man's ears, but he didn't flinch. "You got nerve, I'll give you that. Let the girl go or I'll shoot. I got no truck with kidnappers or rustlers."

"I know you. You don't know me," said Lehi. "A lifetime ago, I swore to serve the Trickster and his slave, the Master Mahan. They granted me powers beyond the white man's gun."

"Enough! Let the girl go, or I scalp you from the inside out."

Lehi grinned, revealing terribly big teeth, a jaw that jutted bristling with fangs. It grew wider and wider, impossibly huge and fearsome.

Port wasn't sure he was seeing correctly.

The old man's nose twitched and stretched. "You see what only the dead have seen."

Port sent a round through Lehi's chest. The old man flinched upon impact but no blood came, and his face stretched further. Port shot a second round and a third into the monster.

But the transformation wasn't complete. Fine white fur sprung from the old man's body, and beneath it muscles rippled. A howl came with the completion.

Port sent a fourth, fifth and sixth round into the beast, none of which produced so much as a drop of blood.

Grinning devilishly, Lehi tossed the bound girl into the lake behind him.

Amanda Cook screamed from farther up into the tree line, as she dashed downhill for her daughter.

"More to slay," growled Lehi, his transformation to skin-walker complete.

Port dove for the girl in the lake but the swift hand of the monster batted him aside.

His pistol knocked from his hand, Port strained for his Bowie. But already the beast took him by the coat and threw him.

The thunderclap of a Sharps rifle, boomed over the lake shore. A tuft of white fur flew, but still no blood came from the skin-walker's wound.

Amanda reached the water's edge and pulled Mary from the weak surf. The little girl took a deep breath, gasping from the cold water.

Then she was thrown back in the lake.

The skin-walker knocked Mary back into the waters while holding her mother like a rag doll. "Danite," it called, emphasizing the 'ite'. "Choose which to save, girl or woman."

Port had the Bowie out, despite how badly his body ached from the blow.

"Throw it away in the lake or I rip her apart, but choose," snarled the skin-walker.

Port knew Lehi was a liar, but he knew it could fulfill the threat. Even a silver slug from the Sharps did nothing against it. Only the Bowie knife Brigham had blessed in Nauvoo could harm it.

The girl was drowning, the choice must be made.

Amanda fumbled one-handed with something in her pocket.

The skin-walker stared cold-fire at Port relishing the Danites painful choice.

Somewhere above, Joseph Rich looked down the barrel of the Sharps, waiting to try another shot.

Mary sputtered in the cold lake water.

Port took the Bowie in hand and threw it true as he had ever thrown anything in his life, straight for the skin-walkers heart. "Lord, guide my hand," he prayed. "Help me end this creature."

The big knife flew end over end impossibly fast. And it seemed for a moment that Port's aim was true and he would skewer the fiend.

It caught the blade with the reflexes of diamondback's strike and sounded out in a cross between a dogs's bark and a man laughing. It arched to throw the knife back.

Port thought it would throw the heavy blade at him. He ran for the girl and drew her from the water like baby Moses. She gasped again her face turning blue.

Looking back, Port expected to be stabbed with his own knife, but the skin-walker reveling waited for Port to watch.

The blade went high and wide of Port, falling into the lake and disappearing in dark waters.

Port watched the trusty blade vanish in the inky darkness, glancing at the shivering girl, he had an idea. Facing the lake he called, "Blue! Blue! Blue!"

The skin-walker taunted, "Calling for your knife's return?"

Amanda found what she had fished for, a small glass vial. She smashed it against the only part of the monster she could reach, its shoulder.

Consecrated oil dripped down the white fur, surprising the beast. Amanda tore free, running to her daughter.

The monster puzzled at her choice of attack. "What is this?"

Granting a thin reflective line down the monster, Joseph Rich took his shot, nailing dead center the shoulder where the holy oil covered.

Deep crimson flowed and the beast howled.

Bare-handed, Port tackled the fiendish beast, punching, kicking and clawing like the monster was the devil himself. The skin-walker resisted until Port jammed a finger in the wound, it let roll a string of wicked curses.

Groaning, it prevailed and sent the avenging angel flying into the cold surf.

Joseph ran down the hill hoping for another shot to present itself, but Porter was too thick in the fray and he dared no take another shot. "Do you have any more oil? It works!"

"I don't," cried Amanda, desperately trying to untie her daughter and run away.

The skin-walker raked at Porter with its claws, but try as it might it couldn't pierce his skin, the sharp edges could not gain access. Yowling, it looked at the lake and dragged Port into the water.

Joseph took another shot, hitting the monster in the back, but missing the oil and nothing happened.

"If I cannot cut you, I will drown you," laughed the skin-walker, holding Port beneath the water.

Kicking, Port strained and fought but the monster was too strong, pushing him into the sandy bottom.

Underwater Port heard a strange set of clicks.

The shaggy white arms let go and Port sat up.

The skin-walker had stepped back away from the water. It beckoned angrily with its right arm, speaking a wolfish tongue.

Behind Port loomed the Bear Lake Monster.

"Blue, I need some help. Get him!" Port shouted, directing the lake dragon's gaze.

The skin-walker's chest began to turn a shade of pale green that was growing in intensity when Joseph shot it again, right where a stream of oil had touched along the ribs.

Wailing of pain and true terror, the skin-walkers glow faded.

"He won't bob off this time. Get 'em, Blue."

The Bear Lake monster lurched forward and swallowed the skin-walker, devouring the white horror entire.

"Chew him up, Blue! Chew him up!" shouted Port. "Wheat!"

An infernal, hollow cry sounded from within the beast, dimming and fading to silence.

Blue opened its cavernous maw and let its tongue loll out between titanic fangs.

Port patted the tremendous beast's snout and examined its handiwork. "No coming back from that," he said, picking random clumps of white fur that stuck in the monsters teeth. "You did good, Blue. Now back to the lake with ya, old friend."

The monster rumbled a colossal purr and turned to slide back into deep waters.

25.

Amanda watched in amazement, holding Mary close. "He is good?"

"Yes, ma'am. He just needed some help and understanding," said Port.

Joseph ran down the hillside shouting, "What a story to tell. I'll get this posted in all the papers across the country. People will come from all over the world to be a part of our valley and see the lake monster."

"No!" Port stuck a thick finger in the tall man's chest. "You're gonna tell everyone you made it up. No good will come of this tale being told for true."

Confused, Joseph looked at Port and the monster disappearing into the lake.

"You don't want what they'll bring to your valley. You don't want more trouble coming down on Brother Brigham. And you don't want 'em messing with the monster."

"I'll say I made it all up," said Joseph Rich, rubbing the sore spot where Porter had pushed. "I can't take back what has already been printed. But I can say now that it was all a wonderful first-class lie."

"Good. Some stories are better off that way."

## THE PROBLEM WITH MAGICK

"Master."

"The problem with magic, is that it's pure chaos," said the master to the apprentice.

"Master . . ."

He waved the boy off, "But it can bestow the most powerful of change and leverage the entire world or it can dissipate if you forget the slightest ingredient. It's a fickle lover."

"Master . . ."

"What? I'm trying to teach!"

"The circle. It's broken."

The master had time enough to look down at his own sandaled foot which had wiped a smear in the protective circle, then up at the single amorphous eye and toothy tentacled maw of the demon opening wider before them.

## STUMPS

The forest, or what was left of it, always made Will and his friends uncomfortable.

Stumps usually make one think of purposefully cut trees, but these were the remnants of a forest fire twelve years gone by. They sprouted black from the mountainside like the magnification of a chin cut with a dull old razor. The stumps haggard and broken, were of varying lengths, ranging from four to twelve feet tall. A few had branches or gnarled knobs reaching like crippled malformed hands. Some looked accusing.

The boys were too young to remember the fire though their parents spoke of it sometimes and how close it had come to taking their homes. It was generally accepted that the one thing that had saved the town was the prayer circle.

When the blaze began on a Sunday, during Sacrament, word spread that an evacuation was imminent considering the dryness, elevation and high winds. An impromptu prayer circle was quickly held in the gymnasium and the parents spoke often enough years later in testimony meeting of how powerful the spirit was that day and through the fear and anxiety that a peace held strong as the Iron Rod.

Things would be okay.

The wildfire swept across the mountain from south to north and by all rights should have taken the town, but miraculously enough it halted right at the borders merely singing the outermost homes and only destroying old man Johnson's place.

The boys joked that it was because he hadn't been paying his tithing. Bad luck was always associated with not paying tithing.

Moving around the town in what could only be divine intervention, the fire spared everything else. Once the smoke cleared many fell down on their knees saying it was the greatest miracle to happen in their lifetime. But the beautiful forest that had surrounded them all across the western slope was nearly eradicated, only blackened stumps remained.

The boys took the trails to the canyons to fish, shoot and camp.

Daily they passed by the dark monuments of miracles long since past and wondered.

Or at least Will did. "You guys ever think about what it would have looked like if we still had woods here?"

"I've seen the pictures. It was nice."

"Look at it this way Jensen, there will never be another bad forest fire in our lifetimes here."

"Oh, that's real comforting Ralph."

"Shut up Toby!"

Will continued, "I'm just saying it seems like it changed everything. Not just the woods but the people too."

"You think too hard Will."

"It happened when we were babies, how can we know what it was like before?"

Will stopped in the middle of a hairpin turn on the trail. "My Dad said before the fires, half the ward didn't come to church but now they do."

"That's a good thing isn't it?"

"Yeah, even old man Johnson comes and sits in the back, that old cuss."

"My Dad said the fire taught old man Johnson a lesson all right."

Will couldn't get the right words out. He always felt bad that old man Johnson was the town pariah. Leave it to Ralph to change the subject.

"Hey Toby, my sister heard from your sister that you got caught with a Playboy."

"Shut up!"

"What happened?"

"My Mom found it under my bed."

The boys laughed.

"Shut up!"

"Where did you even get a Playboy?"

"I stole my Dad's."

"But he is the—"

"Shut up. Don't tell anyone. Now my Mom is making me read The Miracle of Forgiveness."

"And how do you like it perv?"

"I hate it. Makes me feel like a piece of crap."

"So the perv feels like a piece of crap, interesting."

"Shut up. It did have one interesting thing though. Long time ago this guy was riding through the woods and a giant hairy black man came out of the woods, and started talking to him and it was Cain!"

"I've heard that story before. It's like he was always out there watching and he wanted to make everyone as miserable as he was."

"*Is*. As miserable as he *is*," corrected Will.

"Yeah, anyway then he got out of there. Kinda spooky."

"Hey guys what if Cain came running down the trail right now?" They laughed. "I'd like to see that!"

They heard footfalls coming down the trail toward them and they froze cold as a wet Christmas.

He was wearing bright yellow jogging pants and a red tee shirt, but he was a black man.

"Boys." Nodded the man as he continued jogging past them and disappeared down the trail heading toward town.

They watched him vanish around the hairpin and all laughed nervously. "Whoever heard of a black man up here in Idaho?"

"Does he live around here?"

"I've never seen him before but Bret said a black family moved in up in Waynesboro."

Though none would admit they were all unnerved and decided to camp closer to home than usual, only a few ridges away from town and just inside the tree line at the edges of the burned forest.

Dusk moved in and Will found himself staring at the stumps rising up on the mountainside before him. Dark sentinels against a pale dry landscape.

Toby started a fire and everyone gathered closely around for the false comfort it offered against the twilight and the demons that must lurk there. Still they could hardly resist telling each other scary stories about the fire.

"Did you hear about the demon footprints Carl's dad found in the snow last year?"

"Those had to be deer."

"They disappeared from a circle around the house like they couldn't get in, because the home was protected by guardian angels."

"Shut up."

"They can only come in if you invite them! My dad said."

"Oh really? Well how about I invite them?" said Toby getting belligerent.

"Don't."

"How's about I invite the worst one of all? How's about I invite Cain himself?"

"Toby, don't act like this."

"I can do what I want. Nothing is gonna happen."

The boys went still as Toby stood up from the fire shouting, "Come and get us Cain, if you're really out there, wanting everyone to be as miserable as you!"

"Bad idea, Toby."

"Shut up, see nothing happened."

They swapped insults and laughed trying to forget their nervousness for another moment. Gaining courage that indeed nothing would happen.

Will still watched the mountainside transfixed. Then he saw it.

A stump moved.

"Guys."

"What?"

"Look."

A tall black outline moved amongst the gloomy pillars.

"I am not seeing this."

"Is it a bear? Moose?"

"Too tall, too human."

"Is it a Bigfoot?"

"Who cares?"

"It's coming down!"

They didn't put out their fire, they didn't grab their gear. Ralph didn't even remember his twenty-two rifle. They ran.

Tripping over brambles and fallen logs they ran and occasionally one looked back and screamed that *it* was still coming after them.

The closest home on the edge of town was old man Johnson's. Instead of taking the longer circuit around they cut through. As they managed the barbwire fence, Johnson appeared.

"What are you boys doing?"

"He's after us!"

"Run!"

"Who?"

"Cain!"

They tumbled over each other and through the barbwire and looked back just in time to see the biggest man they had ever beheld. He could have stepped over the fence if he wished.

Tall and broad with a fierce face, cruel as a mothers withheld love; he snarled at them with savagery born of damned millennia.

"Away! I rebuke thee!" shouted Johnson.

"I was invited and they shall pay the price," he said, pointing a crooked finger.

"No! In the name of Jesus Christ and through the power of the Melchezidek priesthood I command you to depart! And come here never again, Amen!" shouted Johnson, raising his arms to the square.

"This place? They don't even acknowledge that it was your prayer and sacrifice that saved the town. They think you a heathen and mock your every move while taking credit for your faith."

"Doesn't matter what anyone thinks of me—Go!"

Cain rumbled again like a thunderhead but he turned and faded into the arms of night.

The boys ran home except for Will. "Thank you Brother Johnson."

"Don't mention it."

"Really, thank you. I never knew it was your prayer that saved the town."

"No. I didn't save the town any more than I saved you just now."

"But you did."

"No, I didn't. I just reminded chaotic elements of who is in charge."

"You know most people don't think you are a very good saint.

But I think you are."

He grinned. "Does it matter what people think?"

"I guess not. But people should know the truth."

"Do the stumps care? Would they listen?"

Will shook his head.

"So don't worry about the stumps. Do your best and go on."

## BAPTISM BY FIRE

Green as absinthe, the recruit stepped off the 737 to a blistering Nevada tarmac hours from nowhere. He was ushered away from the other plain clothes passengers, lab workers and spook military types, toward a corrugated steel Quonset hut with heat shimmying off it like an exotic dancer.

Inside a stern faced captain with a buzz cut, sat on the corner of a table reassembling an M-4 assault rifle. He looked up for a moment, quickly finishing the task he had obviously done ten thousand times. "Only you? Well that's fine as frog hair."

'Yes, sir, I—"

"Save it. You're an effing new guy. I asked for twenty more men for this shift alone and all I get is you?"

"Sorry sir. My orders," he said, handing over the forms.

"Uh huh, call me Cap. Look I gotta give you a crash course since we're sorely understaffed thanks to that damn drone fiasco. Lit up the civilian boards like a Christmas tree on fire."

"Ha, conspiracy."

"Wipe that smirk off your face, peach fuzz. Yeah, conspiracy. You don't believe the Brass are keeping stuff from even us—you gotta get a new line of work. Maybe that will be your name."

"What?"

"Now we have a whole pack of Mulder's children trying to stage a UFO convention down at the gates and I'll be damned if we have a Y-12 vandalism incident here. No eighty year old Nun is getting in on my watch."

"Mulder's children?"

"No need to worry about them, I'll send Danklander, Pampers, Speed Bump and Dumb Smith to shoo them off."

"Who?"

"Mulder's children. That's what we call those damn UFO kids who were conceived during X-Files station breaks."

"Who is going?"

"Listen up Nimrod, I said Danklander, Pampers, Speed Bump and Dumb Smith."

"Uh. My name is—"

"Whoa, listen don't try and tell me who you are just yet. I don't know how you did things in the—wherever you're from. But around here you cannot just pick your own name."

"But my name is—"

"Nope," Cap said, holding his cap over his heart. "We have traditions. We're like the noble Native American warriors of old Mexico. Your name is given to you judging off of something you did."

"Uh?"

"Usually something stupid," he said, nodding.

"I see."

"Trying to pick your own name is just asking for it. Look at Danklefson. He wanted to be called Highlander, now he is Danklander. It could be worse. Pampers asked to be called Viper, that became Diaper. You can see the rhythm to it."

"And Dumb Smith?"

"I always felt bad that Dumb Smith was called Dumb Smith. Then I worked with him. Speed Bump is very good at hiding, maybe too good. During training maneuvers he laid down in the road to avoid being seen."

"And?"

"He was run over by a jeep—twice."

"Twice?"

"Yes, first time broke five ribs and a leg. But that man, what a trooper. He didn't cry out not even once."

"Why not?"

"Well because they would have seen him, the bastards. Come on, in here, I'll show you the secret bunker elevator."

"Secret?"

They ducked inside a spacious hangar with a number of experimental aircraft looking half-finished spread about in the rear.

"This is one of the Research and Development wings. Remember everything you see is classified. Especially the TAV's."

"TAV's?"

"Trans-Atmospheric-Vehicles. They are in various stages of

reverse engineering."

"What?"

"Only the lab people that work down in the bunker labs know exactly what is going on down there. But don't let them ever get uppity with you. Smug bastards. We at least have an idea what is going on in every office and lab, they only ever know what is happening in theirs. That and I'll let you in on another secret, lab people are pretty much like the people of Wal-Mart. Make 'em do YMCA once in awhile before you unlock the doors and let them up the elevator. That'll keep 'em off their high horses."

"I see."

"Do you? Listen, lab people are jumpy, they are usually afraid of Base Patrol, we carry guns and actually know the difference between common sense and theirs."

"Theirs?"

"I have seen them walk through caution tape and fall right into twelve foot deep holes. There is a difference between what they have figuring out rockets and such and pure common sense."

"What if someone causes problems?"

"No problem. If you have to kill someone, just say over the secure link that you have to fill out a 5.56 form," the captain patted his 5.56 caliber M-4 rifle, "and we got your back buddy."

"Uh thanks, but I never said kill."

"You didn't have to."

"So I'm staying here?"

"No. You're going down there," said Cap, pointing at the floor elevator.

"OK?"

"Here is your equipment. I know you are trained on using these. Everything is loaded with secret body shock rounds. Hits harder, less over penetration and collateral damage," he said, handing the recruit the M-4 rifle, a belt with a half dozen loaded magazines and a .40 caliber sidearm also with several magazine loaded and ready. "You good?"

"By myself?"

"What? Aren't you especially trained for this kind of thing?

Didn't you put in a request to be stationed here at the base that does not exist? Doesn't doing this for God, country and the United States Air Force give you an effing hard on? Answer me damn you!"

"Yes sir. I'm just not sure about my duties yet. What am I supposed to do down there?"

"You guard the perimeter. You do not let *anything* pass that should not pass."

"*Anything?*"

"Don't let your imagination run away with you. You probably won't see anything but those damn lab people . . . but."

"But?"

"Stop worrying, get down there and do your job."

"Yes sir, Cap."

He shoved the recruit onto the open elevator platform and hit the descent button.

The recruit looked up sullenly as he strapped his belt on and slung the rifle.

"One more thing. Life down in the bunker can be strange. Being in a bunker for days on end does things to a person. I was once hospitalized for eating four day old chicken, that I swear I just got that morning. Another time when I came back topside I saw the sun rise twice and duke it out with itself. Pretty weird . . ."

The grinding of the elevator drowned out the possibility of hearing anything more. The concrete passage went down a rectangular shaft much deeper than the recruit would have believed. He estimated it was at least sixty feet, perhaps more.

At the bottom, wide twin doors slid open to accommodate almost the entire space of the elevator. Small aircraft would easily fit on the gargantuan pad.

Another guard stood there. "I'm so glad to see you," he said, stepping onto the platform.

"Are you leaving?"

"Yeah, you're my relief. I've been down here two days," he said, as he motioned for the recruit to get off so he could push the ascent button. His beard looked more like a week's worth.

"I'm not prepared to be down here that long by myself. I don't know where anything is."

"It's all right," said the stubble faced guard, grinning like a demon. "The head is right there around the corner and you can commandeer food from the lab people if you have to."

The doors shut out the man's wide grinning face and the grinding elevator lifted away.

"This is crap. You can't leave me alone like this," the recruit said into his radio.

The radio crackled alive with response, the droning of the still rising elevator behind it. "Don't be the weird guy who is always begging people to come down to the bunker to visit you. Everybody will think you're a pervo nut-job. Don't be that guy."

The recruit slumped onto a stool behind an almost worthless two foot by two foot desk. He had a pen and a sign in sheet. There were no names. The walls were bare concrete broken by several wide steel doors. The only thing to read was the 'Absolutely No Admittance' signs emblazoned above them.

He sat for a few minutes and boredom took its toll. He found no flaw along the concrete walls, but the plain white tiled floor had similar grooves almost invisible yet all running the same way. He found three that had been set sideways. It wasn't much, but he found the discrepancy, the alteration to sterile conformity.

A door cracked open.

The recruit looked and wondered. There was no light coming from behind the door though it opened a good inch.

"Someone there? Answer me, I'm base patrol security."

The door shut, but opened again a few seconds later.

The recruit stared and something glossy eyed stared back before fading into the darkness yet again.

"Come on out. I'm not going to commandeer your food . . . yet."

Scaly green fingers, ending in hooked claws reached around the door and scraped the dull gray paint off in long jagged flakes.

The recruit's eyes went wide in disbelief.

The door flung open and four or five bug eyed aliens with rubbery green skin presented themselves in a threatening manner. They had yellow horns coming out the top of their heads and curved claws instead of hands.

"Holy shit!" He opened fire with the M-4 rifle and the aliens jerked about and tumbled back into black space. He let another burst go through the open doorway, before struggling for the radio.

"I gotta file a 5.56 form! A 5.56 form! I need backup!"

A spiky headed alien stuck its head out the door and made a clawing gesture.

Another blast from the rifle emptied the magazine. The recruit quickly reloaded and emptied the next thirty rounds into the beckoning dark.

"This is Cap," crackled the radio. "What seems to be the problem? Just tell those bastards to give you a damn candy bar."

Two aliens scuttled from the gloom, their claws scraping against the concrete.

The recruit screamed as he took careful center of mass aim at the two creatures.

They reacted bodily and retreated back to the open door, but there was no trace of blood.

"No sir! No sir! I have damn aliens attacking me. Big green horny aliens!"

"Copy that, did you say horny?"

"You son of a bitch! I have aliens coming to kill me! Get me the hell out of here!"

"Dammit son, you take it easy. We're coming. Just hold them off."

The recruit found that if he didn't send a burst through the door every few seconds he saw one of the awful things staring back at him. Did he imagine seeing them lick their lips? He wasn't sure.

"I'm running low on ammo Cap!"

"Damn fool! Why did you say that? They can hear you!"

The aliens charged out again.

The recruit spent the last of his rifle ammo on them, again they retreated without sign of blood loss.

"Where are you?"

The radio spat out Cap speaking, "Frost, you go right with the .50. I hit center, Danklander and Pampers go left."

"Hurry!"

"Hold on son."

"Hurry!"

The radio crackled as the Cap and others grumbled. "Frost what's the problem? Elevator stuck?"

"Can I just have a moment of peace before the plan fails and we all die?"

"You sons of bitches! Get down here!"

The aliens charged and the recruit opened fire with his .40 caliber pistol. He heard the elevator opening behind him, its slow grind like a whet stone, but the aliens were already upon him. Slamming him to the ground.

Instead of the burst of machine guns or the slathering jaws of horny toad looking aliens he heard laughter.

"Get the son of a bitch up. He's one of us now," ordered Cap.

Strong arms pulled up the recruit and dusted him off.

"Sorry 'bout that Bro."

"Yeah, sorry man."

"What's his name Cap?"

Looking about, the recruit blinked. The aliens were guards, pulling off horrific masks and costumes.

"Dunno yet. Least it ain't Shat Himself."

"Shuddup."

"What the hell is going on?"

"Now don't be all butt-hurt about it."

On his feet the recruit stammered, "You gave me weapons loaded with weird blanks?"

Cap grinned big as a Great White at Baby Beach Day."Yes I did. Baptism by fire! Had to know what I was working with. I needed to know what kind of metal you are for the sake of what you'll do when you *really* see what we have here. Congratulations maggot, you passed."

# THE DIG

The shifting sands revealed a dead city's bones from beside the upper Nile. Charged dust flew on the moaning winds as the scent of the river clung to the ruins. Workmen crawled over her carcass like scavengers feasting on discarded marrow. No one had discovered a lost city of such magnitude since Bingham stumbled upon Machu Picchu.

But the unearthing of fabled Keshan gave its discoverer, Dr. Andrea Forester, little prestige or recognition. Who had time for a lost metropolis, when the Nazi-war machine rolled over Europe and was spreading leprously to Africa? Still, she persevered, regarding the dig as the fulfillment of a lifetime of study. It stung that credit had to be shared with Dr. Julius Rivers, but it was the only way to get the University to finance the expedition she wanted.

She knew Rivers regarded her as much too pretty, meaning he assumed she was too naive and flamboyant for an archaeologist. In turn she thought him pompous, distracted and even a tad yellow. He had balked at the thought of weeks in the sub-Saharan desert and only took a shine to it when it was related that he could evade service in the civil defense force. He seemed more intent on writing his memoirs than in working on the dig. Forester was pleased, since it allowed her to direct the dig as she saw fit. Teatime was the only time they shared conversation, and even that seemed forced, short words and broken sentences pulled from Rivers constant scrawling.

Tea was prepared within the tents precisely at four. Forester paused a moment, setting the milk back onto the table. A distant rumble carried on the malevolent wind. She stepped outside to glimpse the impending commotion. Rivers followed, still clutching the red leather journal that had scarcely left his shaking hands for the past two weeks.

Tents billowed against the hot breeze as men shielded their faces against the biting sand. Workmen swathed in gossamer turbans, dug sands away from a vaulted stone entry as if fighting an incoming tide. A superstitious lot, they took to all manner of charms and good luck pieces to protect them from the spirits of the desert. Forester found herself combating their cowardly idleness almost as much as directing their work.

The rumble grew louder, sending sand rippling in waves down into the dig site from whence it came. Workmen, gibbering in fear, cast glances about the complex; they threw down their shovels and fled for their tents.

Rivers blinked and removed his glasses, staring blankly at the commotion, wrinkling his forehead. "Superstitious fools!" he shouted into the wind.

Walking between the small yet steep-graded pyramids, Forester couldn't help but feel as if gigantic jaws are about to swallow her. The sands reverberated, bringing a light curse from her lips. But it wasn't an earthquake nor the wind blasting through the haunted ruins which drew her ragged breath. The rumble and rising dust cloud of mechanized cavalry, loomed on the red horizon.

"What is it?" asked Rivers. "Sand storm?"

Forester wiped her brow and squinted, "Italians, pushing up from Ethiopia."

The older man held the binoculars up to his partner. "Perhaps they'll move on."

Shaking her head, Forester sighed, "They'll likely take our fuel and food supplies at the least. Mussolini doesn't supply his new empire so well as Caesar did."

A long horizontal line of camouflaged trucks and tanks edged closer, followed by a dark dust-storm.

"What should I tell the men?" he asked.

It took Forester by surprise that he even spoke. "Not to resist. Perhaps we can get back to our research faster that way."

The leading truck barreled up to the waiting archaeologists and slid to a stop in the sands. An officer with a week's worth of growth upon his face leapt from the cab, looked Forester up and down with some pleasure as he strode to face her. "A woman? English?"

Forester nodded, "I am an archaeologist, Forester, Dr. Andrea Forester."

"And I am Dr. Julius Rivers," said her colleague as he extended his hand, "an Egyptologist of some renown..."

The Italian held up his own sun burnt hand, demanding silence. "I am Capitano Santini." He lit a cigarette offered another to Forester, who declined. Rivers was ignored. Shrugging, Santini smiled, "You are spies, yes?"

"No, we are archaeologists investigating the Nubian ruins of Keshan."

Santini looked over their shoulders. The workmen watched from behind cover as the full bulk of the Italian forces drew up beside the dig. "Dig? For what? There is nothing here, it is all up in Egypt."

Forester smiled, "My colleagues tend to agree with you Capitano, but as you can see there is something here and I aim to learn all I can about this former capitol of greater Nubia." She gestured at the half-submerged gatehouse and farther on the steep little pyramids, beyond those, the peak of a wider-based structure poked through the blowing debris.

Santini gazed over the complex but appeared to give it little thought. "It pains me, but I will need to take your fuel and vehicles. I am sure you will be all right and can get more from your— *University*," he said, as if he had caught them in a lie.

Forester shot back, "I need my vehicles and my fuel. If you take them you may as well shoot us now!"

Santini laughed, "I am a soldier, not a murderer."

Forester put on her bravest face. "And what would leaving us here without fuel be, but murder?"

Looking her up and down again, Santini smiled. "I will leave you one vehicle and fuel, but you will swear not alert the English to my presence for a full day, agreed?"

Forester grimaced but nodded. "Very well."

"See, we can all be friends. Now why don't you show me what is so important here in this wasteland," he urged. "Perhaps Il Duce would contribute to your work when all of this is over."

She gave a condescending grin for that remark, sure that the dictator would steal any precious artifacts back to Rome. Reluctant to show Santini anything of obvious value, Forester took him out to the steep sloped pyramids and mounded structure of stone just poking through the sands. She purposely avoided the mysterious gatehouse that promised to be something special once the workmen cleared the thick copper doors of the sand that kept them closed Instead she focused on what she hoped would bore the Capitano.

"They may have grown a garden here, and the remains of a canal look promising," she said, pointing at an indistinct trench. "Beside the river may have been a pottery center. Many broken fragments were recovered there, would you like to see?"

Santini looked at the aged monuments with disdain. "I have seen better monuments in a latrine."

Rivers mouth fell open but he said nothing.

Forester's flushed with anger at mockery of her life's work.

"My manners. I apologize for my rudeness," said Santini. "I have been with only brutes in the army for too long. What is that?" He asked, pointing at the domed stone.

"We're not sure yet. It could be a monument of victory, or simply a place marker."

"Victory? Over whom?" asked Santini incredulous.

"The Nubians here, conquered and ruled Egypt for generations. They fought the Assyrians to a standstill and held western Africa for more than a hundred years."

Santini snorted. "All I see is pale imitation. Now in Rome, I could show you wonders."

Losing patience, Forester proclaimed, "The wonders here would amaze you. You simply repeat the common misconceptions with your boastful pontificating."

She realized too late that was exactly what he wanted all along.

"Then show me," he said gesturing toward the ruined gatehouse.

"You sir, are a cad," said Rivers, stepping between Forester and the Capitano.

Santini smirked at the chivalric display and shoved Rivers aside.

Fuming, Forester led Santini to the massive copper doors. "They are still blocked with sand. I cannot open them yet, but as you can see from the glyphs and workmanship they had marvelous skill."

"Get your men to work. I would like to see inside."

She hesitated.

"There isn't time," she said. "It will be night in a few hours and you must be on your way."

Santini shouted, "I shall decide when we are on our way!" Calming, he added, "I wish to see the wonders of these savages. Show me."

"Now see here, this is a matter of scientific caution." Rivers objected. "Our boys in the RAF will spot you soon enough."

Not to be outdone, Santini grinned, drew his pistol and, from a distance of less than a dozen yards, shot Rivers in the heart. The older man clutched his chest and fell into the thirsty sands, his lifeblood disappearing swiftly.

"Bastard!" she screamed. Rivers journal rested in the sand beside him, its pages rustling in the desert breeze.

"I told you what I want."

"Why should I do anything for you? You'll kill us all."

"Exactly. I will continue until all of your people are gone. Then I will use my own men anyway. Unless you give me a reason not to waste our bullets. Open the doors. Show me. There must be something precious inside for you to hide it so tenaciously."

"I don't know what's inside. No one has opened those gates in twenty-five hundred years."

"Then all the better we should do it quickly," he said with a laugh, tucking his pistol into his belt.

Forester commanded her workmen to double their efforts, while she herself dragged Rivers body out to the edge of the dig. She buried him in the merciless sands amidst the tombs of forgotten kings that he had never before displayed interest in. It was a harsh irony.

The sun faded while she and the men worked, she covering Rivers, his book, his unfinished work, while they uncovered ... who knew what? Finishing the last shovel full of sand, she sensed Santini behind her.

"You think me cruel? These are desperate times for all of us," he said.

"I weep for your problems, Capitano."

"It's true. If I cannot beat the English, I need something special for Il Duce."

"Murder doesn't grant sympathy for your plight. Save your words."

Taking her shoulder, he spun her around to face his sand-blasted countenance. His gray eyes were cold in the desert heat and flashed with an eerie light. "Know this, I will take what treasures are in the vault. I will give you the credit of discovery, but I must give them to Il Duce. You could come with me. You could be a duchess of Rome." He smiled. His teeth looked predatory in the half-light. "You and I are not so different."

Forester shook her head and backed away. "You're completely mad."

"Come now. We each do whatever is necessary to get ahead in our callings."

Forester challenged, "I have never murdered anyone."

He laughed, "Don't tell me you haven't slain someone academically to get what you wanted."

She couldn't look him in the eye. Being a respected woman in her field meant doing whatever it took to get ahead, to get noticed, to be respected. If that meant stepping upon others shoulders, perhaps grinding them down in the process, then yes, she had done that. But didn't everyone in academia? It was du rigueur.

Santini continued, "I take these treasures from the earth without shame."

"Would the dead be pleased with that?"

"Would they be any more pleased that you took them than I?" He gestured at the gloom-laden pyramids etched sharply against the twilight. "It is the way of the conqueror to take what they will from the weak. My ancestors did it. I do it now. These forgotten people did it to raise up this ruin from the sands. They would respect it."

"I share my discoveries with the world."

"So do I. Have you seen the museums of Rome?"

"It's not the same."

He frowned. "Yes it is. You British are so self-righteous. Calling the Axis war-mongers and worse, while the sun never sets upon your glorious empire. It is human nature to judge personal intent against another's actions. Accept that you are no better than I, and I am no worse than you, and we will be friends."

"Are all Italian robbers so philosophical?"

"Veni, vidi, vici."

The workmen called that they had cleared the sand from the vault.

"Now we shall see what treasures the Nubians stole from the Egyptians," said Santini.

"If grave robbers tunneled in another way, as they do in Egypt, there may be nothing. Prepare to be disappointed Capitano."

Santini waved an indignant hand at that as he strode toward the submerged gates.

Torches were lit against the deep darkness of the desert and it seemed that with the night, stronger winds blew, causing the workmen to whisper fearfully.

The threshold of sandstone was fully revealed and glyphs were carved in relief over the massive corroded doors. Over ten feet tall and seven feet wide, the gates were gigantic. A tight seam ran down the center of the verdigris covered metal. Scraping away at the edges, Forester soon found that the copper was merely an ornamentation over a stronger metal.

She gasped in awe as she tore away a hand sized flake, revealing bright steel. "Impossible. They never worked steel such as this."

Santini questioned, "What do you mean?"

"A slab of steel this size would be worth more than gold in seven hundred BC. No one worked metal of this magnitude. No one."

"But here it is."

"This changes everything we know of ancient metallurgy," said Forester, mainly to herself, as she caressed the cool hieroglyphic covered surface.

"What does it say?"

She turned and frowned, remembering who she was dealing with. "You killed the man who could read it better than I."

"But you can read it? Yes?"

"Something about the temple of the watchers. I don't know any more, but I have books . . . give me time."

"No. Open these doors."

She stood and faced Santini with grim resolve. "You don't seem to understand. These doors themselves are incredible treasures. They shouldn't exist. No one has ever found metal workings so large."

"All the more reason to believe there is a great treasure behind them. If this is only the facade of the doorway."

"You have no idea what ruin you are bringing to this discovery!" she shouted.

"Can you open the doors for me?"

"No. I won't. We need time to examine this, to gently excavate the site."

Santini shook his head. "There is no time. Your army comes this way and will display no more caution than I. I must have what lies inside."

The workmen muttered and fretted, understanding their limited use. Rather than be made examples of like Rivers, they threw picks and shovels against the door, prying at the edges.

"Stop!" Forester shouted in vain.

But they could not make even the seam buckle.

"Stand aside," Santini commanded. Taking a German made MP-40 sub-machine gun, he stood around the corner and emptied the full thirty-two round magazine at the door. The copper plate was blackened and scored in a dozen places but the steel beneath was indifferent. "There must be something quite special here."

Dr. Forester refused to answer him.

Santini shouted to his men who quickly moved everyone back.

Forester said, "What did you say? What are you doing? You can't be serious?"

He grinned his oily smile as the rumbling of heavy machinery answered her.

One of the Italian Fiat tanks pulled abreast of the gates, with a mere dozen yards separating them.

"You could destroy everything inside the vault!"

"A chance I am willing to take. Either I will retrieve what is inside or no one will. I cannot wait forever." The Capitano waved his hand, and the tank fired its shell with a deafening roar.

Expecting the worst, Dr. Forester rushed to see the damage. Most of the copper plate was gone, but the steel was almost unblemished, and certainly unmoved, unfazed.

Santini's wide grin vanished as he saw the doors. "Impossible!"

"Perhaps it is a sign Capitano," said Forester.

He waved her off. "It is a strange hindrance, nothing more."

"Admit it. This Nubian door holds better than the Maginot line."

He laughed at that but shouted more Italian at his men.

"You should let this go. Let me keep studying this thing that should not be. I beg you don't destroy any more of the surrounding facade."

"You should get to cover," he said pointing at a nearby dune.

"What? Why? You have already proved you can't blast it open."

"I have more options."

Soldiers brought explosives from supply trucks and stacked them against the doors. Gazing at the fading horizon, Forester could see some of the workmen fleeing upon their camels and briefly wondered if she should have joined them.

A soldier called out the countdown in a crisp staccato voice.

The blast rocked the night. From behind her arms, Forester saw red flames dancing into the azure sky. Before she could see the doors, she heard them. A groaning creak and the thud of that heavy steel slamming against the sandstone. It took a few minutes for the dust to dissipate before she could see the black gaping maw of an opening.

Santini called for an electric torch and he was first through the gap.

Forester was close behind.

And stopped short, confused. She had expected perhaps gold and sarcophagi, treasures and canopic jars but this? There wasn't any carven stone or earth, everything was steel. An entire tunnel vaulted in steel, stretching away into corridors of gloom. The passageway sat at a slight tilt and they walked down shining the light against indecipherable marks and curious artworks that resembled nothing she'd ever seen before. The most curious thing was the echo that sounded down maze-like passages. The haunting whispers implied there was a vast complex buried beneath the sand.

They investigating passage after passage, little of it making any sense. Rooms as large as warehouses held steel containers that could not be opened no matter how hard the Italians tried. Others rooms had thick layers of dust and sand where tiny rips in the steel revealed stress fractures.

"This is not Nubian," she said at last.

"Then whose could it be?" asked Santini, moving the torch every which way. They had entered a huge room which only appeared to have one door, the one they came through. The light reflected wildly from both steel and glass in the distance.

"Theirs," she said, pointing at a pair of tall glass caskets.

A few of the Italian soldiers made the sign of the cross as they gazed up at the giants inside. The caskets towered over the gaping explorers.

While tall and broad-shouldered, they looked emaciated and shriveled and only slightly more alive than the mummies she had seen in the Valley of the Kings. They each had long red hair and one had a beard. Golden implements crossed their silver clothed torsos as did a few tubes and wires. Exotic jewelry rode on each giant's wrist.

"Atlantis," gasped Santini, "these must be refugees from Atlantis. Your Nubians must have viewed them as Gods and built a temple to them."

Forester glimpsed a chart on the wall. Unfamiliar constellations dotted the surface. This was no tomb, no temple to strange gods of yesteryear, she thought. This was a ship lost in a sea of stars, marooned on a primitive island.

"You will be famous for this," exclaimed Santini.

For a moment Forester forgot her anger. "Me?"

"Of course, this is still your discovery. I care not for the scientific papers or prestige. I only want the treasure."

"This is all treasure beyond understanding," she said. Distracted by her awe she ran her hands over an enormous chair, so large she was like a child in comparison.

"I will just take these and go," said Santini.

"Take what?" she asked as she turned back to him, slowly, unwilling to focus on anything that had come in from outside of the complex.

"The gold. They have bracelets big as necklaces, necklaces big as belts. I will be rich as Midas, maybe even move to America and become a cattle baron." He reached out and placed his hands on the nearest casket.

"You can't take those. You can't open the sarcophagi, we don't know what it will do to the remains."

"We have been through this already tonight." he replied without malice. He ran a hand over the clear caskets and noticed a lever beside them. "Ah, easy access."

"Don't," she whispered.

He pulled the lever down and hush of stale air burst from the cases.

A dull alarm sounded from somewhere in the dark and as Forester, still the only one looking up, watched in horror as the giants trembled. Santini braced himself as if for an earthquake but Forester, shocked into silence, watched as the long sleeping "gods" stirred awake and opened their pale vengeful eyes.

"It's all over," she cried as madness took hold.

DAVID J. WEST

# WHY CROWS STEAL SHINY THINGS

When the Gods first crafted the world they gave life to every spirit. Some were men, others beasts and some were dragons. Each worked in accord with its nature. Their formidable grace and lust pushed dragons beyond the measure of their creation.

Realizing the dragons had been given too much strength, the Gods recanted their sins and battled the monsters for forty days. After much loss the Gods won in blood and fury. The Gods allowed dragons to keep their wings but their nature has not changed.

These tiny black thieves still sup on flesh and lust for their horde.

# TANGLE CROWNED DEVIL

Deep in the ages before old men repeated the stories they were told as children about dying fires; the cannibal demon, Átahsaia haunted the canyon lands above Pariah Crossing. These lands were his and the red man knew not to disturb him . . . but the white man didn't.

\* \* \*

A black scorpion crawled ponderously up Porter's arm. His Bowie sheared the stinger without knocking the creature off balance. He slid the blade back in its sheath silent as sleeping death.

He flicked the crippled creature away and continued watching the rustler's camp from just below the spine of a shadowy crag. He wouldn't take the chance that even the dim web of stars might outline him.

Port was being extra-cautious as of late, quite a number of folks had been taking shots at him lately and he hadn't yet been able to identify them all. The likelihood that it was the rustlers themselves watching their back trail was the most likely explanation, but if that were the case we were they being so careless now?

When the moon dipped behind clouds, he felt his way down the jagged granite boulders and stalked toward the fading orange glow of the campfire. The floor of pine needles concealed his approach and the rustlers slept soundly. Even the watchman, a half-breed Lakota, called Red Cap was resting against a tree, dozing.

The horses nickered at Porter's approach. He grunted softly to them and they quieted, still shying away. The scent of the predator was strong even with the cool wind whipping through the pines.

A horse neighed, waking Red Cap who peered blindly into the palpable darkness. The smoky dying fire gave stark shape to the night, each tree seemed a slender column of rough tiger striped orange and black.

Port knew that old Red Cap saw nothing but might feel his presence and wake the others, he had to move fast.

Red Cap glanced toward his companions, likely taking false

comfort in their nearness. The tree he sat under ran sap across his homespun blanket. The stickiness threatened to trap his hands. He rubbed them furiously against his pants so they wouldn't mar his Sharps rifle.

A soft sound in the needles was all the warning Red Cap had before looking up in time to see Port's snub-nosed Navy colt revolver trained on the his chest.

"Put it down. Quietly," whispered Porter harsh as steel trap. His long wild hair and beard made him look every bit the maniacal gunslinger come feared lawman. For good or evil, people knew him when they saw him. Legend had it that he had shot well over a hundred men, some called him the Destroying Angel.

"Porter, I didn't want any part of this. Honest," Red Cap said, putting down the rifle and rolling away from the tree. "Two-Toes, he said—"

"On your belly."

Port bound the Red Cap's hands with stout rope and then put the man's own dirty sock in his mouth to gag him. Porter then walked to the sleeping men and nudged the closest one with his boot. As the man rolled over angry, Port stuck the snub nosed barrel in his face.

"Shhh. Don't need to wake your friends up just yet."

Port repeated the process until three of the five rustlers were bound up like corn husk dolls. He kicked the last two awake. They yawned and exchanged horrified looks as they beheld the infamous gunman.

"Porter, you son of a—"

"Save the sweet talk for the judge, Two-Toes," said Porter, tossing a length of rope at Two-Toes Turley, the leader of the gang. "One of you tie up the other. And if it ain't a top notch, I'll be making you walk."

That prospect alone was enough to make the two men fight each other over who got to bind who. Once they finished Porter bound the last one and double checked the other.

"My hands, I can't feel 'em," whined Saw-Tooth Roberts.

"That's alright, you don't need 'em to ride anyway," said Porter, picking Saw-Tooth up by his belt and flinging him sideways upon a waiting horse.

With dawn's early light, Porter led the five rustlers and their herd of horses back out the box canyon and northwest toward Fort Kanab. A way out across the vale Port thought he saw a small light brown creature standing on its hind end watching them. It had antlers. He shook his head guessing a shrub must have been beside the creature granting it a tangled crown. He kept riding on, but it was a strange sight.

It wasn't yet noon when a boy of perhaps twelve or thirteen came riding from the east at a furious pace.

He was calling for Porter before he even hit earshot. "Mr. Rockwell! Mr. Rockwell! I found you! Right where Mr. Lee said you'd be."

"Easy son, give that horse a breather before she keel's over on you. What's got you so riled?"

The boy nodded and got off his horse, stroking the panting creatures neck. The affection he had for the animal was plain. "Mr. Rockwell, sir, I'm John Worrell, Hezekiah Deacon's nephew. My uncle has rich claim of a mining camp on the other side of Lee's ferry. We're down a box canyon that he discovered."

Porter listened and took a swig of Valley Tan whiskey from his dusters side pocket. "So?"

"We need help, something is a murdering at night."

"Claim jumpers? Ute's?" Porter took another swig.

The boy shook his head vigorously. "No sir. My Uncle could handle other men."

Porter squinted at the boy against the sunlight. "What are you saying?"

"It's a monster sir. Kills with its mouth and antlers."

The rustlers bound and uncomfortable as they were, chuckled at the boy.

The boy glared at the rustlers. "You tell them to keep their traps shut...sir. I'm sorry, but this thing is real. It may sound like a story but 'tain't."

"Monster huh? How big? Big as a man?" asked Port. Holding

his hand up to gauge height. "This high?" The boy shook his head. "This high?"

"No, it's a lot bigger."

"This high?"

"No, bigger."

Porter grinned, "Lot bigger huh?" He took another swig of his whiskey. "What are you all mining in this canyon your Uncle discovered? Pyrite? Mercury? Guano?"

"You don't believe me do you? Uncle says you're the only one that can help us. He said you've dealt with monsters before."

"Maybe I have, but I got a bounty I aim to collect on these rustlers. It's gonna pay twenty dollars a head. I don't have time for something that your Pa ought a shoot himself. Probably just a bear or panther."

"No it isn't. Its killed good men," protested the boy wiping away a tear. "My Uncle said."

"My uncle said, my uncle said, look kid. I haven't got time. I'm riding to Fort Kanab."

"Uncle Hezekiah said you might say that. Said you might not remember him from the old days back in California, back in Murderer's Bar, but he remembers you. Said he knew what would motivate you." The kid reached into his saddlebag.

Porter, ever wary, kept a free hand near his gun.

The kid pulled something small enough to be concealed in his hand out of the saddlebag and tossed it to Porter. It glittered, capturing sunlight across its face. The rustlers saw it too, nudging each other in excitement.

Porter caught it and his eyes grew wide. A gold nugget bigger than any he had ever seen, even in the days of the gold rush no one had found one this big.

"There's more where that came from, if you will come."

"You could buy an army with this. Why's it need to be me?"

"Bullets can't kill this monster."

"Course not," said Porter. "What am I supposed to do? Grin it to death?"

"Everybody in these parts knows that Porter Rockwell can't be harmed by bullet nor blade. That a holy man blessed you like Samson of old. Your long hair and you lead a charmed life. You coming with me is our only hope of killing what can't be killed."

Port admired the nugget again asking, "Am I supposed to keep this for the job?"

The boy nodded. "It's to pay you to believe and have a little respect."

Port glanced at the rustlers behind. "Two-Toes, Red Cap, Saw-Tooth and you others, *if* I let you boys go...you leave the territory and I never want to see you again. Do we understand each other?"

The rustlers who knew they were facing a hanging, all nodded. Porter cut the bindings on the lead rustler and then the rest.

"You're gonna listen to this kids tall tale and leave us out here? What about our horses?" grumbled Two-Toes.

Port wheeled. "You ain't got horses anymore. Get going 'fore I change my mind."

"You're a gonna abandon us without guns or horses? Why that's practically a death sentence."

"I could *use you up* right now Turley," Port snarled, emphasizing the slang for killing.

"We ain't forgetting this." The rustlers shook their heads and begrudgingly started walking.

Whether they meant that in a positive or negative light Port no longer cared. The nugget was big enough to be worth twenty bounties and if Two-Toes and the others tried any more rustling, he would just snag them again for possibly a higher bounty. Things have a way of working themselves out.

Porter ushered the pack of horses after the kid down toward the southeast. They rode the better part of the day, all the while Porter asked the kid for more information.

"So why don't bullets work?"

"We've tried shooting it, cutting at it, nothing penetrates the skin. Uncle Hezekiah lit some bonfires a couple nights back. It stays away out from the fire but the box canyon don't have much wood left. And when the fires die down it comes back and feeds."

"Feeds?"

"It's a murderer, a cannibal, its eaten seven men and one woman," said the kid, looking away to wipe a tear. "A monster killed my pa!"

"Your pa?"

The kid nodded. "I wanna kill that bastard so bad, but there's nothing I can do . . . yet."

"Alright, answer me this. Why not just leave?"

"You saw the nugget. My uncle and the others won't leave. They keep pulling the gold out of a fissure the river must have cut open this last spring. Uncle says by next year the river may change and we'll never get back. He's rich and crazy as Midas. Me? I just want revenge on that murderer."

Port nodded, "Can't say I blame ya."

As Port watched his back trail he saw the little antlered creature away out in the distance and this time he was sure there was no brush or shrubs to give illusion to the diminutive abomination.

The kid looked back and grinned.

"You seen those before?" asked Port.

"Jackalopes? Yeah, some reckon they are lucky, others say an omen of death."

"What do you think?"

"I know they are."

They reached Lee's Ferry on the Colorado River by late afternoon. Porter arranged for his newly acquired herd of horses to stay there while he and the kid would be ferried to Deacon's camp across the river. Once across what was known as Pariah's Crossing, they followed a narrow trail upriver, half of the time in the river it seemed. Porter marveled at the stark canyon walls, they were carved deep red, streaked black and burning orange like fire in stone.

"I've been here before kid and there ain't no canyon like you're telling me."

"There is. You just have to know where to look. It's not far now."

Sure enough, just around a long bend in the river a wide wet sandbar opened up along the cliff face and tucked into the slanting golden shadows of this Grand Canyon was a slot canyon no wider than six feet. It reached up hundreds of feet to the mesa above. The closer Port looked, it didn't seem to be a force of erosion, instead it was a great crack in the high desert tableau; the birthing pains of an earthquake not long ago.

Beneath the musky scent of the river, Porter smelt the stink of death. This unhallowed natural hall reeked of grim loss and decay. The horses threatened to bolt and each rider was forced to dismount and lead.

At one point Port looked back and saw the jackalope again. He guessed it had to be a different one because there was no way such an animal could have crossed the wild Colorado. He wasn't superstitious but he started to wonder about omens.

They walked through the serpentine canyon for only a few hundred yards when it opened up to the oblong size of a few square acres. Sunlight only touched down from the high canyon walls in a few spots. The ground was river rock and sand. A variety of tents, makeshift huts and lean-to's were scattered throughout and a few mangy horses stood in a dilapidated corral made of rope and driftwood. The men looked worse. Haggard and hollow-eyed, like beaten dogs they watched Port fearfully.

Port's gut told him they were up to no good but considering few if any were gun belts, he didn't figure they could be much danger.

A man with yellow hair fading to grey came forward to take his nephew in his burly arms. He then faced Porter. "I'm Hezekiah Deacon, I want to thank you for coming."

"'Lo, but I haven't done anything yet."

Deacon smiled saying, "But you came. I was telling the men about that incident in Murderer's Bar and I told 'em you were the only man who could take care of this."

Port looked shrewdly at Deacon. "How do you know about any of that?"

"Bloody Creek Mary told me, after you left following the incident with Boyd Stewart." He grinned at that, knowing full well it was more than just an incident. Porter narrowly escaped being hung following a thousand dollar shooting match--which he won.

"Don't tell me you're friends with that polecat Stewart."

"No, but Bloody Creek Mary said you killed some monsters.

Scariest things she ever saw."

Port grimaced, recalling the event brought no pride or joy, just nightmares. "I was in the wrong place, wrong time. We were blessed to escape alive."

"I take it my nephew told you what we need here?"

Porter's eyes caressed the hollow, taking in every feature where something could hide. He had suspected a trap, but the broken look of the men and stink of death spoke that this was no trap for him.

"He told me enough. When can I see this thing for myself? Has it got a lair?"

"It must, but we've never seen it. Lives somewhere up the canyon, possibly up top, we don't really know. No one has dared follow the beast."

"So it's a dumb animal?"

Deacon's face went serious as the grave, "It ain't dumb, Lord no, this thing thinks and it hates and it relish's what it does. It's an evil spawn of Cain himself."

Porter rubbed a broad hand over his forehead and adjusted his hat. His hand instinctively felt for his pistol and the deadly comfort it gave. He had never heard of a beast that couldn't be harmed by flying lead, though the creatures in California were damn close. What could this be? "If I take care of this . . . beast?"

Deacon wrinkled his face. "Didn't the boy give you the nugget?"

"He did, but I wanna hear it from you."

"You're right, *if* the monster can be killed. You deserve more. We just ain't been able to mine more because of that thing."

Port folded his arms nodding, then pulled his Valley-Tan from his duster. "What makes you think I can take care of this?"

"You've got a charmed life, especially for a gunfighter and lawman. Word is no one can harm you with a bullet or blade, you're a modern-day Samson. If anybody can face this thing it'd be you."

"I been hearing that a lot lately, though I've had some folks trying to test that."

Deacon grunted and shook his head. "Straight up that wash, is where we think the beast is. Night will be the best time to try and trap it for you to kill...somehow. It only comes out at night"

"I only use the same tools as any man," said Port gesturing to his navy-colt and Bowie. "But sometimes you need a steady hand at the wheel."

"You certainly do."

"I am tuckered, wouldn't mind a bit of shut eye before twilight."

Deacon showed Port to his tent and said, "We'll holler when we're ready."

All of it made Port uneasy but he was dog tired from scoping out the rustlers all night and he truly wanted to make things right for the Worrell kid. Why did that name seem familiar? He drifted off to uneasy dreams and the heat seemed to climb making him sweat more than he should have this time of year. Jackalopes danced in his dreams, slapping their feet against the naked desert. A warning that something was coming?

Specters haunted his sleep and something stole over him until...

"Mr. Rockwell, its time."

Port roused himself and felt for his gun belt, it was gone! As was his Bowie knife.

Nothing to do but meet this challenge head on.

Stepping outside dusk washed blue black to the horizon that barely retained a shade of blood. Stars like serpent eyes blinked overhead and Port could swear that he didn't recognize the constellations for a brief moment.

A handful of small fires blazed in a wide circular pattern and Port wondered at the devious mannerisms of Deacon and his men. "What's all this?"

"We've called out the beast to take care of you."

Port furrowed his brow. "Did I hear you right?"

"You did murderer!" accused John Worrell, his voice almost cracking to splinters.

It was then Port looked at the ground and where the fires were placed. A great pentagram was drawn out on the ground surrounding him, alien glyphs written in blood were spaced between the dark stars points and Port was in the dead center. Alone.

"Now we've all heard the tales on how you cannot be harmed by bullet or blade. I never believed them myself, but hell we've been taking shots at you for three weeks now and haven't been able to hit you once," laughed Deacon as if it were all in good fun.

"What'd I ever do to you?" said Port stalling for a moment as he eyed the canyon walls watching for a way out.

"You killed my Pa! Frank Worrell!"

Port rubbed his chin. "Yep. Got him right in the belt buckle. Thought your name was familiar."

Deacon continued, "And we can all see now you're unrepentant son of a bitch too. No remorse for your killing!"

Port chuckled, "I ain't never killed anyone who didn't need killing. Frank got what was coming to him. Everyone always does."

He might have taunted them further waiting for an opening to make good his escape when an unnatural chill fell on him like the mantle of winter itself. It was a cold full to the bone and it drained any love of life Port held. Only a dim recollection of what he cared for remained, drowning in a sea of emptiness and despair.

Then he saw the eyes.

Eyes crimson and full of hate, crowned with sharp tangled antlers.

From out of the ethereal abyss the demon jackalope stood before Porter with a wide twitching nose. His matted fur was a slain brown and long black claws hung from his paws. An orange aura hung over the demon looking like flames about ready to boil over in stark contrast to the overwhelming cold emanating from this forgotten specimen of hell.

"The Zuni's call him Átahsaia, and we decided that if you couldn't be killed by mortal means we would summon a demon to do it for us."

"Jackalope demon, that's diabolical."

"Indeed it is," confirmed Deacon. "I was able to summon and control him through this book of black magic I stole from a man name of Godbe. I reckon I'll get better use of it than that Brit."

"You make a deal with the devil you're gonna pay more in interest than you ever bargained."

"Don't lecture me murderer. We got you! And you're gonna be

the one to pay!"

"Want your nugget back then?" Anything to buy some time, Port hoped even angering them might give him something to work with, but not this time.

"Átahsaia destroy him!"

The monster lunged and Port dodged, but the wicked claws still tore his jacket to shreds. Trying to roll away, Port was slammed to the ground, the air bursting from his lungs under the titanic pressure.

Port swept a leg out to trip the demon, but it merely hopped over his attack.

The treacherous men laughed at the spectacle calling out Átahsaia to slay their hated foe.

The Jackalope dropped down on all fours and tried to gore Porter with its hideous antlers, but Port grabbed the furthest one out and used the momentum against it, driving the monster into the ground.

Back legs kicked out sent Port reeling. Before he knew it Átahsaia was on top.

Turning blue from the pressure of a bear-sized creature on top of him, Port dazedly thought he saw a small typical enough jackalope slapping the ground with its big foot. No, it was scraping its foot along the ground, clearing a fresh trail of earth over the old. And Port understood.

Crushed down, Port's boot cut across a portion of the pentagram's circle. A whirlwind rushed through the gap and the monster sensed freedom turning its attention from Port to its unbidden masters outside, those foolish mortals who had dared try to command it.

"Now you boys messed up. I know the secret!" Port wiped clean a wide swath of the blood-soaked ground opening the door.

Like slick lightning Átahsaia was through the gap.

Taking a precious breather for the moment, Port marveled at the look of shock and fear wafting over Deacon and his men like palpable smoke.

The monster took one of Deacon's men by the neck and

throttled him. Another was impaled by the antlers and flung away, jets of blood spraying the already tainted ground.

Gunshots fired birthed in chaotic abandon, but nothing harmed the demon.

Porter scuttled out of the damnable pentagram toward the canyon wall where the little brown jackalope had been.

It was gone, but Port sensed it had stood there for good reason. Sure enough his Bowie knife, gun belt and cartridges were lying there.

He checked the revolver, loaded and prepared to take whatever presented itself.

But all was now silent and gone. Deacon, Worrell and their handful of haggard men were all on the ground, bleeding out from voracious wounds.

Átahsaia was nowhere to be seen, but that vile cold still filled the camp.

Shadows moved out in the gloom and Porter prepared to give it his all against the devils jackrabbit.

Things swept in, surrounding. Chuckles and haunting whispers came and dread footfalls washed over the blood soaked sands.

Voices crept and the dying hellish flames only made Port blind to the encroaching mass. A figure moved into the half-light.

"Told you we wouldn't forget," said Two-Toes with a jutting grin.

Port then saw Red Cap leveling his Sharps rifle and Saw-Tooth his scattergun, the others close behind. "I never doubted you Turley."

"How'd you kill all these feller's? And where is that nugget I saw and more? Speak or Red Cap and Saw-Tooth are gonna open you up."

"You boys should run."

Two-Toes Turley gave a charity chuckle. "You ain't immortal. You can't *use us all up.*"

"No, but he can."

Átahsaia loomed behind Two-Toes and rammed his blood-red antlers into the rustlers back. Rearing up, it flung his body away into the night.

Red Cap's Sharps rifle sang out once before he died but Saw-Tooth only screamed.

The others full of terror ran gibbering a brutal moment before Átahsaia bound after them silencing them swiftly. The bone-crunching savagery lasting but a few seconds.

Porter held his ground, waiting for the demon to return, all went still and though the darkness was hard as obsidian, nothing materialized and the feverish cold vanished.

Looking down, Porter saw the little jackalope beside his leg, standing on its hind quarters. He reached down to its eye level and said, "Thanks."

\* \* \*

The next day as Porter gathered his horses from the corrals at Lee's Ferry, old Lee called out, "Will you take a look at that?" He cocked his rifle and took aim at a jackalope standing out on the flats beside the river.

Port put his hand on the barrel. "Oh no, John. That's a friend that is and good luck to boot. Don't ever try and shoot one and that's the God's truth."

# DAVID J. WEST

## THE CRY OF CARRION BIRDS

Some may think me cruel and unseemly, but I only did that which was expected and proper in light of events such as they were . . . as maddening and unbelievable as they are. If black nightmares come spiraling out of the sky and reveal themselves as a true yet hidden reality . . . who are you to judge me? I believe you would take a shovel in hand just as quickly as I.

* * *

After the grotesque attack involving the madman at the University, upon my once beautiful wife, Tabitha, it was decided we would take the early retirement pension and move far to the western end of the state. We wanted to get away from the noisome city, backstabbing friends and her interfering family. I could also no longer tolerate society's eyes gazing at her frail features, always lingering upon those scars that cut jagged like lightning bolts down her pale cheeks and lips, ending in swirling vortexes on the throat where life nearly ended. She should not have to relive that horror with every awkward glance. I grew weary of my knuckles turning white upon my trusted cane with every leer and whisper.

So my wife and I searched for a secluded home in the mountainous Pintler range, so very far from the heavy footed paths of casual callers and unwelcome visitors. A place where life would be simpler, reclusive, quiet as we imagined it had been in the days of our noble ancestors. I had but to pour over the maps and find the least populous areas, those places almost overlooked in the westward expansion of our nation. What some might call grim and foreboding, I welcomed. Who would stare at her here? Nothing but rolling hills, turbulent rivers, forests of supreme pine, gnarled oak and the occasional aboriginal collection of scattered and ruined stone.

Beyond the dank marsh and lowlands, far up into the hills and towering mountains beyond we found there a massive old two-story cabin with four gables, wrap-around porch and a river rock chimney. The residence was owned by the Davis family; who had fallen upon hard times and now sought whatever financial gain they could before losing the property to the revenuers. The cattle fields of their bourgeois ancestors had been reclaimed by the encroaching forest, and as I had no desire to ranch it seemed the perfect place for us. The home was stark. It had no mirrors hanging on the wall nor any telephone. The climate was cool, even in mid-summer and we knew to expect a harsh winter.

All of this was fine. Only one thing bothered me the propensity of chattering crows that lingered about the property. The owners were more than pleased to sell, since they lived more than two miles to the south in a crooked house of their own construction. Its lumber never properly dried and had warped in the months after it was built, giving the appearance of a structure ready to fly apart; and the windows were always dark, reminding one of the black secretive eyes of its inhabitants. It all seemed a reflection of the souls of these furtive beings who resembled human weasels. I made my appointments with them brief and to the point, disliking how they, too, leered at my wife through the windows of our car until the murder of crows drew our attention once again.

"Can't abide them crows myself, but nothing gets rid of them," said the elder Davis.

"Wouldn't a scarecrow frighten them away?" I inquired.

"No, there aren't even any fields here for them to sup on, they jus' claim the place."

"What do they eat then?"

"Whatever they can find I 'spose," he said grinning. "It's your lan' now but I woul't recommend wandering too far off into these haunted mountains, not too many folks who did, ever came back and those that did t'were never the same." He pointed at himself, "I've seen things make a preacher cry."

Spying his offspring staring at my wife, I coughed and gestured, arresting his nonsensical jabbering. He called his children away and we finished our inspection of the property.

For a very fair price, they sold the colossal cabin and surrounding property to me with but a handshake and visit to the local bank. They were very happy they did not have to sell to other townsfolk, whom they considered beneath them. Though I would be damned if I could tell the difference.

Brooding forests and mountain peaks blockaded the pretentious kindred's and cowardly curious I feared would call on us, here we would be safe from prying eyes and gossiping vulture's eager to speak of the wretched victim of that deranged slashing monster.

My wife's sister called us mad to move out to the desolate country, oblivious that she was a leading cause of our insanity. I was so terribly pleased that she would never venture from the civilized east to visit us here, that she would not be present to remind us of what was once normal life, to speak of the balls and parties we would never again attend. I had my once beautiful bride and would keep her safe from the world. I alone could do what everyone else failed in.

Besides my pension, I found through correspondence and investments I could still make a decent living, and with a postal service visiting twice a week at the fork in the county road we had no worries of keeping contact with the few people that mattered. Thirty miles from the nearest small town and all of it down a dirt road made us feel like golden pioneers carving out the frontier from a desiccated wood.

I paid a Davis boy a reasonable sum to deliver groceries for us twice a week and thus my devastated wife never had to leave the home for sundries. In the country we had surprisingly few expenses and were able to order fine things from the catalogs and yet still I could hear her crying late at night, remembering the horrors inflicted upon her. Though she would deny it in the morning that I had heard any such thing, tear-stained pillows do not lie. I dread the thought of how terribly unhappy she would be if I had not taken her away from the city, what further embarrassments would be inflicted upon us.

After six weeks of gentle secluded life, I was shocked to find Tabitha answering the door herself when the Davis boy came calling with his weekly delivery. They had been speaking softly and I was angry as I had told him specifically to only give me the grocery order. I cuffed him severely on the ear and was to strike him again with my cane when Tabitha begged I let him go, that it was her fault, she had answered the door. He fled and again Tabitha wept at her horrible condition and the memory aroused of her brutal attack. Holding her as tight as I could in my arms and still she could not escape the fear and sadness at her shattered life, she even deliriously cried to return to our former home and her family. But I knew those vultures would only try and reveal her hideousness to the world, a sick way of bearing themselves up at our wretched misfortune.

When came dusk, the elder Davis pulled up to my property in his ancient jalopy and I met him on the porch. Upset over his bruised son, it took but a moment of speaking to him as his better, as a man of science and reason, for him to understand my position. He smiled and replied that he was sad or sorry and saw how things were very well, and that his son would indeed continue doing deliveries for us but that he would not again speak to my wife without my permission. He asked in his colloquial manner of the weather, the turning season and of the crows which had become naught but background noise to me. Or as I soon discovered they had been gone for some time, that was why I had not heard their incessant chattering for days now. He again advised that I stay clear of the woods and left after negotiating a slight payment increase for his son.

Tabitha watched from the windows and once Mr. Davis had gone, she stepped outside to watch the evenings crimson glow depart. We stood there for a long time before she spoke.

"I think I want to go back, visit my family, the letters by themselves get terribly boring." She sighed and looked away.

"What of your humours? The physicians recommended you to not allow stress to overwhelm you," I reminded her. "You don't want the gossip and looks to sting, I don't want that for you. I gladly sacrifice to be here and keep you from that embarrassment," I said, putting my arm around her.

"You don't know me," she said, with tearful lunacy.

She threw off my gentle hand and holding her skirts up, dashed into the thick dark wood, branches and splayed twigs immediately obscured my vision. I called and pleaded at her to stop for dusk took full flight over us with cumulus wings. I worried what would the neighbors say if they could hear such a spat. I could not keep up with her pace and she knew it, the limp I received from the war kept me at half her speed and she soon disappeared in the bleak, odiferous forest.

Giving chase, I tore my tweed jacket and trousers, Phoenician red bruises formed upon my legs where stones and brambles waylaid me and it seemed the ghoulish forest itself attempted to hinder my righteous pursuit. What insanity took the woman to run as she did at this late hour?

The chase rambled uphill over dense underbrush and bloodthirsty insects seemed to swarm overhead with a nauseous buzzing, bites swelled and bled, the streaks of crimson mingled with sweat and stung. My air was running short and I was near to fainting from exhaustion and shouting for Tabitha, when near the zenith of the fiendish mount, colossal shapes loomed overhead.

Stark grey dolmens of stone, alien to this landscapes geology, erected by the hands of some lost race surely raised these. I certainly knew that the local tribes of Indians never worked in such ghastly marvels. These must have stood over twelve feet tall and there were more than a score of them in a loose circular fashion. In the gathering gloom I could not see Tabitha but knew she was nearby, the roots and leaves left a wake of her trail akin to a ship rolling through a glass-smooth bay.

The leering moon shone through the trees revealing sadistic glyphs that were not carved into the stone but were curiously embossed in some impossible fashion. The half-light clearly made them stand outward and I marveled in silence a moment before hearing a shriek from Tabitha not more than a dozen of paces from me through the circular altar of stone. I raced stumbling in the direction I believed her to be, when a sound like Tabitha laughing came from my far left, but Tabitha never laughed with such an ominous mocking tone. I was briefly afraid of what affect this ancient observatory had upon her, during a time like this, when witches may have gathered and held covens under stars that were not right.

The laugh came again, this time far to my right, a ludicrous speed for Tabitha to have made through the sloping surrounding woods. I called to her and received nothing in return. Angry and fearful, I glanced about as it seemed the tops of the stones swirled and ebbed against the starry night overhead, I could not recognize the constellations and knew I must have us away from this unhallowed place.

Grateful to have the security my cane, a single primal weapon if needs be, I stumbled to the far edge of the circle and just as suddenly Tabitha appeared. She was smiling from behind one of the towering dolmens, her pale hand caressing the grooved monument.

"We must depart for home, its late, and I fear gas may leak from this hillock," I told her.

She laughed looking into my soul with her bright blue eyes, she nodded and put her arm in mine. "We should go to your home," she said.

Struggling down the hideous mount, I tripped many times but Tabitha stepped carefully as if she could see better at night than I ever could. I saw her look back at the nexus of stones several times and wondered at her curiously fright-less behavior. What changed for her in that mindless flight to make her so unafraid?

At the cabin, she still looked in the direction of the ruin, though no trace of it could be seen from our home. We made ready for bed and with my bites and scratch's attended, we lay down and to sleep.

I could not possibly say how long I had been asleep but it must have been several hours as the light from the moon had crossed a portion of the room. And out in the cold distance of night, I thought I faintly heard a scream. A scream full of unchaste horror such as I had not heard since the madman's razor slashed across my beloved. Tabitha's scream.

My first thought was to leap to my feet and take the forgotten rifle out into the night, when I paused and saw she still lay there beside me, sound asleep, her white skin slightly heaving with even breaths. Standing at the window, I waited a moment longer and heard nothing more.

Lying down, I once again began to drift away to heavy slumber and the dreams came and sat at my feet and entered in. I thought I heard Tabitha scream again far out in the forest, but no, she still lay beside me with cool summer skin.

The dreams lay and hatched and I saw Tabitha running through the grim wood pursued by flapping onyx shapes, formless as the void but palpably hideous and evil. She called my name again and again, and each time, I awoke and looked, she still lay snoring evenly beside me. I wondered at the strange mountain ruins, and pondered if gas would explain the nature of the feelings I had, or perhaps a toxic insect bite, maybe I had a fever from the exertions of the night. Again I heard Tabitha scream, but no, she is still beside me, sleeping peaceful as the cosmic serpent wheeled overhead.

I put the fears away, there were many possible explanations, it could be any one of them, and I needed sleep. And the nightmares came and knelt at the foot of my bed and laughed, for the stars were not right.

I awoke at the cackling of a murder of crows, the damned black vermin had returned. Tabitha lay sprawled across the bed, a light snore escaping her once beautiful lips. Looking to the window, I saw the morning carrion birds spread across the ground, bunched and jostling here and there over a form of curiously familiar color. My instinct prickled as dread reared up again at so eerie a collection beside the trees.

Stepping outside, I threw a stone at the nearest crow. It hopped a few paces farther away, and the others answered indignant at my presence, as if I was to attempt to steal their hard won prize.

Then I saw.

Pale legs stretched out frozen and still upon the merciless ground. Blonde hair wafted over the unholy soil and I knew those lips, those scars, that once beautiful face of Tabitha, my wife.

This could not be, she was asleep in bed, but here she lay before me, dead.

I gasped and vomited. Rushing back inside the house, I raced up the stairs and threw back the door. Tabitha was spread across the bed, her sleeping breast heaving.

Outside, the crows picked at the corpse and in a moment of panic, I made my decision.

Taking a shovel, I hurried and dug a pit there on the edge of the vile wood, and I cast this impostor's warm corpse into it.

I will make no venture of explanation for the cursed midnight hour that cast this insanity at my feet, but I will hide it and forget the whole thing in time, once the blank stare of this false Tabitha's eyes exit my horrified memory. They did not flicker, I remind myself as I cast the dirt into the grave, I did not see them flicker, nor the mouth open ever so briefly. I did not see them flicker.

This was the proper thing to do, you bury a dead body, especially that of an abomination from some witch-haunted wood, it is what anyone of you would have done in my place.

I had just finished placing the last shovel full of dirt upon my own new mound when the real Tabitha stepped from the door, still clutching her silken bedding. I peered into her eyes, never noticing before how black they were, like dark windows of some awful abode.

She asked, "What are you doing?"

Only the carrion birds know and I shall not answer for them.

## DAVID J. WEST

# THE MAD SONG

*According to legend, the most sinister and destructive of musical instruments, the Pipe of Mahmackrah, was crafted near the dawn of time by Goonayn the Enchanter, who was also credited with creating the occult sciences of metallurgy, alchemy, and music. Soon after its creation, and with a terrible blood sacrifice, the Pipe itself was dedicated to the lion-headed fire god Mahmackrah. Whether such a god exists and accepted the sanguine tribute remains a mystery. What is known though, has been recounted in the Vedja of the Imam's in far off Kathul, the accounts of the Sen-Toku Admiralty, and the holy writ of the historian monks in Tiburon, each considered beyond reproach in their record keeping.*

*After centuries of being used merely as symbol of status among the wealthier Dar-Alahamran's, the Pipe found its way into the possession of a minor band of robbers known as Kardik's Men. By chance Kardik sacked the caravan which was transporting the Pipe of Mahmackrah. Intrigued by the ornate and double-barreled pipe, Kardik deigned to play upon it. Something was summoned.*

*A maddening scourge seized upon Kardik at once and proceeded to infect and contaminate all his band, the few that fled to the nearest city-states across the desert soon found themselves only spreading the pestilence to larger populations. In a matter of weeks the subcontinental realm of Dar-Alahamra was overrun with a sonic plague. The sorcerous infection was contained because the coastal Sen-Toku Empire blockaded the harbors, forcing the small desert continent to embrace its fate and die.*

*In a fit of cannibalism and murder, the entire subcontinent was depopulated and remained a haunted landscape for generations. Ships did not dock for decades, but from a distance the sailors described hideous shambling monstrosities that only vaguely resembled humans. Eventually the abominations were seen no more and a few brave souls explored, colonized and rebuilt until a new people dwelt over the face of the land and the dead were nearly forgotten but for their Cyclopean ruins. Though an intensive search was made for such a destructive instrument, the Pipe of Mahmackrah itself was never found.*

*The nomads who populate the hinterlands whisper that if a man goes mad in the night he must have heard the pipes call* — from the writings of Niblyus

† † †

The gossamer-shrouded caravan rolled lightly over unhallowed sands. Silk-clad maidens and armored horsemen alike cast furtive glances down at the shifting sands, half expecting withered and rotted hands to rise—for beneath the surface lie the supposed remnants of a lost and cursed civilization.

It was not uncommon for some ancient cup or brooch to be found along the trail. Anywhere else such a trinket would be but a trifle to recover, the work of a moment to step down and be rescued from the ever-present heat and wind; but here in the Vale of Desolation, near any item would be left alone, as it was said by the wilderness nomads to bring some ill luck upon the traveler that gambled to keep it.

Such was the superstitious bearing of this caravan, too. An alchemist leapt from his seat on the wagon to pick up a brass goblet half-buried in the sands. A scolding from his wife coaxed him to softly toss the relic away. No point in waking the dead, she chided, for the damned know what is theirs and what is disturbed.

The sun bearing down with the ferociousness of a blast furnace granted some courage to the superstitious, while black-winged vultures circled overhead, patient as the decayed mummies rumored to be interred below. Mile after mile of rolling dunes broke and gave way to outcroppings of fractured, red stone that gradually formed into spidery canyons and ravines, and for those sheltered stony mountains the caravan made all due progress. Whips struck the hind ends of oxen in anticipation to be out and away of the Vale. Flanking the treasure and spice wagons were row upon row of mounted Yanissary bodyguards, their long, curled mustaches and wide, flaring turbans bouncing in time to their camels' steps. Next came the perfumed seraglio carriages with women's laughter hovering overhead, then the overloaded acting company's coach, the alchemist, apothecary and water/food supply wagons; lastly, the exotic animals in a half-dozen stinking carts lined with bars of bronze, painted in stripes of flat black and lustrous gold. Azure banners fluttered in the chaotic breeze, and the more fearful even blamed the weather on the Djinn and bane of the desert.

So wary were these merchant princes that, when a solitary rider crested a dune, they formed a defensive circle, expecting an attack.

The stranger galloped his roan horse to within a hundred yards, then slowed to a canter with arms upraised in the universal sign of peace. "Hold, I bear a message," he shouted.

A nervous Yanissary loosed a long-flanged arrow.

Unblinking, the stranger watched the shaft as it was about to strike his breast and swiftly, though almost casually, leaned aside, letting the missile bypass within a hairsbreadth.

"That's speed of a viper and will of iron, there," said a merchant.

"Or stupidity," said another.

"Damn you! I said I come in peace with a message!" shouted the stranger in a thick foreign accent.

The Yanissary commander smacked the overeager bowman over the head, and only then did the stranger trot his horse closer.

"Give me a moment that I may hear you," he said.

The Yanissary commander nodded, beckoning his welcome with palms outward, the sign of peace and truce in the desert kingdoms.

The stranger tore the turban from his scalp as he approached, revealing a shaven skull. Only stubble remained upon his crown and face. His face and exposed hands were sun-burnt, painting him red-bronze. He wore faded black leather breeches made of a multitude of patches sewn together. The ox-hide boots were dull and cracked, and his open vest and sweat-stained linen shirt were not much better. The only articles in fine shape were his weapons: a sturdy horn bow, a light Valchiki shield of woven leather and reeds; and a broadsword and matching brazen spear from his homeland over the sea, snow-clad Vjorn. Such items were well crafted and bore the marks of frequent, and likely bloody, use. He had everything a fighting man might need, save armor. But in the heat of these desert hinterlands, none wore armor, or if he did, he wore very little.

A white-bearded man in a bright yellow tunic pushed to the forefront of the crowd, saying, "I am Vareem, master of this caravan. Who are you? And what lord sends us this message?"

Halting only a dozen paces from the gathering guardsmen and posturing merchants, the stranger answered, "I am Khyte of Vjorn, a veteran sell-sword. I fought for the emperor of Sen-Toku in the War of fifty-two against the Bhustani's, and then later in fifty-seven against the Galinese city states, and now I want an ear and respect for what I must say." Khyte's eyes darted about, watching everyone and everything, not in the fearful manner of a craven, but that of a wary hunter, ever vigilant and tensed.

The Yanissary commander, decorated with several badges of honor, stepped forward. "I am Barzelai, the Yanissary captain. We have fought in the same wars and paid the same price. Apologies for my foolish underling firing upon you. Who is your lord?" He beckoned for Khyte to continue.

"I serve no lord, but was riding due east to sell my sword in Scalia or Avaris when I passed over your trail."

Vareem grimaced. "Your rudeness belies your lack of critical thinking. You have halted my entire caravan for pointless pleasantries. What do you want, outlander?"

"You have missed a crucial detail in your journey," he said, keeping a vigilant eye upon all before him, as if he didn't want to miss a single response.

"Why tell us this?"

Khyte leaned forward in the saddle, squinting against the sunlight. "On account you don't know that there is also a band of forty-plus men moving parallel to you. They have for the last few days, just out of site beyond that ridge."

One of the junior officers broke in. "And why should they wait to attack us?"

Another jeered, "And how do we know this man isn't one of them spying upon us?"

Khyte scoffed, "They already know your numbers and tactics.

They don't need a spy."

"But why wait?"

Gesturing out to the rising red cliffs and canyons, Khyte said, "Because we're farther out into the uninhabited wilderness and away from all possible help. Likely we're much closer now to the lair where they may hide up their treasure. You saved them the trouble of hauling it. I expect they plan to attack by morning, kill all your men, loot the valuables and take the women for slaves."

"And what is your advice, outlander?"

"Don't get into that Notch yonder. They might have more men planning to fully ambush you there."

Vareem sniffed again as he took a pinch of snuff, "And why would you suggest such an ambush?"

Khyte grinned. "Because it's what I would do, if I had not changed my ways."

"Are you saying we must sit and wait, rather than traveling on?"

"Yes. Build defensive positions tonight and be prepared for more tomorrow."

Barzelai shook his head. "You are an outlander and cannot fully understand. We dare not camp overnight in this cursed valley, but must press on."

"They are swifter than this caravan. Running won't solve this," said Khyte. "Perhaps they are as superstitious as you and won't be eager to attack here. But they will eventually, and this might be the best place to wait them out. Soon enough they will run out of water. They are all on horseback and have limited supplies."

"That is sound logic. But why should you, an outlander, do this for us?"

"Because it is the way of the desert to help another in need; and I am nearly out of water myself, plus, I don't care much for bandits."

Vareem leaned in and whispered in Barzelai's ear. The Yanissary commander nodded. Though he still eyed Khyte suspiciously, Vareem admitted, "I agree that if what he has spoken is true, it is the wisest council. But first I will consult the seeress and roll the bones. If they support him we shall do as he advises."

"But here?" asked a short fat merchant, "in the Desolation of the damned?"

"We have no choice," snapped Vareem before disappearing into a silk shrouded wagon.

Khyte furrowed his brow. "What is in this valley? There is grass just yonder for the livestock. I have seen nothing of danger but the bandits."

"Slake your thirst with this outlander, while I explain," shouted Barzelai, tossing the wineskin as hard as he could.

Khyte caught the swift underhanded throw with the speed of a striking asp. He stared hard at the commander, scrutinizing his behavior.

Barzelai's eyebrows raised in satisfaction. He nodded, saying, "Vareem said you were quick dodging that arrow. I wanted to see how quick up close."

Before guzzling the strong Yanaian brew, Khyte said, "The arrow was quicker. Any more tests?" He finished the skin, then tossed it back.

His jovial face darkening, Barzelai answered, "Aye, there will be tests enough when we see what these raiders shall do. In the Desolation between city-states men are always tested, but those that make it through will be richly rewarded. Judging by your poor accouterments, I suspect any amount of pay will do you well, eh? That is old equipment you bear, indeed, outlander."

"These have served me well enough," he said, patting his sword hilt.

"I need your sword on this journey. What do you say?"

Dusting his worn clothing, Khyte dismounted, then nodded. He stared intently at Barzelai to be sure that he read each word across his lips right.

"Then you are no longer an outlander, but my friend. So tell me, Khyte, you closely watch us speak. Are you still grappling with our language? So different from the Northern wastes, I am sure."

"Yes, I am still learning. Tell me more about this place. Why do you fear it?"

"Fear? No, it is a healthy respect. This valley that we travel upon is named the Vale of Desolation, and it must be traveled over before nightfall. You mentioned grass that our animals might eat? No, it is upon land where much blood has been spilt. To let our animals graze there would invite much bad luck. I might add it is rumored to be laid over the top of a legendary city of old Dar-Alahamra, back before the madness seized that great civilization and the desert swallowed it. All accounts say it was one week's travel from the coast and upon the edge of the red-canyon lands. So it is safe to say that it is beneath our feet even now."

"Words and superstitions," said Khyte.

"No, my new friend, no. Many times I have crossed this desert myself, and each time I have seen strange and hideous things. Many times we have found the remains of caravans bleaching in the sun."

"Nothing strange about bandits raiding."

"These bandits, as you call them, are new in our land. It is the younger generation that has no respect for their elders that turns to the dishonorable practice. No, when I was a boy, no one would raid the caravans—yet still they would be taken."

"Now who is being naive?"

"I did not say no one did evil things, but merely that my people did not become raiders. These caravans would be found in the desert still loaded with gold, jewels and spices. Superior vintages of wine left to bake in their kegs. No, no one was raiding for goods, my friend. It was the ghosts of old Dar-Alahamra returning to evoke their madness."

"I guess I believe in ghosts. And I agree that they don't drink wine, nor take treasures of the earth." Khyte gazed out over the windswept bleakness. "But they don't kill people, either."

Barzelai shrugged. "I am only telling you what I have seen with my own two eyes. Treasures were left to rot while their owners where torn to pieces and desiccated under an invincible sun."

"Now, that's something different. I thought you were saying they just up and disappeared."

"No, my friend. They were eaten . . . at least in part."

"Ghosts, by definition, don't eat."

Barzelai leaned in, serious as could be. "I know what you will say. Vultures like those above us, eh? No, my friend, no. I have seen able-bodied Yanissaries and fair caravan maidens whose faces were blackened by the long sun, frozen in horror. Though every drop of their blood was drained and dried from them, making them appear as so much driftwood, I could not mistake the terrible claw-marks upon their faces and torsos. Something devoured their hearts and drank their blood, and it was no vulture nor jackal."

Khyte nodded. "You're saying if we remain here tonight, we invite death as much as we do from those bandits?"

"One is as certain as the other, my friend; but I would rather have my death be upon the hot steel of a bastard's *tulwar* than in the belly of a cursed beast."

✝ ✝ ✝

They waited while Vareem rolled the bones and listened to the seeress in her myrrh-scented carriage. When he exited a short time later, men made jokes and whispered behind his back that it had not been nearly long enough to couple with her, while others argued that to remain a seeress she must remain pure as the driven snows of Vjorn. Either way, tongues wagged and Khyte wondered whether any useful decision could be made in such a hotbed of rumor and gossip.

Vareem prepared to address the anxious throng. Just as they had moments ago laughed behind his back, they were now compelled to follow whatever decision he proclaimed. "Attention, attention. I have spoken with Vashti and she has seen that we are to move on. So let the caravan continue, and if there is indeed any danger we will have the fortifications of the cliffs about us that we might hedge up the way of the raiders ... if they exist," he muttered at the last.

"I couldn't have heard you right. Were you calling me a liar?" Khyte shouted, narrowing his gaze at Vareem from across the way.

"I called you nothing, outlander. I merely do as the gods insist." Several of the Yanissaries moved in concert to protect Vareem from the hinted assault betrayed by a bitter Northerner's gaze.

Khyte tensed, preparing to duel. Always his eyes scanned every direction for danger, as his other three senses flared to catch the scent of a well-oiled scabbard, touch of a treacherous hand, or taste the hint of nervous fear on the wind.

Another pair of Yanissaries moved in to flank Khyte, their glinting swords at the ready.

"Enough of this! He is one of us now!" shouted Barzelai.

The murderous situation would have lasted longer, but for the sudden cry of a harem girl standing beside the commander. "Look there, above the dunes! As the outlander said!"

A trio of men on horseback watched from the bluff. On each side of the darkly mounted men another rider appeared, until they lined the entire horizon upon the bluff like dark buzzards. As Khyte had warned, there were at least forty of the grim-faced bandits.

"As I have mentioned, these naughty children, they grow bold these days," said Barzelai, thumbing the edge of his scimitar.

"I suspect that because we stopped, they are puzzled and may attack us even now," grumbled Vareem. "We must away!"

"Khyte speaks the truth. They will run us down if we flee."

"Do you wish to tempt fate staying upon this accursed ground?"

"No, but—"

"But nothing. We move."

Khyte interrupted, putting his weatherbeaten hand on Vareem's shoulder. "Tempt fate? We know what those bandits will do. They will ride us down and pick us off one by one. You must see that? Let us stand and fight!"

"Take your hand from me, outlander!"

Barzelai edged between the two. "He is caravan master, my friend. We follow his orders. As I have said, I know what one enemy may do, but not the demons of the desert. We ride."

Khyte grimaced. "I am with you, but I'll hang back. I'd rather face death head-on than have them creep up my backside."

Barzelai clapped Khyte on the shoulder and laughed heartily, "Together we'll send those devils back to hell! My spear!"

The caravan slowly rolled away, sand running from the wagon spokes and fearful glances from the civilized and pampered occupants. The red cliffs pitted with dark spots loomed ahead, granting somber welcome.

Sweat beaded from Khyte's forehead as he squinted at the still-waiting bandits. "They aren't moving yet."

"So we have a head start, my friend," laughed Barzelai.

"I doubt it. I think they want us to move into that canyon."

The caravan crawled on with a pair of Yanissaries leading the way. The remaining twenty trailed behind with Barzelai and Khyte.

"Are your men better than an average bandit? Maybe twice as good?"

"I would say so, my friend. They have each been trained with the sword from childhood. To wear the turquoise sash of a Yanissary denotes the finest of schooling in fencing. All but three sport the long mustache of a veteran. We could meet those forty at a head and leave them bleeding enough to think better of it." Barzelai followed Khyte s roving gaze. "Why do you ask?"

"There're more."

Howling like wolves, twenty riders came in fast, flanking from the east; their scimitars catching sunlight on honed edges.

Half of the caravan froze while the others took the whip to their animals and sped away in chaotic abandon.

Khyte saw the original forty on the bluffs, save three, charge to join their brothers in the fray. Drawing his bow, he loosed and took a raider in the chest.

The Yanissaries joined in, dropping a dozen of the attackers or their mounts. Several bandits, having lost their horses, drew their sabers and ran forward like devils to complete their assault.

The bandits were swift and inside the caravan's circle, spoiling the shots of all but the most skilled bowmen. They slashed at the Yanissaries and merchants alike, even crippling several of the horses and camels.

Khyte charged an especially large raider and sent his spear through the man's leather-studded tunic.

Another bandit swung wildly and broke Khyte's spear's maple shaft.

Barzelai rode in and brought his horse into the fight, letting the well-trained beast kick a bandit from the saddle and trample him.

A woman gave a silent scream as one of the shrouded wagons

took fire. Black smoke belched into the sky quicker than Khyte would have believed possible.

Barzelai shouted at Khyte, but the outlander could not hear the captain, so beset was he by a pair of bandits. Throwing his helm in a raider's face, Barzelai distracted the pair enabling Khyte to slay them.

The blazing wagon roared with a devouring green witch-fire, sending smoking black tendrils across it. Wretched fumes spewed from a score of canopic jars into the sky, roiling on their way up. The alchemist and his wife, on foot, ran blindly toward the cliffs.

Khyte turned in the saddle just as Barzelai knocked him off his horse and slammed him to the ground. The wind whooshed from his lungs and Barzelai lay atop him.

He coughed, "Are you mad?"

Barzelai said, "Stay, my friend, stay."

Khyte panicked, seeing a handful of bandits circling them only a few paces away, swords raised.

But Barzelai held him down, covering almost all of Khyte's body with his own greater bulk. "Stay, my friend, stay."

An explosion ripped the atmosphere. Hot air slapped Khyte in the face. The foes that had recently stood so near, ready to deal death, were swept away in a green flash.

Barzelai went limp.

Khyte easily pushed the bigger man off. He blinked and wiped his eyes, trying to catch his breath. A fine, black creosote coated everything.

Barzelai was dead, his back ripped open from the blast and pin-cushioned with shards from the wagon.

"I am indebted, my friend, and will honor your sacrifice," whispered Khyte.

It took a few moments for Khyte to adjust his sight beyond the few feet near him. Nothing moved but taunting smoke and dancing wisps of flame. At least a score of blackened bodies lay strewn about. One was a woman, her doll-like face shielded by a dead horse.

Khyte struggled to stand.

The black blast of creosote reached fifty paces out. A bandit, thrown from the explosion yet lived. He struggled to crawl away dragging his useless, shattered legs behind him.

Leaning upon his sword a moment, Khyte rested, then smote the enemy on the neck.

The headless body raised on its hands, struggled for breath, then fell still.

Gazing across the desert, Khyte saw a handful of raiders retreating from the scene, though the caravan had fared little better. The half that had stopped with the alchemist where char as well as every man and woman near them. Those that fled on foot were almost to the canyons now. They looked to have been running at least ten minutes to be as far away as they were.

He wondered at how such a sudden explosion could have stolen so much time.

Looking to the bluffs, Khyte could almost see the fury in the bandit chieftain's bearded face. Loping to catch the rest of the caravan, Khyte watched his back. The figures remained on the bluff a moment longer.

† † †

Within the shade of the deep canyon, Khyte felt a bit cooler and energized.

The caravan had taken a left turn among the many slots available and ended in a box canyon.

Situated among the sheer, red cliffs were a number of stone ruins and fallen monuments. Toppled pillars and weathered friezes caught the eye, as did guardian statues of lions with bearded human heads and eagles' wings. What once must have been golden fountains now pooled naught but fine, red dust.

"We should not be here," lamented Vareem.

"What is this place?" asked Khyte.

Frowning, Vareem answered, "You still live? Are the rest— dead?"

Khyte nodded.

"Very well. We should continue on. We cannot stay here."

"But it is almost dusk, and a storm approaches," responded a merchant.

"We must stay the night at least. The bandits are regrouping. They know we were as damaged as they, if not worse, in the explosion."

"We have no choice. We must travel at night. I only led us to this place in hopes that—"

"This is no time for superstition."

"Listen, outlander, we have no water. Those supply wagons were destroyed in the blast. I hoped there would be water in this canyon. Rancid water, even, to fuel the horses, but no. We must reach the Arcane Wells before we run out of the meager supplies we have left."

"So, you suggest that we blindly flee in the night to get water that is at least three days away?"

"You were the one who said to wait out the raiders because of water, and now we have none."

"Neither do they. But surely there must be something amidst these ruins?"

Vareem countered, "If the cursed valley outside is the grave city of Dar-Alahamra, a home for the damned, then surely this ruin was its temple and we would be fools to remain. No debate. We go now."

"Then this is where we part ways."

"You were hired to guard the caravan."

"And the man I gave my word to is dead. Gave his life for mine—out there, and you haven't said a word about the sacrifice of those that are gone."

Vareem spoke flatly. "Yanissaries are paid to die. They did their job. My job is to lead the rest to Avaris as intact as I can. You wish to honor the fallen? Then get the rest of us safely to Avaris."

Khyte felt his neck tense, but admitted, "You're right. We go tonight. But we may as well wait for full sundown to rest the horses and oxen; let me look to see if there is any water hidden among these ruins."

Vareem gave a curt nod and cried, "Sundown, we depart."

Khyte posted a pair of Yanissaries to guard the canyon's mouth and keep a lookout for the bandits while he and most of the others searched the ruins.

† † †

Khyte clambered over the decayed monuments and lifted what flagstones he could in hopes of a well or cistern. Such a desert complex must surely have had a cistern somewhere, he kept reminding himself. He looked for depressions or central areas that would belie such necessities, but these ruins were alien in any sense of useful function. The close canyon walls, perhaps only a few hundred paces across at the narrowest point, precluded the use of stargazing except for the narrow slot of heavens above, a veritable visored helm's view of a full sky. Useless, unless you only cared for certain constellations.

A discolored pale marble tile caught his eye. He flexed his back and legs to the utmost, pulling up the wide square stone. Beneath lay nothing but sandy fill and annoyed centipedes. Khyte then noticed an olive-skinned woman standing a few paces away. "Hello?"

"Now you pay attention?" She wore a deep V-necked gown with a golden girdle that amplified her womanly features. A flared tiara held back long, dark hair and accentuated her wide, cocoa eyes. Her pursed lips, while full and red, looked cruel in the half-light. Altogether she was one of the most beautiful women Khyte had ever seen.

He stood and dusted himself off. "You were speaking?"

"I was—but you were so intent on your work you didn't hear me. I said that you will not find what you are looking for."

He smirked. "You must be the seeress. Why don't you tell me where to look for a well, then?"

She gave him a cool look. "I am Vashti, seeress of the Rose, and chief confidant to the Princess Esmeralda, may she reign in time."

"Yeah, listen, about that well—"

"There will not be one here. In ancient times water flowed freely and there was no need for such things."

"Here? In the desert?"'

"The land was not yet accursed."

"You can understand if I have to try," he said, turning over another stone.

"And you can understand that some things are futile."

He stopped turning over flagstones and strode up to her. "No fate but what we make."

"A juvenile expression from a people only recently raised to the level of barbarian."

He gave a lopsided grin. "Is there something you wish to say to me?"

She pointed at the rapidly darkening sky, hues of red and maroon graduated quickly to a bruising purple. "A storm is coming. We won't leave tonight or ever."

"You are as beautiful as you are depressing."

She returned the half-smile, though with decidedly more sarcasm.

Khyte asked, "If you can see all, why did you tell Vareem that we should move out of the valley and into danger. Whose side are you on? Why even come on this magic caravan?"

She ran her hand across his shoulder and down his arm, feeling the muscle. "I don't often throw myself at anyone, but your heroism and stupidity are intriguing."

"Answer my question and I'll answer yours." He would not admit her scent was intoxicating.

"I asked you no question, outlander."

"My name is Khyte and I don't have time for this."

She grasped his hand when he turned away. "Wait! No man has ever refused me."

Khyte laughed. "I'm not playing your game, precious."

"I can tell you what I see." She waited for him to stop before continuing. "I offered myself this last evening so I might know some pleasure before we meet our fate."

"Tell me what you see. What makes you so sure this is it? I've made it through a lot of rough scrapes before."

She swirled her gown and sat on a fallen pillar. "I see images of night, here in these ruins. Madness takes in thrall all those that hear the call of the pipes; they are damned to eternal waking horror held close to the breast of the desert."

Haze from the coming storm swirled high in the atmosphere, creating a malevolent design in the sky like cloaked death.

"You think we should just roll over and take it? Just let it happen and die?" he spit.

His grimace took her by surprise. She answered, "In our lands we know the gods have already set the board, played the game and moved the pieces where they lie. It only brings pain to go against such things. I am more merciful than the gods with my own cursed gift; at times I grant the mercy of ambivalent mystery to those whose doom is about to fall upon them. I sometimes tell only what people wish to hear, perhaps only what they can bear. I saw that we should die tonight, whether we stayed in the valley or came here."

"Maybe you only see glimpses of what will come to pass, but it doesn't mean it's always so. I believe in choice and chance both. I've escaped enough things that I never should have, lived through wounds that have killed bigger men and drunk enough poison that you should watch your kisses; and yet I'm still standing. I'll take on your ghosts and demons and leave this desolate place far behind."

"If such gives you peace of mind, then believe it."

Khyte gave her another lopsided grin. "Tell me, did you see Barzelai die on the valley floor with that explosion from the alchemist's wagon?"

Vashti turned away. "Yes."

"And me too?"

She shook her head. "I—I don't know."

"He gave his life for me at a moment's notice. I don't know if someone as selfish as you could have seen and understood that about him or not. Maybe all your skill is just chance, too."

"Are you quite through humiliating me?"

The wind whipped over the cliffs and gave them each a face full of biting sand.

"I haven't even started. Let's get to cover. I got a feeling we won't be leaving in this storm." Khyte pulled Vashti up to get her moving.

"Leave me be, outlander. I spoke the truth that we will not leave and you mocked me. Now you act as if you had foreseen this."

He let go of her arm and she ran away with a shawl over her face. Whether beneath the moon in every dark continent or under the sun shining across all the bright lands, women made no sense.

† † †

The sky grew murkily yellow as clouds of sand obscured the sun and bit the face. The pair of Yanissaries huddled together against the storm. They wrapped their scarves about their faces and took turns peering up and out into the blasting weather.

A hundred paces away, in a cleft of rock hardly shielded from the sun and sand, Khyte watched the canyon's entrance. He took another tear at his tough camel jerky as one of the Yanissaries suddenly became animated and the other dropped to his knees.

Khyte could not make out the man's words, but the kneeling Yanissary fell over while the other waved his arms as if shouting against the storm before he, too, sprouted a javelin full grown out of his back. Spitting out his jerky, Khyte put a hand on his sword pommel and dashed down the rocky path.

Out of the blazing dust-cloud came two dozen or more of the bandits, using the swirling concealment. They were wrapped like mummies in banded rags, as well as being colored akin to the storm, caked in fine red-brown dust. Khyte might have thought them the legendary ghosts of Desolation had he not seen one trip and fall on his face. They were indeed just men—bastard killers, but still just men.

Khyte drew his sword and ran down the path Vashti had taken moments earlier. He caught her by the wrist right before she entered her wagon. "Take cover in the ruins. The bandits are here."

"There is no fighting fate."

"Then it won't matter if you hide yourself away while I slay these dogs!" he shouted, turning his head to watch the incoming tide of doom.

Vashti looked as though she would argue again, but furrowed her brow and pulled from his hard grasp. "I understand now. You weren't ignoring me. You, the pipe cannot touch."

"Just go!"

She said something again as she disappeared into the haze, but Khyte could not hear her. All that mattered was that she ran into the ruins and away from the fight.

It was too late to warn others. Already the bandits engaged the few remaining Yanissaries and cut them down.

Vareem offered spangles of gold and a great ruby necklace, but he spat crimson into his white beard as he was met with a saber in his gullet. The valuables were taken without need of his bargaining.

A pair from the acting company valiantly tried to fend off a trio of bandits, but their fencing skill was no match for the bandits' hard-won brutality.

Striking with a serpent's speed and a panther's grace, Khyte cut down a bandit before the robber knew a superior foe was there. Another was slashed across the back and face as he turned to face his killer.

Diving behind a carriage, Khyte avoided the gaze of several bandits sweeping in to see why their dog brother had cried out.

They muttered and cursed at whoever had slain him, but were quickly pulled away by their greed.

A slim, goateed bandit attempted to ravish a subdued maiden. Khyte's sharp edge slit his throat. He pulled the shivering girl to her feet and directed her to the tumbled morass behind the caravan.

She ran only a few paces before another pair of grim bearded faces leapt at her.

This fourth raider was beheaded and the fifth disemboweled but cried out to Libnah, god of thieves, alerting the bandit chieftain of Khyte's counterattack.

"Run, girl! That way!" Khyte shouted at the frozen girl.

She remained still another moment until Khyte lunged toward her. She ran to the cover of stone.

It was too late for anything but vengeance for the others. Still,

Khyte saw no reason to charge in and needlessly die; he was practical. He hid beneath a wagon to await a devil's chance to turn about his luck. He scanned for a horse, but most had already been spirited away.

Bandits ran past in fruitless attempts to head off the last of the resistance. None looked down.

From beneath the wagon, Khyte saw the chieftain shout, "Hold, wolf brothers! There is a lion among these sheep. Work together as a pack and we shall take him!"

"What if he is a desert spirit sent to punish our wicked ways?"

The chieftain struck the penitent bandit across the mouth, sending him reeling to the ground. "He is but a man that we can slay, the same as any other."

"And the others?"

"Kill them all. We need no hostages nor slaves."

The bandits regrouped against the sand and wind, glaring like frightened vultures while they moved in concert between the wagons, ignoring the whimpering of the slave girls and moans of the dying. Even the haunted wind was beyond heeding when such a dangerous opponent lurked.

Khyte rolled out from under the wagon and vanished into the whipping sands.

The bandits believed that Khyte must be hidden behind the final carriage and the dozen of them raced around to find no one. They glanced at a low defile abreast of the wagons, but saw only the twisting, dancing sands of tuneless dust devils.

The bandits gradually inched outward from their demanding leader. They searched both above and below the wagons. They looted and tossed trunks of fine silks and expensive spices to the ground, but of their quarry they found nothing. Soon they had more wealth than they could possibly carry; enough to remove or at least blur the memory of their comrades' slayer.

The screams of those being murdered were soon lost in the arms of the waiting wind.

↟ ↟ ↟

Clutching the girl across her chest and clasping a hand over her mouth, Khyte inched away from the bandits' unseeing gazes. His slow stealth coupled with the blazing sands concealed both himself and the struggling girl from the raider's vision as they tore apart the caravan looking for treasure.

He rounded a colossal boulder and relaxed his hold on the girl.

She spun about to face him. "Did you rescue me just to satisfy yourself?"

He shook his head and put a finger to his lips.

Sands swirled and threatened their eyes. She held a hand upward to shield her vision and glanced low around the side of the stone. Facing Khyte, she said, "They can hear nothing in this storm either."

He motioned to keep moving farther afield of the bandits. She nodded and they retreated over the chaotic landscape for several minutes, looking for shelter before climbing down into the sunken and tumbled ruins of an ancient temple. It was oval with light gray flagstones, sand couched into the crevices and blasted into heaps a foot deep upon the south side. Grotesque figures were carved into seemingly random effigy upon the wall, some resembling men, some far from it. Despite the heat, a chill washed over this place as if unseen forces blinked at their intrusion.

Any rooftops had long since fallen in this wreck of a complex. A huge, dried and desiccated wooden doorway lay at the far end of the exposed temple foundation. A precarious Cyclopean archway protected the aperture from the ruin of a merciless sun.

"Let us shelter there while I come up with a plan."

"What plan? You only slew four of them."

"Five."

"Five. And there are still twenty more! They will take whatever wealth there was, horses, camels, food and water. Even if they don't find us, we are dead here without."

"I have been through worse and survived."

She shook her head. "Well, I haven't. I know what comes in the night." The wind whipped all the more bitter and she gave a satisfied look as if the weather itself proved her point.

"Tell me what comes at night and tell me your name. I am Khyte."

"I know who you are, outlander."

He found it hard to give his usual smirk against her belligerence and tone of 'outlander'. "Why does everyone on this continent insist on calling me that? And you still didn't tell me your name."

"Why ask my name? That you might know something of me? To hold over me?"

Khyte shook his head. "I told you mine freely enough without fear or judgment."

"I am not fearful. I am Tisha, and though I am just a handmaid in the court of pleasure, I know the true way of the world. If we don't flee this place the ghoul shall have us."

"What ghoul? Those were just bandits."

"Not them, you fool. The ghoul of the desert, those who have heard the call of the pipe."

"Pipe?"

"Yes, the Pipe of Mahmackrah. The most cursed of all evil instruments."

"I am not familiar with such tales."

She rolled her eyes. "And that is why you are a foolish outlander. You have no respect for our ways. You don't listen to half of what I say. You have no understanding that we may know more than you about our very own land."

"I never said that."

"You didn't need to, I know how you are. I have served many mercenaries from across the sea."

He took her by the shoulders and held her at arm's length in a firm grip. "Not all men are like those you have met in the pleasure houses. Not all men must tread upon flowers to appreciate them."

She smiled, saying, "Oh, you are a smooth one. But I warn you, I will still charge full price."

He pushed her away. "Strumpet, I denied Vashti; surely I would not pay for you!"

Tisha looked shocked at that revelation. "But her powers demand purity. If she was willing to give herself even to one such as

252

you, then she must surely have seen that we are doomed!"

He scowled at that while she closed in on herself and dropped to the ground, cringing.

"You spoke of ghoul. What are they?"

She buried her head in her cloak.

He knelt and shook her until she looked up wide eyed and afraid. "What are they?" he demanded.

"I already told you."

"Tell me again!"

"Don't you listen? You will see them soon enough. At dusk."

"But what are they?"

"Must I repeat everything for you? They are the damned souls who have heard the call of the Pipe of Mahmackrah. They are murderous and will feast upon our souls as well as our flesh. If Vashti would give herself away ... we are lost, there is no chance for us." She trailed off, crying into her cloak, and Khyte could understand nothing more from her.

The orange sun yet shone, but sudden shadows warped and hung over them in the stillness of the archway, and for a moment he wondered if dusk had already fallen when Tisha startled.

Vashti appeared. "They are here! Take them!"

A dozen bandits leapt and tore at Khyte as he struggled for his sword hilt. Brutal hands beat him down as he fought to rise up against the tide of bodies.

Vashti watched, the wind grasping her silken scarves and skirt like so many unseen lustful hands. She stood imperious over them upon the foundation stones as the bandits bound Khyte and Tisha, together within the sunken temple.

Khyte snarled at the seeress. "Slut! Turn-cloak! Does not fate punish terribly such as you?"

Her face gave no emotion or hint of guilt as the bandits lifted their prisoners overhead and carted them off.

"To the altar with them!" cried Vashti.

☥ ☥ ☥

At the far end of the canyon, where the shadows lay deep as doomed man's conscience, the bandits bound Khyte and Tisha to a wide, black obelisk. Squared and altogether short, it reached only as high as a tall man. Its dark features were pitted with more than age. Short, straight gashes along the surface revealed a violent sacrament to hungry gods.

Vashti stooped in front of Khyte and whispered, "These bandit fools worship Mahmackrah and think that by sacrificing you they will be allowed the power of the Pipe—that they will be conquerors and ruiner's both."

"They have it?" gasped Tisha.

Vashti ignored her and continued. "When I hid for a moment I was granted the vision of salvation for my people, and I will assist that, though I may die a maddening death. Such is the only reason I betrayed you—for the greater good. Promise me, Khyte, that you will kill me when the time comes. Kill me and destroy the Pipe."

"Let me loose and I will gladly," he grated, straining against his bonds.

Tisha whimpered unintelligibly.

"You still don't understand. I have saved your life with my own and have given you the opportunity and the duty to save my nation, my people."

"With your own? You just asked me to kill you."

"Your sword and kit are just beyond that rock wall behind me. I know you can reach it in swift moments when you are freed."

The black-robed bandit chieftain strode up to Vashti's side and rubbed a lecherous hand over her graceful form before turning his attention to Khyte. "You are the outlander who slew so many of my men."

"I am Khyte of Vjorn. I don't recall you introducing yourself ... as is custom in these lands."

"My name is my own and I need not share it with the likes of you who are about to die."

"Do the gods of this land not say, 'A man who whips his horse will pull his own cart someday'?"

The chieftain gave a half-smile. "You know the customs and

tenets of my people well, but I worship the god of fire and death, mighty Mahmackrah. He cares not for weakness, and I shall honor him by sacrificing you upon the raising of tonight's harvest moon."

"And what of the ghoul?"

The chieftain laughed. "You know of them? Few outlanders do. My people are usually reluctant to speak of them to outsiders. But they are the children of Mahmackrah, too. I have watched them, you know. I have been in the wilderness many years now, since I was a boy. And I have seen from a distance the ghoul dance in the night. Always under a bright moon, like tonight. Naked as newborn babes, yet withered as old men, the ghoul dance in exultation of Mahmackrah, and soon enough I shall command them."

"You're mad!" shrieked Tisha.

The chieftain's face reddened. He slapped Tisha across the mouth, yet whispered angrily to taunt them. "I have found the pipe! It is no dream." He produced from out of the folds of his robe an exquisitely carved ebon pipe. Shaped like an inverted V, it had note holes in an alternating, semi-spiraling pattern fit for no human hand to play. "I alone found it, only a fortnight ago, in that temple you tried to hide in. Praise be to Mahmackrah, the seeress and I were destined to be together. Without her I would not know the song to play. This journey, your death, and my triumph were foreordained."

"You would blow upon it and summon the madness I have heard tell of?" asked Khyte.

The chieftain nodded and grinned a sly, venomous smile.

"If he did not, he would not be the chosen of Mahmackrah," said Vashti, as boldly as she ever had yet. "He must play the song of old Casmir, and only then claim his kingdom!"

"But you just asked Khyte—" Tisha's words were cut off as Vashti slapped her across the face.

"Silence, whore!" Vashti snarled, as she put a gag into Tisha's soft mouth.

"The seeress knows how to handle a slave girl," chuckled the chieftain. "Know this, outlander, I will play the mad song at eventide, and the ghoul will show themselves and bow in servitude to me. The seeress has seen it. You will be the first to die in honor before I conquer the whole of the world."

"I killed a score of your men. Wouldn't you rather I serve you?"

"Ha, good—good. I credit you for your clever bargaining, but what need have I for any, even great, sell-swords, when I will command the invincible army of the ghoul? The ghoul will grow until the whole of the world are one with them and ghoul themselves. Only we few who command the respect of Mahmackrah will remain untainted."

"What of your men?"

"Small, superstitious minds who may yet better serve me as ghoul. They are not immune or worthy, they are irrelevant."

"And how did you learn all these things?"

The chieftain grinned with wicked teeth and wrapped an arm about Vashti. "Why, she told me, of course. She saw in vision that I had found the Pipe, and knew she must guide me to use it. In my heart I always knew I was destined for greatness; I always did."

Vashti nodded and winked as Tisha raged.

"Your companion does not share in your understanding of my vision. No matter, her bitterness will not sour in a ghoul belly." He laughed cruelly at that and strode away.

Vashti turned to follow, whispering, "Remember." As she dropped a needle like hair-pin at Khyte's feet.

⚡ ⚡ ⚡

Khyte patiently reached with his foot, dragging the pin over to where he could not grasp it, but Tisha could.

She strained against her bonds and finally plucked it up with swelling fingers.

"Toss it to where I can reach it."

She mumbled through her gag as she tried to saw and poke at her own bindings.

"Fool girl! With some subtlety, or those bastards will see."

This only brought about a more frantic sawing and stabbing motion from the girl. She might have screamed aloud if the gag were not suffocating her cries at the multitude of times she jabbed herself.

"Tisha, slowly."

She mumbled her assent and tried again and again. One cord of the dozen about her wrists began to fray.

"Keep working at it. I'll keep watch."

"Too lates for that's, I'm afraid," said a snaggle-toothed bandit, as he rounded the obelisk. He reached down and took the hair pin from Tisha's weak grasp. "Lookit that, you mighta hurt yourself withat," he drawled.

The bandit had a pervasive stink that recoiled Khyte. Upon his beard rode newly looted food, and Khyte decided the man was drunk on Vareem's wine. He would use what he could. "Why not take her and have some fun before your master kills her?"

Tisha turned to look with wide, angry eyes at Khyte and screamed through her gag.

The dirty bandit grinned and stroked Tisha's cheek. "She ist a looker."

"Go on, take her," Khyte prodded.

The bandit looked from Khyte to Tisha, and finally in the chieftain's direction. "He mights kill me if I moves hers."

"Then take her right here. He won't see."

Tisha's eyes flared at Khyte and her muted screams grew more frantic.

The dirty bandit pondered a moment, put his wineskin down on the flagstones beside the obelisk and got down on his knees to begin his business with the girl.

Khyte's bound legs flew up and came crashing down on the bandit's skull.

Reeling yet still conscious, the bandit had time to look once at Khyte before both feet, still tied together, slammed down, pulping his sour face.

Khyte kicked several more bloody times to be sure the man would not stir.

Tisha still screamed silently, though perhaps now because of the carnage seeping toward her.

"Can you reach his knife?"

She shook her head.

Reaching, Khyte brought his foot beneath the bandit's armpit and inched the carcass a half-pace closer. "Now?"

Tisha mumbled that she had the knife. Her nervous breathing doubled its pace and she awkwardly tried to cut her own bindings first.

"If you can't cut your own then pass me the knife."

She grumbled at that remark and kept trying. A moment later her hand was free and she tore the gag from her mouth. "You filthy cur! Offering me to that dog!" She slapped Khyte across the mouth.

"It all worked out. Cut me loose."

She yanked and cut the bindings from her own feet. "I should leave you here! I should—"

"Yes, you should," said the chieftain. "You are both troublesome souls, but there is a need for you as well."

Tisha slashed wildly at the chieftain.

He laughed and easily disarmed her before striking her across the face. Glancing at her neckline, he pulled back a strap, revealing a blue-ink tattoo placed just above her heart. He raged, smacking Tisha across the face yet again. "I see the tattoo upon your breast. I know you are from my own clan, and yet you defile yourself as a pleasure girl?!"

"What does it matter? You wish to make me a ghoul! You are the true betrayer!" she cried.

Several of the bandits looked on, agitated. Tisha's cry made them nervous that indeed what the chieftain planned for the prisoners would invoke doom for them as well.

The chieftain stuffed the gag back into Tisha's mouth as he again bound her up. "And you, outlander—even bound you kill my men. Truly Mahmackrah will be pleased with eating a warrior's heart that is this worthy of his honor."

"I hope he chokes."

"Hope is dead," answered the chieftain. He gave Tisha one last slap before walking away and shouting at his men again. "Dispose of Ahmed's body! Pay no attention to the ramblings of that trollop."

"That could have gone better," mused Khyte.

✝ ✝ ✝

A dusky, old bandit, absently chewing on a twig, waited while two other bandits hauled Ahmed's body away. He mumbled quickly under his breath, "What know you of ghoul?"

"Nothing," said Khyte.

The bandit shook his head, watching carefully that his companions were out of earshot. "That does not ring true. I heard both of you mention ghoul to the chieftain and I want to know why. It's ill luck to speak of them so openly."

"I have nothing to say to you."

"Is no trick." He held his palms outward as the sign of peace and trust in that part of the world, such a maneuver was held inviolate, even by bandits. "I wonder, do you know the legend of the ghoul?"

"No."

He pointed at the ruins within the canyon. "Long ago the ghoul and men worshiped the same gods. But man, he think he know better, think he know progress and civilization, he made new gods and abandoned the old."

Khyte chuckled. "Is this supposed to warn me about jealous old gods coming for revenge?"

The old bandit returned the smile but shook his head again. "No, the old gods are dead or sleep, they care no more. But the ghoul—they care. They are insulted that men abandon the way. They are made from the dark magics of hate and bitterness. The ghoul want to punish men for leaving the faith."

"The faith?"

The old bandit nodded. "Once all worshiped at the same altar of the creators, but in their inner darkness men abandoned the true path."

"You a religious man?"

The bandit chuckled now and shook his head.

"What about the Pipe?" prodded Khyte.

"What Pipe?"

"The one your chieftain found. Of Mahmackrah. He showed it to us."

"Impossible. If he found it, he would have told us. Would he lie?" The bandit asked himself.

Khyte rolled his eyes hardly containing a full laugh at that. "No, I expect not."

The old bandit grinned without mirth. "The legends say the Pipe can create ghoul."

"More? Are there any now?"

"Oh yes, they are very real. You doubt?"

Khyte shrugged. "What do they do, when they aren't devouring wayfarers."

The bandit frowned at Khyte as if he had asked a stupid question.

"Answer me!"

"They build cities underground and grow and grow, but if the Pipe is blown and everyone hears the call—well then, then all of mankind would suffer as they take over and rule."

"Build? Rule what?"

"Legends of my father's say the ghoul have cities buried under the sands. Kingdoms in dust. They wait for when the stars are right."

"Right for what?"

"To attack, to reclaim the world and rebuild it in their own perfect image."

"Were they once men? Or another creation altogether?"

"Who knows which was first? Perhaps it was the ghoul who were defiled and became men?"

Khyte jerked his hands as far up as he could reach. "You need to let me go."

"No, I cannot." He shook his head adamantly. "Those are just stories. No one knows the truth anymore."

"We need to stop him before he plays the Pipe. He will make you all ghoul."

"No, the magic must surely be as dead as the old gods. I was just telling stories," he said nervously. "Khalem Khan found no Pipe. And even if he did, he would not dare play upon it."

"You want to take that chance? Why hasn't he shown you the Pipe? Cut me loose."

The bandit looked at Khyte, then toward his chieftain's ox-hide tent. "That I cannot do. Khalem Khan will sacrifice you in the old ways. If I went against him, my dog-brothers would cut me across the manhood and leave me staked to an anthill. Accept your fate. Farewell."

"Then why do you fear the ghoul? Why does your voice quaver at their mention?"

He struck Khyte full across the face, splitting his sun-burnt lips. "Do not insinuate that I am a coward. Khalem Khan is my Shah and I will not betray him."

"Even to your own doom?"

"Fate is fate." The dusky bandit walked away after a few choice curses in his native tongue.

"I thought for sure that would work," muttered Khyte.

Tisha looked on, her mute screams were damned at the horror of the words she had just heard.

⸸ ⸸ ⸸

The moon rose and shadows materialized on the canyon walls and Khyte thought he recognized the mythic gathering foe. Leprous, gray movement along the cliff face gave awful images to his mind's eye, and he wondered briefly if he was letting his imagination run away with him in this terrible place.

The chieftain, who Khyte now knew as Khalem Khan, left his tent as the moon stood out strong, hanging above the coarse canyon walls.

The bandits huddled close, for Khyte was not the only one who had noticed the monstrous gesticulations in the gloom.

Calming their fears, Khalem Khan shouted, "Fear not! For I have the power to rule them."

Vashti appeared beside him. When she saw Khyte and Tisha still bound she grew visibly disturbed. She mouthed, *You should have been free by now.*

Khalem Khan strode up to the elevated outcrop. The bandits moved closer as he revealed the Pipe. "With this I shall take back what has been stolen from us!"

The old, dusky bandit looked back toward Khyte, fear etched between the lines across his face. "My lord, no!"

Khalem Khan grinned. "There is no denying my power!" He brought the double-pronged Pipe to his lips and blew an eldritch song. A song unlike anything heard in millennia blasted forth.

After a brief few resounding notes, some of the men reacted badly. They shook as the haunting music pierced their souls. Some vomited at the resonating power of a low rhythm that was far too powerful for the size of the instrument in the khan's hands.

Then Khyte saw the ghoul lurking in the shadows slowly creeping forth, taking tentative steps outside the gloom. It wasn't a slow, ponderous gait; no, these were creatures of speed and cunning purpose, they merely waited for the shadows to stretch so they might be covered awhile longer from the harsh gaze of moonlight. The speed with which they moved along the cliff walls would put a panther to shame.

At least it should be a speedy death.

Khyte struggled at the bindings, but though the dried rawhide gave, it wasn't nearly enough. He stretched to reach with his teeth that he might gnaw his way to freedom, but he was held too closely behind.

Beside him, Tisha strained. She had at least spit out the gag but had even less success at worming her hands free. Tears streamed from her eyes as the panic washed over her like a drowning wave.

"They're coming, they're coming," she wailed.

But Khyte paid scant attention. He wasn't ready to die yet. Barzelai's words echoed in his mind, '*Better to die with the hot steel of a bastards tulwar in your guts than in the guts of some foul beast.*' If he could just go down fighting instead of as food.

In the surrounding chaos, Vashti ran with a stolen falcata and sliced through Khyte's bonds and then Tisha's. She dropped to her knees at the ominous, powerful sound, retching. "Only you can stop this."

Glancing toward Khalem Khan, Khyte saw that he still blew upon the Pipe, but something was wrong. Khalem's face was turning blue.

It looked as if he could not stop blowing.

"Cover your ears as best you can," Khyte ordered the women.

All the bandits were now driven to their knees as Khalem Khan still blew the Pipe as his dusky skin turned a sickening purple. What appeared as a fine blue mist wafted from the Pipe and held the bandit chieftain like a dominating lover.

"Your promise," struggled Vashti. "Slay me . . . that I should not . . . become ghoul."

Tisha screamed, rocking her head to and fro as the reverberation of the Pipe rocked the canyon.

Khyte held the short falcata, but he could not yet bring himself to strike down the suffering women.

The Pipe's mad song seemed to inflict awful pain on everyone but Khyte and the encroaching ghoul.

Khyte bolted at Khalem, slashing several of the bandits as he strode past.

Khalem Khan himself fell to the ground, still blowing the terrible artifact, though his lungs contained no more life-giving air. He glanced up at Khyte with wide eyes full of maddening fear and desperation begging for death.

Khyte raised the falcata high and slammed it against the Pipe.

The blow knocked against Khalem's body but the Pipe would not break, it would not be cast from his lips.

The hollow notes grew in strength and Khyte felt the ground shake. He struck again and again, beating the chieftain across the ground for the power of the hits, but the Pipe was unbreakable.

Then the ghoul were upon him.

Savage faces twisted in a mockery of what were once men.

They tore with clawed fingers upon Khyte's back and snapped their gaping jaws, famished for his flesh.

Khyte struck back in a whirlwind of Damascus steel, slaying several before realizing these were the transformed bandits. Men made into monsters of an eldritch muse because of the still-blowing Pipe.

The few bandits left were then augmented by naked savage forms, more monstrous than their own. These true ghoul looked feral and primeval beyond reckoning, like unholy hybrids of jackal and man. Elongated mouths and drawn-back ears with eyes that were slits of cold fire. Taut muscle writhed beneath gray, mottled skin as the monsters leapt.

Khyte screamed in fury, slashing across the black-blooded demons.

He hammered at the foes, crushing skulls and raining what could only be entrails of the long dead, and still the dread music played.

Knowing the ghoul had no end in their legion of slathering jaws, Khyte turned back to the Pipe itself. He was sure that his only hope lay in that relic's destruction.

Khalem Khan's face was nearly black from asphyxiation, yet he still blew upon the Pipe, as if the blue mist wrapped about him was a demon-god forcing air through him as a mere vessel to be toyed with. His hands, too, were black, clutching each barrel of the pipe in a death-grip.

Ghoul roared and launched upon Khyte, only to be cut away and cry their grief and hurt.

Khyte's righteous wrath brought his blade down and again in brutal assault. Instinct born in the frozen north landed here in the boiling south and fought a battle as old as time.

Granted the slightest respite, Khyte launched against the Pipe yet again.

Bringing the blade down with all his possible strength, still gave nothing but heartache.

The Pipe played on, indifferent, if not perhaps taunting.

All Khyte saw turned to brown and red as he was further surrounded by the dead.

Khalem Khan's pained eyes still looked out, begging forgiveness, begging for an end.

The ghoul held back a moment in full circle about Khyte. He knew there was no strength left to slay them all, no strength left to slay ten of their damned number.

Tisha and Vashti now stood among them, in terrible counterfeit of their former selves; once-graceful, lilting hands now bore claws with death written upon them, beautiful lips had given way to slathering jaws.

The malevolent song of the Pipe played on.

Khyte looked down at Khalem Khan's blackened body and raised his falcata one last time and chopped the hands from the Shah's body, freeing the Pipe from undead lips.

The song which had been burning through the air, shaking the ground, swirling sands into the air, abruptly stopped. The blue mist faded.

Without the mad song echoing through them, the ghoul screamed and dropped in fetal positions on the ground—writhing, howling like damned souls before they, too, went silent and still.

Khyte dropped to his knees spent.

Khalem Khan's lips moved silently until Khyte looked at them head on.

"Outlander . . . outlander . . . outlander."

Some weak color returned to the crippled Khalem Kahn and Khyte looked down at his pathetic form. "Last words dog?"

"How . . . did you . . . resist . . . the power . . . of the . . . Pipe?"

"I'm deaf."

† † †

Aboard the comfort of a rolling ship sailing over fresh seas, Khyte raised a toast to the shades of Barzelai, Tisha, and Vashti, and dropped the Pipe of Mahmackrah into bottomless ocean depths.

**THE END**

# AFTERWORD

One of my great joys is haunting old book stores and finding some dog-eared old jewel with a lurid cover and equally byzantine-titled tales throughout promising exotic adventure, nameless fear and violent intrigue. Stories with roguish anti-heroes, clever heroines, demonic villains and voluptuous hussies, tales with sinister creatures and frightful monsters from beyond, all told with a decidedly purple prose and enchanting hush between yellowed pages.

I couldn't say how many times I have gone hunting for such books, I probably always will, for there is no end to fantastic books in the world.

So I am quite the fan, nay connoisseur of old-school pulp fiction. My stories contained herein are inspired by those I deem the masters, Robert E. Howard, H.P. Lovecraft, Clark Ashton Smith, Fritz Leiber, Karl Edward Wagner, C.L. Moore, Dashiell Hammett, Louis L'amour and many, many more.

Pondering on who I was really writing so many of these tales contained herein for, I determined that these mark a part of my life that is about appreciation and fascination for the above named writers, and as such these stories weren't so much a letter to anyone in particular living (unlike other work I have done –my wife, the kids, GAN Warriors and friends) this collection embodies a desire to reach out and be kindred spirits with my departed mentors. I'd like to think I did that.

Thanks for reading.

David J. West
Los Angeles
June 2nd, 2014

## ABOUT THE AUTHOR

David has been writing as long as he can remember, winning a number of secretive awards too prestigious for you to have heard of. He currently lives in Los Angeles with his wife and three children. Among his other published works are *Heroes of the Fallen, Bless the Child, Whispers of the Goddess,* and the sci-fi horror collections of *Space Eldritch 1 & 2*

You can visit him online at:
http://david-j-west.blogspot.com
https://twitter.com/David_JWest
http://davidjwest.tumblr.com/

*Garden of Legion* was originally published in Wandering Weeds

*The King in the Wood* was intended for The Green Man collection but rejected, I'm still surprised

*Gods in Darkness* was originally published in Space Eldritch

*I Once Heard the Pipes of Pan,* was intended but never submitted

*Fistful of Tengu* was originally published in Monk Punk

*A Good Home for the Spoon* was originally published in Dark Eclipse #17

*Lovecraftian Haiku* was originally published on twitter/Lovecraft haiku contest

*Peace in the New World* was intended for a flash fiction millennial project

*Make A Monkey Outta Me* was to be published in Heavy Metal Horror but the collection was cancelled

*Echo From The Abyss* was intended for a Lovecraftian Diversity project but never submitted

*One Thousand One Nights Unseen* was intended for a Weird Warfare collection but was cancelled

*Curse the Child* was originally published in the Lovecraft Ezine #4

*Fangs of the Dragon* was originally published in Monsters and Mormons

*The Problem with Magick* was originally published in Another 100 Horrors

*Stumps* was written for the Mormon Litz Blitz of 2012, it lost, but I still like it

*The Dig* was originally published in In Situ

*Baptism By Fire* was written for Unidentified Funny Objects, it was rejected but I still think it's funny

*Why Crows Steal Shiny Things* was originally published in 100 Worlds

*Tangle Crowned Devil* was originally published in Unnatural Tales of the Jackalope

*The Cry of Carrion Birds* was to be published in The Evil Twin but the collection was cancelled

*The Mad Song* was originally published in Artifacts & Relics: Extreme Sorcery